PLAINS

OF

GOLD

NICHOLAS PETERS

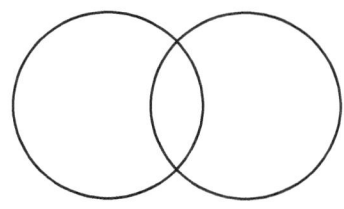

PLAINS OF GOLD

Library of Congress Cataloging-in-Publication Data has been applied for.
Peters, Nicholas - Plains of Gold
FIRST EDITION

ISBN: 978-0-9973381-1-9 (Softcover Edition)
ISBN: 978-0-9973381-0-2 (eBook Edition)

Book Editor: Lory Peters Ph.D., J.D.

www.plainsofgold.net
www.nicholaspeters.com

For Lory
and our Goldens

Part I

1
The Rogue Planet

T HE BIGGEST EVENT in Martian history began with a five-sentence kicker at the end of a late-night television newscast.

And finally tonight, astronomers say a rare event will take place this fall. The planet Koya will pass near Mars on its 412-year orbit around the Sun. For more than a month, Koya will be visible in the nighttime sky. But don't worry. We're told that Koya poses no danger to our planet.

With some newsy-sounding music fading up in the background, the newscaster wished his audience a pleasant evening and the station switched to late-night programming.

By the next day, everyone had forgotten about Koya. The planet's arrival wasn't mentioned during the early morning news shows or the evening ones, either. There were bigger

stories, more urgent ones, that took priority over one more
rock passing through the solar system.

In the northern hemisphere, the winter and spring
seasons had been unseasonably warm. Now, it was mid-sum-
mer and the heat was almost unbearable. Temperature records
were shattered every day for a month, with the heat wave
showing no signs of letting up. The planet's electrical grid
sagged under the demand for air conditioning. Making things
worse, a decade-long drought had emptied most of the planet's reservoirs, forcing Martians to get more and more of their
drinking water from the oceans. Removing salt from seawater
takes huge amounts of electricity, which only added to the
strain on the power grid.

At this point, a bit of planetary history might help put the
plight of the Martians into perspective. The first four planets
of the solar system – Mercury, Venus, Earth, and Mars –
formed at the same time, about 4.5 billion years ago. Each
has an iron core and a mantle made primarily of silicates. The
Earth is the biggest of the four. Mars is much smaller – about
a quarter the size and one-tenth the mass of Earth.

As the planets cooled, they were bombarded by millions
of asteroids that roamed in the same neighborhood. Many of
them contained water ice. Mercury was too close to the Sun
and the water evaporated. The same was true for Venus. The
third planet, Earth, was perfect for holding onto its water,
with mild temperatures, strong gravity, and an atmosphere
and magnetic belt to protect the water from the Sun's intense
rays. Mars got a lot of water, too, but the water should have

stayed frozen. The planet is too far from the Sun and too cold for liquid water.

But Mars caught a break. Even though it gets less than half the solar radiation of Earth, what it does get is held tightly to the surface by a thick atmosphere of carbon dioxide. Mars was a working example of a *beneficial* greenhouse effect.

Like Earth, Mars is tilted on its axis, giving it seasonal variations in temperatures. The difference between the warm and cool air established a complex planetary mechanism that regulated the climate. Most of the ice melted, forming oceans that covered forty-percent of its surface. Mars was ready for the next phase of its evolution.

As on Earth, the water that came to Mars contained amino acids, the building blocks of life. Heat and light from the Sun warmed the oceans, making an inviting, mineral-rich soup for the amino acids to form into more complex proteins. They reacted with the Sun's energy to start the evolutionary life process. The planet's smaller size, combined with its tranquil, carbon-rich atmosphere, gave it a head-start on Earth. On Mars, the first single-celled organisms arrived a half-billion years before the same life processes started on Earth.

Once life began, evolution did the rest, creating new forms of plant and animal life that adapted to the warm conditions on Mars. About ten million years ago, the first hominid species emerged. They shared many of the attributes of human ancestors - bipedalism, stereoscopic vision, and fingers to make tools. This species came to dominate the planet and, as they evolved, their brains grew larger. About a half-million years ago, they emerged with the intellect and creativity to form a modern Martian society.

On Earth, human cells are damaged and replaced in a natural process that eventually ages the body. That building and repairing process gives humans an average lifespan of about seventy years. But on Mars, due mainly to its carbon dioxide atmosphere, cell destruction and repair was much less. Lifespans got longer as living conditions improved. By the time of Koya, an average Martian could expect to live 500-600 years.

Low mortality and a high birthrate meant that Martians were soon sharing a very crowded planet. As they cleared the forests to build more houses, the delicate mechanisms that supported life began to change. Because Mars is only a fraction of the size and mass of Earth, every change in the planet's ecosystem was magnified. By the time of Koya's arrival, the planet's greenhouse mechanism seemed to be stuck on high. Even more troubling, scientists said that without immediate and drastic changes, Mars would soon reach a tipping point, when the planet would become too hot to support life.

On Earth, in places where land is scarce, buildings get taller. The invention of structural steel allowed builders to imagine ever-taller buildings. In cities where a few used to live, thousands could now live and work. In Asia, Europe, and the Americas, taller and taller buildings, using steel-framed construction, represent the state of the building art. So far, there doesn't seem to be a limit on how high builders can build.

But for Martians, building taller wasn't an option. Their atmosphere had almost no oxygen to support fire – the heat necessary to turn iron and carbon into steel. And even though the Red Planet got its nickname from the abundance of iron in its soil, without oxygen, large furnaces could not be built to take advantage of this natural resource. Metals that were available were made in small batches, using oxygen-fed kilns. There was enough metal for electronics and precision tools, but not enough to build the long, structural steel beams required for high-rise buildings.

This scarcity of metal limited Martian society in other ways. Aviation and space travel were impossible. While they understood the science of space travel and had even designed propulsion systems that could take them across the galaxy, without the metals that humans take for granted for everything from cars to can openers, space travel was impossible.

So, here was the paradox of Mars. Its citizens were as advanced as any society in the galaxy. They had solved the theoretical mysteries of time, space, and matter. The Martians safely harnessed the Sun's own fusion process to provide almost limitless, pollution-free power. And their medical arts, computer technology, and manufacturing abilities were centuries ahead of what humans can do, even today.

Yet, at the time of Koya's arrival, 1.5 billion Martians lived on a crowded planet that was giving every indication of an imminent environmental collapse. But for the lack of one particular molecule in their atmosphere, they couldn't use the abundant iron that would have given them more flexibility to set aside large, natural spaces that would have protected the planet's delicate ecosystem.

And as the citizens on this small, crowded planet baked in the heat, Koya was out there.

And, it was coming for them.

2
The History of Koya

I N THE WEEKS following the announcement of Koya, news about the planet was limited and vague. If anything was written at all about Koya, the story was usually a one paragraph squib buried on the inside pages of the newspaper. On television, Koya was mentioned during the two or three minutes that the weather guy was given to talk about the hot weather and extreme drought conditions.

But while the public remained ignorant of Koya's intentions, in the scientific community, Koya already had a reputation as a troublemaker. The planet was discovered by Martian astronomers eight centuries ago. Astronomers at an observatory atop the dormant *Olympus Mons* volcano spotted Koya while studying the inner planets of the solar system. As they analyzed the orbits of these planets, astronomers saw another planet-sized body enter their field-of-view. It was Koya, a solid ball of iron, roughly the same size as Mars.

Koya was a rogue – not an original member of the solar system. Its home was probably a star that went supernova, kicking Koya out of orbit and setting it adrift across the galaxy. Koya could have stayed that way forever. But Koya wandered too close to the Sun, whose gravity pulled it into the solar system.

Because it joined the solar system later, the shape and angle of Koya's orbit were different. Unlike the roughly circular orbit of the other planets, Koya's orbit was elliptical. Inbound, it would speed up as it neared the Sun. Then, it would slingshot back out into a wide arc at the fringes of the solar system. Just about when it was ready to break free of the Sun's pull, Koya would slow down again, and then turn back in for another roller coaster ride toward the Sun.

Koya's other oddity was its orbital plane. The planet orbited the Sun at a forty-degree angle from the orbital planes of the other planets. Each time it revolved around the Sun, Koya would cut across the orbits of the other planets. What's more, because of its size, mass, and certain aspects about Koya that astronomers did not yet fully understand, Koya's orbits were erratic and unpredictable. Each visit near the Sun found Koya at a different spot when it crossed through the orbits of the other planets.

When Martian astronomers first discovered Koya, they watched as it just missed hitting Venus. Although the two planets did not collide, Koya's dense gravitational pull changed the orbit of Venus, pulling it closer to the Sun. The extra solar radiation from the closer orbit changed Venus forever, altering its atmospheric chemistry and making it a hot and cloud-covered place that would never support life.

On its return, 412 years later, a new generation of astronomers with vastly better telescopes were waiting. Scanning the general neighborhood of Venus, Koya was nowhere to be found. But as they swung their telescopes in wider and wider arcs, they found Koya. On this trip, instead of threatening Venus, Koya was bearing down on the planet Earth.

On Earth, at the time of Koya, Genghis Khan was building his empire across Asia. The Magna Carta was signed in England. And in China, the first rockets were being built – the very beginning of mankind's quest to reach outer space.

For months, astronomers tracked Koya as it neared the Earth's orbital plane. If it struck, they would be witness to the planet's annihilation. Fortunately, by the time Koya arrived, Earth had already passed on its orbit around the Sun. But given its mass, astronomers calculated that if Koya had struck the Earth, both planets would have been destroyed. Today, the remnants of Earth would be yet another asteroid belt orbiting around the Sun.

Now, it was time for Koya to make another trip through the solar system. With hundreds of telescopes across the planet, finding Koya should have been easier this time. But Koya was nowhere to be found. For two years, astronomers crossed the sky again and again searching for the dark iron rock. Four months ago, an astronomer happened to point his glass straight up. A black spot appeared to blot out the stars in a small portion of the sky. Each night, the black disk got a little larger. That growing disk was Koya, heading straight for Mars. Koya was still too far away to predict how close it would come to Mars, but this much was certain – Mars would be in the neighborhood when Koya crossed its orbital plane. And like its encounters with Venus and Earth, there was a small probability that it could hit Mars.

As astronomers watched Koya, they were frustrated by their inability to determine where Koya would be when it crossed the Martian orbital plane. Martians are a precise people and error is not easily accepted. But for whatever reason, Koya was proving to be a most difficult subject for analysis. Calculations changed daily and each new set of numbers raised or lowered the probability of an uncomfortably close flyby of Mars. No one had yet suggested that the two planets might strike each other, but there were certainly whispers among astronomers and physicists about the possibility.

Going from summer to fall in the northern hemisphere, observatories watched Koya tumble and wobble as it got closer and closer to Mars. Distant photographs of Koya hinted at wisps of steam or gas being ejected from vents on the surface. Inside the planet, Koya's iron core was still hot, still generating heat and instability from radioactive decay – the same forces at work today in the Earth's core and the reason for earthquakes and volcanoes around the world.

Three months before Mars and Koya would cross paths, the big telescopes confirmed what scientists had suspected. Active volcanoes were pushing steam and gas into space. The planet's crusty iron surface throttled these eruptions through small vents. The effect was to create powerful, highly focused bursts of thrust that pushed the planet in random directions. This fast-spinning, high-speed iron rock with its own jet pack was like an out-of-control freight train. And although the odds that two objects in three-dimensional space would occupy the same space at the same time, when its intermittent wobbles were factored in, it did seem possible that the planet had its sights on Mars.

As information about Koya started leaking to the press, the story took on new importance. Reporters covering the story noticed the way the scientific community began parsing its words when asked about Koya. Most denied that Koya posed a threat to Mars. However, a few scientists were now openly speculating that this rogue planet might strike Mars.

To counter speculation in the media about Koya, the government stepped up its own public information campaign. News releases from the government maintained that there was no scientific evidence that Koya was a danger to Mars. The government's reports quoted the most eminent astronomers, who insisted that Koya would pass close to, but would not strike Mars. But behind the scenes, more and more members of the scientific community were sounding alarms as their own calculations began to narrow the approach angle of the planet.

As the scientific community wrestled with the question of how close Koya would come to Mars, astute news junkies began noticing a subtle shift in words that the government used to report on Koya. Definite words were replaced with more vague-sounding declarations. Each news release sounded a bit less certain than the last one. The public was sensing that something was wrong. Maybe that grinning, late-night news anchor last summer was wrong. Maybe Koya would be more than just another interesting object in the nighttime sky.

3
The Underground

AT THE TIME of Koya's arrival, a visitor to Mars would find a modern planet, brimming with life, and built shore to shore with low, single story buildings. Manicured parks, playgrounds, and walking paths were everywhere. There was no honking traffic because there was no metal to build cars. This was a pedestrian-friendly planet.

The people looked healthy and happy, well-fed, and prosperous in a material sense. The Martian world before Koya was the realization of thousands of years of careful planning to make it look and work exactly like it did.

But after time, a visitor would notice what was missing – the means by which the Martians were able to enjoy their comfortable lifestyles. There were no factories to make the clothing, electronic devices, and the thousands of other goods that require complex materials management and assembly. Inside the stone homes were televisions on the walls, refrigerators filled with processed food, and all of the comforts of a modern society. But where were these things being made? And with so much food, where were the farms?

The answer was simple and elegant. Martians couldn't build higher, but they could go below-ground.

Beneath the surface is another world, known to Martians simply as the Underground. The Underground is a vast network of thousands of kilometers of tunnels, crossing the entire planet – under the land and the oceans. Everything needed for Martian society to function was there – power generation, manufacturing, and the planet's entire food production system. An efficient electric rail network crisscrossed the planet, delivering to the surface everything the Martians needed. Each day, millions of Martians commuted to the Underground to work. And each night, they came back to the surface to enjoy life under an open sky.

Interestingly, the beginnings of the Underground came when early miners began searching for raw materials. Maybe it was in their genes to dig or maybe it was gold fever, but it seemed that early Martians were hell-on-wheels when it came to tunneling. For half of their existence – a quarter-million years – miners dug tunnels everywhere, from pole to pole and in concentric rings that circled deeper and deeper into the planet. They searched for the same things miners on Earth have always sought. By the end of its mining period, after all of the gold, silver, platinum, and gemstones had been found, Mars had nearly as much space below-ground as it had on the surface.

But as the population soared, a land shortage made it harder and harder for citizens to find housing. By the beginning of Earth's second millennium – about 960 CE – the building industry announced that Mars was officially "built-out," meaning that there was no more undeveloped land on which to build. The planet's prosperity was threatened by a chronic housing shortage, with generations of Martians sharing the same small houses. Mars was becoming a very crowded place to live.

What's more, the planet's environment began to rebel against the loss of natural habitat. Mars needed more housing, but it also needed more green space. So, in an innovative attempt to reset the planet's environment by setting aside more natural space, the citizens decided to move their economy to the Underground.

The first to move to the Underground were factories. Large chambers were hollowed out of the rock and installed with thousands of manufacturing lines that produced everything from toothpaste to computers. The factories were automated with robots handling everything from the loading of raw materials at one end to the packaging of the finished products at the other. The manufactured goods were loaded onto electric trains that carried them to elevators, where they were delivered to the surface.

The empty spaces where factories used to be were cleared and replaced with parks, lakes, and natural habitats. It was an innovative and successful example of Martians working together for the common good. But it wasn't enough. Housing was still in short supply and even more green space was needed to keep the environment in balance. It was agriculture's turn.

As plans were made to move the farming sector to the Underground, agronomists developed new strains of crops that could thrive beneath the surface. Miners and engineers built special chambers for farming, layering the floors with a mixture of surface soil and nutrients from below ground that plants had long-ago exhausted on the surface. The atmosphere in these chambers was amended with nitrogen – an element scarce in the Martian atmosphere, but one that provided crops with more nutrients and more growth. Automated irrigation, lighting that mimicked the Sun, and robotic harvesters created an agricultural system that was efficient and immune to the variables of rainfall and temperature.

Crops thrived in the new environment and food production doubled and doubled again, producing an abundance of fresh vegetables, grains, legumes, and fruits. Martians, who had always been vegetarians, never had so much to eat. They were gaining weight and their kids and grandkids were getting taller and stronger.

To offset the seasonal rise and fall of lakes and reservoirs, a water storage system was also built in the Underground. Huge cisterns, capable of storing billions of liters of fresh water were connected together and to the surface reservoirs to replenish the lakes or to withdraw water during times of heavy rains. Mars also had a backup supply of water – the northern polar ice cap – that could be used during water shortages.

Energy had been the biggest barrier to Martian economic development. Mars has almost no concentrated hydrocarbons in the form of coal or oil. And even if it had these things, its carbon dioxide atmosphere would snuff out any attempt to burn them to make electricity. Early power stations relied on water power and wind, but the amount of electricity generated was too little. About 150 years ago, physicists discovered the formula for cold fusion, the same process that the Sun uses to make light and heat. But unlike the Sun, their process could produce nuclear fusion at a much lower temperature than the Sun – at just a few thousand degrees. It was the breakthrough Martian society needed – safe, clean, and almost unlimited electrical energy.

Hundreds of fusion power plants were built, the reactors located in the deepest levels of the Underground. Built in clusters of four to eight reactors, these power stations were connected to a planet-wide power grid, allowing all areas to be served with electricity even when some plants were shut down for maintenance. Unlike the farms and factories that were mostly automated, the fusion reactor network was staffed with trained technicians who monitored the units and maintained the delicate balance of heat and pressure needed to keep the fusion process working safely.

The final piece of infrastructure to move to the Underground was something Martians never had before – a way to quickly get around the planet. Using the existing tunnel network, high-speed rail lines were built. For the first time in their history, Martians could travel anywhere on the planet quickly and easily. Before the Underground rail system, there were few transportation options. Small electric vehicles could carry them short distances. But, there wasn't enough room on the surface to build highways or rail lines and all the bridges and support systems needed to maintain a large surface transportation network. Even in places where it had been tried, the transportation system had fallen into disrepair as the shortage of metals became chronic.

At the time of Koya's arrival, about one in five citizens worked in the Underground. But nearly everyone used the Underground transportation system to commute to jobs or to travel around the planet. The move to the Underground allowed businesses that once operated in small geographic areas to expand planet-wide. The economy prospered in this dual world, where the surface was used for living and the Underground served as the engine and support network for the economy.

And yet, try as they might, every attempt to build affordable housing in the Underground failed. The benefits of a modern transportation network, dining and recreation, and even the latest technological innovations in housing construction, were not enough to convince Martians to move there. Maybe it was claustrophobia or a genetic need to see the sky and grab what little light they could get from the distant Sun – but whatever the reasons – Martians would never willingly live in the Underground. And that would complicate things for the Martian government in the months ahead.

4
Naira's Inspection

THE STAFF ON Level 9 Northwest was buzzing with excitement. The President of the Martian Administrative Council, Naira Tuparnac, was visiting the Underground this morning. They knew the reason for her visit. For several weeks, thousands of team members on L9-NW had been logging double shifts to complete a secret project that Naira had ordered. The nature of the project and even the smallest details were kept secret from the population – even from the other members of the Council. But under the circumstances, Naira believed that secrecy was the best course, given the magnitude of the problem the planet might soon face.

Naira and her staff were met at the surface station by the director of L9-NW, a young woman named Sela Jaran. Her responsibilities in this sector included managing six fusion reactors. Sela welcomed the president and her staff before the group boarded an elevator for the eight kilometer ride down to Level 9.

The elevators that connected the surface with the Underground were so fast that riders initially suffered from motion sickness. But in recent years, the elevators had been updated to minimize the effects of the rapid descents. Sensors and servo-motors in the elevator car adjusted the floor to counteract the sensation of falling. The clear glass walls and doors changed to a white translucence to mask the movement of the car as it passed through the planet's crust. The atmosphere and pressure were adjusted as the riders went deeper into the planet. The combined effect was an elevator ride that took less than ninety seconds and produced almost no sensation of movement.

Naira had been to the Underground many times in her more than 500 years of life on Mars. A hundred thousand years ago, members of her line were among the miners who dug these shafts. She thought about the backbreaking toil of working in the dark underground, extracting the scarce minerals in the Martian crust. Many died building these shafts. Now, with Koya on the way, how terribly ironic would it be if this was the last refuge for the citizens of Mars?

During the ride down to Level 9, Sela provided a summary of the work that had been completed since Naira gave the order to start construction. The project was on schedule, she said, and aside from some power interruptions, the only part of the project that was falling behind was getting the fresh water they needed to fill the storage cisterns. Everyone was aware of the chronic water shortage on the surface and if water was diverted to the Underground, it might arouse suspicion. Sela said that she and the other district managers had a plan to tap into the polar ice cap reservoir to top-off the fresh-water supplies. They expected to have the engineering specifications ready for Naira to approve within a day.

As they approached Level 9, the elevator car slowed and adjusted pressure and floor tension to minimize the effects of inertia on the passengers. As the car eased to a stop, the glass walls became clear again, allowing Naira a 360-degree view of the station that served as a hub for many tunnels extending like spokes on a wheel to the horizon. The station walls were finished in a smooth granite. Shops and restaurants served commuters and workers – although for the time being, commuters were being routed to different stations to maintain the project's strict secrecy.

The place was bustling. Trains arrived and departed, delivering materials. Workers, in groups of three and four, hustled down corridors, carrying blueprints and a variety of hand and power tools. The air was dusty with construction material, but the ventilators were running full-blast, sending clean and cool air into the tunnels. Catalysts reworked the chemistry, mixing-in a jolt of oxygen, which seemed to have a positive effect on Martians working in the Underground.

As Naira stepped off the elevator, she was greeted by the applause of a large group of workers, who were dressed in white coveralls and hardhats. Naira walked toward the group, facing them with a smile and modestly waving off their applause. She greeted each one of them, shaking their hands and thanking them for their work. Then, she moved to the center of the group, which stepped back a few paces to give her room.

Naira was a legend on Mars, championing many of the economic and cultural changes over the past few hundred years that improved life on the planet and gave more people the opportunity to pursue their passions. She thanked the

group and praised the work they had done in completing the
project in such a short period of time. Naira also acknowledged that most of these workers had not seen their families
in weeks. But she assured them that their sacrifices would
make a difference as Mars prepared for the possibility of an
impact with Koya.

Sela added her own thanks and, as the group dispersed
and went back to work, she escorted the president to a waiting
train that would take them another ten kilometers north to
the purpose of her visit. Naira was quiet during the ride. She
tried to imagine getting millions of reluctant citizens to come
down here. *If Koya struck Mars, could they even survive? And
if they did, how long would they be stuck here before returning
to the surface?* There were a lot of unknowns, but Naira was
sure of one thing – the Underground was the only chance
the Martian people had to continue their civilization if Koya
struck. And this experimental station would prove that, if
necessary, citizens could live here.

With each passing day, the Martian government was
coming to the conclusion that Koya would strike Mars. The
public had not yet been told because Naira still didn't have
a definitive answer from the Director of the Astronomical
Society, her old friend, Dr. Tal Anak. He had the unenviable
job of collating all of the disparate information about Koya
that was coming in from observatories all over the planet.
In a call earlier in the day, Naira and Tal agreed that there
would be a go or no-go decision made this afternoon. Unless
he could absolutely assure Naira that Koya would miss the
planet, she would order full-scale construction of emergency living quarters across the planet. During her visit to the
Underground, Naira held tightly to her mobile phone, waiting
for word from Tal.

The train ride north lasted only a few minutes. It stopped in front of large doors that opened to a wide hallway, connecting a series of large chambers – sixteen in this cluster. Each chamber was 30 meters high and 500 meters square. Inside the chambers, thousands of housing units had been assembled, built with varying numbers of beds – from two to as many as twelve. Around each housing unit, rigid silicon wallboard was assembled for privacy, complete with wired lights and translucent windows, giving the space the appearance of private living quarters. The ceilings remained open to allow for light and ventilation. The beds were stacked in twos and each bed was equipped with drawers underneath that were large enough to hold a month's worth of clothing and personal effects.

The group walked up and down the aisles, inspecting the living units. Each had a table and chairs, as well as upholstered furniture, and a small computer. At many intersections, play areas were built with jungle gyms and other playground equipment. Park benches and picnic tables were everywhere – familiar references to the public parks on the surface.

Naira smiled at Sela. She was very pleased with the work that had been done.

"Sela, how many citizens can you accommodate in each of these chambers?" Naira asked.

"Each chamber can hold 4,000 citizens," Sela answered. "So this pod of sixteen housing chambers would be able to accommodate as many as 64,000 citizens."

"And how many pods are operational?"

"Well, I can speak only for Level 9 Northwest, but all eight pods are finished.

"So your total capacity would be?"

"More than a half-million citizens."

"Excellent work," Naira said, smiling. "May I see the dining facilities?"

"Of course, Madam President," Sela said. They walked out of the housing section and crossed a pedestrian bridge over the train tracks that ran down the center of the tunnel. On the other side was another set of large chambers, but these were outfitted with dining furniture. Glass counters were constructed every eight tables in a lattice that formed throughout the dining hall. The design allowed anyone sitting at the tables to be no more than a few meters from the nearest food station. Overhead, conveyors delivered food to the serving stations.

Naira noticed the little touches that Sela and her team built into the design. Plates and utensils were whisked away on return conveyors, eliminating the need for waste cans to be emptied. At the food stations, some of the beverage dispensers were set at half the normal height to let children get their own drinks. Large ventilators removed the cooking odors, keeping the dining room air clean and fresh.

Naira looked in amazement at all that had been done. She couldn't even imagine the effort that Sela and everyone working underground had devoted to this project since Naira gave the order. She turned to Sela and gave her a warm hug.

Crossing over the bridge, Naira took one last look at the living quarters. If she had any doubts about an evacuation to the Underground, Sela's team had dispelled them. *Yes. Yes! This will work!* she thought, as she boarded the train back to the central station. There, she and her aides would get on another train, this one bound for Arens, the planet's capital.

During the inspection, Naira's phone buzzed. It was Tal Anak, giving her the news she dreaded. He said that there was a seventy-percent chance that Koya would strike Mars. She instructed her aides to call the Administrative Council for an emergency meeting that would be held tonight. At its conclusion, Naira would expect the Council to approve construction of evacuation shelters like these, all over Mars. Tomorrow, after the Administrative Council made its decision, Naira would go on television and tell everyone about Koya.

So, it is really coming. In a month, this place will be filled with terrified citizens. She lowered her head and closed her eyes as the train began moving.

Naira raised her head again and leaned closer to Sela.

"Will you please contact the other district managers and tell them to begin construction?" Naira whispered. "Tell them you have authorization from the Administrative Council."

"So it is really happening?" Sela asked with tears welling in her eyes.

"Yes, my dear," Naira said, putting her arm around Sela's shoulder. "What you have done here will save millions. Now, we must carry on."

Sela wiped her tears and put on a brave face. By tomorrow, construction plans would be in the hands of every district manager on Mars. The Underground would be made ready for the hundreds of millions of citizens who would soon need to evacuate.

As Sela pulled herself together, Naira gently squeezed her hand in a final gesture of appreciation.

5
The Administrative Council

AFTER A HALF-MILLION years of civilization, Martians had worked out most of the kinks of living together on a small, crowded planet. Behavior that damaged the fabric of society – war, violence, and prejudice – had long been eliminated. Much of the change in Martian thought and behavior was evolutionary. Survival favored cooperation over competition. But there was another reason. It was something that seemed to be part of their genetic makeup. Everyone was in the same small boat – or in this case – the same small, resource-poor planet, where self-serving behavior would not succeed.

The planet had no police force because there were no property crimes or acts of violence that required rules and enforcers of rules. The occasional minor disputes were settled in arbitration. More often, these conflicts were settled by the individuals directly. It's hard to stay mad at your neighbor when you might be living next to each other for centuries.

On Earth, the Roman empire had been dismantled after a thousand years of conquest and absorption. Filling the vacuum were the great seafaring nations – England, Spain, France, Portugal, and Holland. Their wooden sailing ships circled the globe, and the mere planting of their flag on whatever land they reached gave them legal claim of ownership, despite opinions the locals might have to the contrary. Wars were fought to hold or expand the territorial riches of their monarchs.

Mars never had a similar epoch of empires or nation-states, fighting for land, resources, or for ideological reasons. The planet's small size, and the fact that its single continental land mass could be traversed without crossing over any oceans, prevented the formation of tribes or distinct ethnic groups. Without borders, Martians continuously moved from place to place in search of a better life. Through intermarriage, the citizens were shaped into a single, homogenized people, with no geographic or ethnic loyalties through which leaders could rally citizens to take up arms against each other.

By the time of Koya's arrival, the Martian government had devolved into an administrative body. As many citizens liked to say, the Administrative Council's job was delivering the mail and keeping the lights on. Actually, managing the underpinnings of a society of 1.5 billion citizens was much more complicated than most realized. Although Mars didn't have a centrally-planned economy, the government had a large role in managing the environment and the planet's natural resources. It also served as a backstop for private enterprises, untangling knots in the supply and distribution systems that kept goods and services moving across the planet.

Most importantly, the government served as a protector of rights, ensuring that every citizen had access to the same resources, whether it was education, work opportunities, or the distribution of food, water, and consumer goods. Good governance, as defined by the Martian people, was protecting the population so that they could perform at their best, in whatever work they chose.

But after tonight, the definition of government would need to be amended. There was a threat out there – an existential threat of a kind that Mars had never faced before. And the only sitting authority capable of dealing with it was the Administrative Council.

The Council had eleven elected seats, chosen at-large. This meant that members did not represent a region or a particular constituency. The term of office was for life. And, since the lifespan of a Martian could be 600 years, some of the members of the Council had been at their posts for a very long time. Each member was well-known to the public, although their higher profile in Martian society was more about respect for the office, rather than the star-power of the individual members.

The council was not a full-time assembly. There was no need for a standing legislative body because the rules and regulations governing the planet could fill a three-ring binder. Instead, the Council met when needed – called to order by any member.

The day-to-day functions of government were handled by a layer of well-qualified managers who reported to the Council. Their areas of responsibility were changed every five years to give them broader administrative experience and to prevent the formation of alliances or cliques through which personal agendas could be pursued.

The council met in Arens, a city of over a million citizens, located on the Martian equator. Long ago, this place had been the junction of trade routes that crisscrossed the continent, so placing the seat of government here made sense. Meetings took place in the Assembly Building, an ordinary-looking, one-story stone structure. Walking by, one would never know that the planet's government was based in this modest structure. The building had few inscriptions and no ornate columns or other grandiose appendages to indicate some sort of enlarged importance of government in the Martian culture. Martians had little tolerance for pomposity or self-aggrandizement, and the design of the Assembly Building reflected the small role that the government played in the lives of the citizens.

Inside the Assembly Building was a large theater, used mainly for public events. Across from the theater was a conference room with a circular table that was used when the Administrative Council was called into session. The 600-year-old stone building also had a number of smaller rooms where managers could meet with their staffs. No one, not even the President of the Administrative Council, had an official office with their name on the door.

In the hallway that divided the theater from the conference room, the stone walls were covered in relief carvings, depicting the history of the Martian people. In exquisite detail, artisans over the centuries created these panels, which were assembled like a jigsaw puzzle on the walls. Each panel was made by a different artist and depicted their interpretation of an historical period of Mars. Walking the hallway, visitors to the Assembly Building could view the progress of Martian culture, from its early days as a nomadic people, to the building of modern cities. Many famous artists had their work here, but each was given only one panel. By the time of Koya's arrival, the hallway was nearly filled. Only a few spaces remained empty, waiting for future artists.

Naira walked alone down the hallway to the conference room. Aside from a brief nap on the train after her inspection tour, she had slept very little in the last two days. It was unlikely that she would get any sleep tonight, either. *No matter,* she thought, *my work will soon be done.*

She stopped for a moment to view one of the reliefs. This panel, depicting an early agricultural settlement, was carved by her husband Kalay – a gifted doctor and artist who died sixty years ago. Their marriage produced only one child and one grandchild, a youngster who was destined to do great things for Mars, if only she could save him and the rest of her people.

Naira entered the conference room where the other members were already seated at the large, granite table. An agenda was set in front of each of them. It had just one item of business – the evacuation of the planet. Staff members and stenographers were already in place. Food and beverages were available at tables along the walls. It was going to be a long night and Naira knew that the council members always worked at their best on full stomachs.

The meeting was called to order promptly at 6 p.m. As the Council's president, a position she held for the past seventy years, Naira's main job was to push meetings to conclusion – something not easy with ten other members who each had at least *one* opinion on any subject. But among these, one member reigned supreme. Sitting directly across from her was Dr. Karal Malik, a philosopher and teacher by training and a pain in the ass by choice. It was said that the brilliant and irascible Malik had been on the Council since the planet first cooled. Malik saw his role as the Council's equivalent to the loyal opposition in a parliamentary system of government. The phrase, "Just one moment, Madame President," was seared into the brains of everyone sitting at this table.

Naira smiled warmly at the members and gave Malik a wink, a seductive gesture in the Martian culture, which only served to make him even more ill-tempered than usual. Naira told the Council that Dr. Malik was celebrating a wedding anniversary tomorrow, a feat, she said, that was difficult to understand on many levels. Considering the man, she wasn't far from the truth. The Council laughed at the remark and she even got a slight smile out of the old man himself.

A holographic projector rose from the center of the table. It came alive with a detailed image of Mars and the fast-approaching Koya. Lines, arrows, and text popped up and over and around the images, providing additional information about the inbound planet and its projected heading.

As Mars spun benignly on its axis, Naira began a measured and deliberate presentation of the situation. On the ride to Arens, her staff had been in touch with Tal Anak, who provided them with his final report on Koya. Naira's staff distilled the report into a dozen or so three-dimensional slides.

No one at the table spoke during Naira's presentation. Electronic copies of the slides were delivered to their handheld devices the minute the presentation was over. Although they had been briefed daily since Koya was first detected three months ago, it wasn't until tonight that the Council learned that, in a little more than one month, Koya would likely strike Mars.

The projector blinked off and disappeared below the table surface. Naira rose to deliver her summation. A lawyer by training, Naira had long-ago given up her law practice. Her profession was obsolete, as citizens settled into a new order that no longer required legal services. But her training in

oratory still served her well and she was determined to move
the pilot program she inspected earlier today into full-pro-
duction before Koya arrived.

Allow me to summarize what you have just seen, Koya
will strike Mars in thirty-two days. We don't know
whether the impact will be direct or whether Koya will
strike Mars in a glancing blow.

Naira moved around the table as she spoke, standing
between the seated members in a physical show of solidarity.

If the latter happens, there is a reasonable chance that
we can save a large portion of the population by evac-
uating them to the Underground. I believe the living
areas that you saw in the presentation will be adequate
to house our people for an extended period during
surface recovery and repair.

As she moved around the table, she watched the expres-
sions on the members' faces. Everyone was in shock.

In the opinion of the team working on the pilot project,
the Underground has more than enough room to house
everyone who will want to evacuate. Manufacturing
lines have been re-tooled to produce beds, furniture,
medical supplies – everything citizens will need.

Naira finally reached the seat of her nemesis. Malik stared
straight ahead, not looking up at Naira as she concluded her
remarks.

Tonight, in what might be the last formal session of the Council, I ask for your votes to approve this plan. May I see a show of hands of those who agree?

Naira walked back to her seat and sat down. The tension in the room was palpable. None of the staff moved as the Council members sat stunned, trying to get their minds around everything they had just seen. Naira's logic was perfect. There was no other choice. Evacuation was the only way to save the population from an event over which they had no control.

With Naira's hand already raised, other hands started to rise. First one, then two more, and then three others. After a minute passed, ten hands were raised. There was just one dissenter.

It was Malik, of course. Someone once remarked that if the Council were to vote to make him Emperor of Mars, he would still need a week to think about it. Then, he would vote *no*. And here he was, staring into the abyss, unable to put aside his penchant for argument, when the answer to the problem was so clear.

"So, we have ten votes in favor. Dr. Malik, you are not voting in favor of the proposal. Is that correct, sir?" Naira asked.

"That is correct, Madam President," he said. "I cannot agree with this plan."

"May we know the reason for your objection, Dr. Malik?" Naira was being as respectful as she could, but was also determined to pry a *yes* vote from this man before the evening was concluded.

"First, I strenuously object to your working independently, spending treasury resources without the Council's approval," Malik said, as he smiled sarcastically at Naira.

"You are right, Dr. Malik," Naira replied. "What I did was wrong. I acted on my own. But if that is the only thing stopping you from voting *yes*, I will resign from the Council tonight," Naira said, placing her political head on the chopping block. It was a small price to pay, considering the magnitude of the problem.

Malik stared at her for a moment. He inhaled sharply as if to argue the point, and then exhaled without responding. A second or two later, he did reply.

"No, that is not the reason." Malik stopped talking and lowered his head.

"It is our only hope, Karal," Naira said quietly. Her eyes grew kinder as she waited for Malik to express what each member of the Council was feeling – a great sadness in the loss that was to come to their planet. Instead of arguing, Malik sagged in his chair, staring off blankly, unable to speak. Finally, he pushed his chair away from the table, stood, and started walking toward the door.

"Karal, wait," Naira called out.

Malik stopped but kept his back to the Council as he tried to regain his composure. He turned and walked over to Naira's seat.

"I am sorry, Naira. We have had many differences over the years. But your motives have always been pure." Malik stopped and his head drooped.

"What is it Karal?" another member of Council asked.

"It's the loss of all of this," Malik said as he looked around the room. After a moment, he spoke again. "Yes. I change my vote to *yes*. But I will not evacuate. I will stay here, in the capital, to do whatever needs to be done."

"And I will be here with you," Naira replied.

"You are not going to the Underground?"

"No, I am staying here in Arens with you."

"And me," another Council member added.

"I will also," a second member declared.

All of the members raised their hands. Everyone would stay in the capital. The Administrative Council would not allow an iron rock from who-knows-where to dictate the duties of their offices. The Administrative Council would operate as long as there was a planet to run.

Malik stared back at the table of raised hands and saw the smiles each one was showing him. His eyes were filled with tears. For the first time that anyone could recall, Malik returned the smile. "Thank you. Thank you. Now, if you will excuse me for about an hour, Madam President, I have an urgent matter to attend to."

"What is it, Karal?" Naira asked, causing Malik to stop in mid-step.

Without turning, he said, "I have to go out and buy an anniversary present for my wife. Until you reminded me, I had forgotten the date."

The room burst into laughter as Malik started walking again. Naira called out to him as he opened the door. "How many times has that happened?"

"Every anniversary, I think," Malik said, as he turned and smiled at the Council before leaving.

6
The News Conference

TWO MONTHS TO the day after the first mention of Koya on a late-night television newscast, the Martian government called a news conference in Arens. Although Mars had an active and thriving media, news conferences at the Assembly Building were rare. The reporters were not given a reason for the news conference, but most believed that it had something to do with the heat wave and the water shortage.

None of the council members got more than an hour or two of sleep after their overnight session. Even Malik came back after patching things up with his wife and making reservations for a belated anniversary dinner tonight.

By the time reporters arrived and started poking around, all evidence of the Council meeting had been removed. They were guided into the theater, which usually had some sort of staging for a play or concert. But this morning, the stage had no set – just a deep purple curtain across the back. In front was a long table with eleven seats facing the audience. Microphones were placed at each seat, along with folders that seemed to have very little paper inside.

Naira stood off-stage, peering through the curtains at the audience. With only a minute or so before the conference was scheduled to begin, Naira stepped away and sat down in front of a computer. She typed in some numbers to make a video call. The call went through and her daughter, Tamara, picked up on the second ring.

"Mom?" Tamara answered, rubbing her eyes, trying to focus on the screen. "Is everything all right? Shouldn't you be preparing for your news conference? When does it start?"

"About a minute ago," Naira answered, laughing with her daughter. It is a universal truth – politicians don't like reporters and making them wait for news conferences to begin is one of the little pleasures of public office.

"Listen, honey, this news conference – it's going to be big. The biggest thing in our lives. I just wanted to call to make sure you are home and safe and that you have Kai with you. Is he there?"

Just as she spoke, a little blur flew into the picture. It was Kai, just a toddler, climbing up on his mother's lap to look into the computer screen. He was wearing a helmet, the kind that a miner might use. Only this one was way too big for his head and it flopped forward, covering his large black eyes. He pulled it off to look into the screen.

"Grannie!" Kai squealed with delight to see Naira on the screen. The two talked nearly every night and shared a very special relationship. "Want to see the toy I just built?" Kai asked, holding up a chunk of silvery material, attached to some glued paper and sticks. It resembled nothing she had ever seen before.

"Yes, I can see your toy, honey. Can you tell Grannie what it is?"

"It's a spaceship. Isn't it neat?"

Tamara grinned at her mother from behind Kai. "Yes, Kai, I think that would make an ideal spaceship," Naira said. "Where do you plan to go in it?"

"Dunno. Some place way far away. Maybe the Sun. Hey, let's go together?" Kai replied as he tinkered with his invention. He was already losing focus and going back into his own reverie, no doubt dreaming of space travel. "I know! I'll be the first Martian to walk on the blue planet, the one with all the water."

"Maybe you will, Kai," Naira said, holding back a flood of tears that had been waiting for days to be released. Only, not right now. Not with Kai looking at her.

Tamara sensed her mother's anguish. "Kai, Mommy has to talk with Grannie for a second. Grannie will call you tonight," Tamara said as she put Kai down. The kid was gone the minute his feet touched the floor. "Bye, Grannie!" Kai shouted, already sprinting into another room.

Naira and Tamara laughed for a moment, but Tamara remembered what her mother said when she first called. "Mom, you look very tired. What's going on?"

"Don't worry, honey. But, Tamara, please hold Kai for awhile. It will make me feel better knowing that the two of you are together," Naira said, her eyes starting to well-up. "Look I have to go or old man Malik will shuffle on-stage and try running the meeting himself. Talk to you soon."

With that, Naira closed the screen and joined the rest of the Council, preparing to take the stage. Tamara would learn soon enough what was going on, but Naira wanted to make sure the extremely bright and impressionable Kai had a backstop to answer questions as his grandmother spoke. Even at his young age, Kai would understand most of what was being said. An extraordinary child in a world of extraordinary people, Kai was a once-in-a-generation child – even if only his grandmother thought so.

The room got quiet as the eleven members of the Council walked single file to their seats on stage. As they sat, they avoided eye contact with the reporters. After a few minutes of hushed conversation with Malik seated on one side and another council member on the other, Naira tapped a gavel that was placed in front of her and adjusted the microphone. She was glad that she didn't have to stand.

Taking a sheet of paper from the folder placed in front of her, Naira began reading a prepared statement. She spoke slowly and carefully.

The Administrative Council welcomes you to the capital this morning. We are here to make an announcement regarding the planetary object known as Koya.

Naira stopped reading for a few seconds. This was no orator's trick to build tension. Rather, viewers could see that she was visibly shaken by what she was going to say next and needed time to gather herself. She finally looked up again and continued reading.

For the past three months, the scientific community has studied Koya, a planet in our solar system that arrives every 412 years. Koya is unusual in that it cuts across the orbit of Mars and the other planets in the inner solar system. Until now, we assumed that it would pass safely behind Mars as our planet orbits around the Sun.

Reporters were shifting nervously in their seats, getting a hint of what was coming next. This was more serious than a few hot summer nights.

It has been difficult to plot Koya's exact course, because the planet does not behave in ways that are consistent with normal planetary mechanics. But, we have finally determined Koya's course.

Naira paused again for a few seconds, now looking directly into the pool camera that was providing the same video to all of the networks. The camera's red light blazed in her eyes, reminding her that more than a billion Martians were watching. What she would say next had never been spoken on Mars. For this, she no longer needed a script.

Thirty-one days from today, Koya will arrive. There is a high probability that it will strike Mars. We believe that the two planets will brush alongside each other instead of hitting directly. While any contact with Koya will cause destruction, we believe that our civilization can survive if we evacuate to the Underground. Preparations are already underway to provide living quarters for everyone. There is abundant food and water and we are working to make the time in the Underground as comfortable as possible.

The theater's acoustics bounced her last words back into her ears. All over the planet, Martians stood in front of their televisions, stunned as they listened to Naira's words. She paused for a moment to let the audience catch up with her. Then, she continued:

Evacuation will begin in one week. Each citizen will receive an electronic communication, providing a registration code and instructions for evacuation. Depending on the severity of the impact, we believe that we can return to the surface to start rebuilding in two to four weeks. The Council urges all of you to make preparations to evacuate as soon as possible.

Naira was nearly done. But she needed to speak directly to those who would not evacuate. The Council estimated that a third of the population would rather perish on the surface than go to the Underground. There was no way to know exactly how many until registrations began. Naira understood that each citizen had the right to evacuate or not. The only thing she could do was to use the power of her office to try to persuade those who were undecided.

As a free people, each of us has the choice to evacuate or not. But let me be very clear. Anyone who is on the surface at the time of impact will die from the searing heat and the shock waves that will follow the impact. The Administrative Council strongly urges you to evacuate. Now, we will take questions.

The room exploded with voices, each trying to catch the attention of the president. Naira pointed at one particularly energetic reporter.

"Madam President, how long has the Council known that Koya would strike Mars?"

"We learned this last night," Naira said. "Koya's course has been difficult to plot."

"How can you be certain that Koya will strike the planet," another reporter shouted out. This was no time for decorum.

"We are not certain," Naira said. "The scientific community places the chances at seventy-percent."

"So it could miss?" the reporter asked.

"Were you not listening?" Malik jumped in. There were times when his temper was appreciated. "The Council President just told you that there is a seventy-percent chance of impact."

The young reporter withered under Malik's glare. Few could go more than a round or two with the old man before leaving the ring.

"Madam President, how sure are you that Koya will only glance the planet instead of hitting it directly?"

"We're not sure," Naira replied. "If Koya does hit Mars directly, there is little chance that we will survive. All we can do is prepare and hope that Koya will miss or graze us as it passes by."

"What will happen when Koya arrives?" another reporter asked, almost innocently.

Naira looked down the table at Dr. Pao Tama, a retired physicist, who had been the conduit for information about Koya between the scientific community and the Council.

"Koya will appear larger in the sky each night," Tama began. "Soon, you will be able to see it even during the day. As Koya enters our atmosphere, friction will produce heat so intense that no one who is still on the surface can survive. Then, when Koya strikes, shock waves will destroy most of the buildings." He looked back at Naira who nodded in approval at his stark depiction of what would happen. It helped make her case that everyone should evacuate.

Silence returned to the theater. There wasn't much more to ask. Naira wanted to end the conference and allow viewers the opportunity to process the information and to respond to the electronic communications that were now being sent to every household on the planet. She looked at the members on either side of her and nodded that it was time to leave the stage.

With that, the Council members rose in unison and walked in single-file off the stage. Television reporters, still broadcasting live with their anchor teams, turned to their cameras and recapped what the Council had just presented. Back in the television studios, producers scrambled to find experts who could speak about Koya in more detail. The scientific community had been uncommonly quiet over the past few weeks, a fact that was conveniently disguised by other breaking news of the day.

One of the networks, based in the capital, was able to lasso Dr. Isi Wayna, a prominent astronomer who taught at Arens University. The professor appeared calm as he sat under the television lights, waiting to take incoming fire from the anchor team. But there was a reason for his calm demeanor. He and every other member of the scientific community had a head start in preparing for the reality of Koya's arrival.

Before going live, the studio producer told Dr. Wayna that he would have an almost unlimited amount of time. She said that he would be asked to explain the details of Koya and its effects on Mars. After a commercial break, the anchor introduced his guest and asked him to provide some background.

Dr. Wayna summarized Koya's history, its unusual orbit, and its likely origin as a rogue planet. He explained that this irregular-shaped ball of iron weighed a great deal more than Mars and was big enough to turn Mars into rubble if it struck directly. But as the Council said, Koya would graze Mars, not hit it directly.

"So, Dr. Wayna," the anchor interrupted, "What will happen when the two planets *graze each other*, as you described it?"

"Well, without getting into the physics of it all, what happens will depend on Koya's speed, its angle of attack, and how much of the surface of the two planets is placed in physical contact," Dr. Wayna explained. "Also, gravitational forces will be at play and we're not sure how the two planets will react to the force of the other's gravity."

"So, you really don't know the outcome of the impact, do you?" the anchor asked, hoping for more detail. But since Koya refused to reveal much about itself, there was a lot that astronomers still didn't know.

"All that we can say is that a glancing impact is certainly preferable to a direct hit," Dr. Wayna returned. "But nothing like this has ever been observed, so we really can't predict the final outcome."

"Well, is evacuation really a viable option?" the anchor said, suggesting that evacuation might be futile, in direct opposition to what the Council had just recommended. Dr. Wayna and his family planned to evacuate and he did not want the anchorman to contradict what most members of the scientific community believed was the best option for survival.

"As the Council President stated..."

"Yes, yes, we know, Doctor," the anchor interrupted. "We heard what she said at the news conference. My question to you is this – are you really going to evacuate?"

The professor's eyes flashed with anger. This anchorman was looking for a controversy in a place where there was none. Koya was real. The effect of the impact was not known. Evacuation didn't guarantee anything. The planet might be destroyed. Those were the facts. Nothing he could say would reveal some deep secrets about why it had taken so long to discover Koya's intentions and why the scientific community still couldn't tell with certainty what the outcome would be. Dr. Wayna decided that he didn't want to play anymore.

"Yes. I will be evacuating," he said. "And while I hope that you evacuate as well, it is my fervent hope that you will be as far away from me and my family as possible." Some of the crew behind the cameras laughed. Dr. Wayna stood up, removed his microphone, and walked off the set – the camera following him as he left the lighted stage for the darkness behind the cameras.

There was a pregnant pause as the flummoxed anchor tried to figure out what to do next. The floor director snapped her fingers to alert him to the active camera that had pulled in on him. He switched on his official anchorman grin and said, "Well, I guess we'll be back after these messages."

7

The Astronomers

TAL ANAK MUTED the sound on his television. He had just watched his old friend Naira tell the rest of the planet what he and other astronomers had known for a while – that Koya was coming and that it would change Mars forever.

Like everyone else who watched this morning, Tal simply stood in front of the television while Naira spoke. She called him just a few minutes before walking out on stage, grasping at one last straw of hope before going on-record. Tal broke down when he told her that he had nothing more to add to what he sent her yesterday. Koya was going to hit Mars.

Through his tears, he asked Naira to forgive him for not having something more hopeful to offer. Like the great leader she was, Naira was comforting him when it was he who should have been giving her strength to go out on the stage and tell everyone what was about to happen. She ended the call by telling him that she and her husband had always loved Tal and his wife and hoped that she would see both of them in the Underground.

Ten minutes after the news conference ended, Tal received another call. This one was from one of his deputy directors, a bright and dedicated astronomer who had been living for weeks at the huge telescope complex atop the dormant *Olympus Mons* volcano. The observatory had some of the best glass on the planet. The astronomer called to report that Koya had just made another course adjustment.

The news wasn't good. In fact, it was the worst. He told Tal that Koya's new course would be a direct hit on Mars, not the bump that the government was depending on. Koya's new heading would destroy Mars.

Tal sat down at his computer and watched the stream of data and images being sent by his colleague. Koya wobbled again, with long-streams of gas shooting from massive geysers on the side of the planet. There was now proof that volcanic activity was responsible for Koya's erratic motions. This planet had its own set of built-in thrusters. Tal cursed at this flying death machine that almost seemed intent on destroying Mars.

As his deputy continued speaking, Tal could only shake his head as he read the data. Everything Tal told the Council last night was wrong. There was no need to evacuate because no one would survive – above or below the surface. How could he possibly call her now with news that was even worse than before – that evacuation was futile?

Tal thanked his young colleague for the update and asked if he would assemble his team in front of the computer so that Tal could speak to all of them. In less than a minute, four astronomers stood within view of the computer's camera. Each was wearing the same kind of white coat Tal wore over 400 years ago when he was on duty at the very same observatory, tracking Koya the last time it passed through the solar system. Never did he imagine that he would be alive to witness its return, let alone its intent on destroying his planet. It was the cruelest of ironies that Tal was going to correct immediately after he completed this call.

"My dear friends, I am going ask a great favor. I am going to ask that you not share this new information with anyone else." Tal could see the surprised looks on the faces of these scientists he had trained. Understanding their confusion, Tal asked them to consider the larger picture – the psychological effect on the population if their one last hope had been dashed. Wasn't it better to leave things as they were?

"Can I be assured of your promises of silence?" Tal asked pointedly.

The four stared back at their boss, the most esteemed astronomer on the planet. He was breaking the first rule of science – always seek the truth. But sometimes, seeking the truth can be separated from telling the truth, and such was the case now. Each of them nodded their assent, then folded their hands in front of them and bowed in respect.

"Thank you all. Please make your own decisions on whether you will evacuate," Tal said. "I wish for each of you, peace and comfort. Farewell."

Tal returned the bow and turned off the connection. He got up from the computer and walked slowly back into the living room, where he sat down in an old chair. It had been days since he slept. His wife, Rayen, had been in the Underground for the past week, working on the housing construction program. They spoke frequently, but he missed having her here with him, feeling her warm embrace.

Tal called his wife, but she did not pick up. They argued the last night they were together, after he told her that he would not evacuate. She begged him to reconsider, saying that she couldn't understand why he would want to die and leave her behind. The ebb and flow of persuasive reasoning went back and forth well into the night. The next morning, Rayen received a call that she was urgently needed in the Underground. Rayen told Tal that it was unlikely that she would return to the surface before impact. Again, she pleaded with him to evacuate.

Tal walked with his wife to the Underground station. As she waited for an elevator to take her below, they embraced. Tal kissed Rayen softly and whispered that he would join her as soon as the announcement had been made by the Administrative Council. She hugged him tighter and gave him one last kiss before getting on the elevator.

But there were no bags packed at the front door when the news conference ended. Tal sat motionless in his chair, listening to Rayen's soft voice on her voice mail as she asked the caller to leave her a message. He hesitated leaving a recorded message, but there was no time left. He explained that he still had some data files that needed to be processed before he could evacuate. But, he promised that they would have dinner together tomorrow night. He ended his message by telling Rayen that loved her and would always love her.

Tal hung up the phone and picked up the small bottle of pills that he placed on the end table last week after seeing Rayen off. Nearby was a half-empty glass that contained a very potent alcoholic beverage made from fermented legumes that grew in the southern hemisphere. The portion he drank during the news conference was already starting to affect his judgment, but not so much as to prevent him from doing what he had planned to do next.

Tal could not evacuate. Try as he might, and weighing everything that he would lose, he could not will himself to evacuate. Koya broke him and he would never forgive himself,

somehow believing that he could have done more to prevent
what was to come. Even if no one would allow him to accept
any blame for what would happen, Tal reconciled himself
with the thought that, even as a young child, he was destined
to study the universe. Underground, without a night sky over
his head, Tal saw no further reason to live.

Tal opened the bottle, which hissed with the sound of gas
escaping. The ten blue pills had been sealed to preserve them.
But once opened, as a safety measure, the user had only one
minute to consume them before their ingredients became
inert. This was designed to prevent an accident or to protect
someone who might have second thoughts about suicide. But
Tal had no doubts. In one swift movement, he poured the
ten blue pills into his mouth and followed them with a long
swallow from the glass he held in his other hand.

The drug was pain-free and incredibly fast-acting. In less
than a minute, Tal was dead. The empty bottle fell to the floor
and Tal's head settled sideways on the back of the chair.

The phone rang. It was Rayen calling him back. But he did
not pick up. Nor would the phone be answered as she continued calling for the next twelve hours. That night, she got word
from a neighbor who had brought Tal some dinner. Her team
refused to allow her back to the surface.

The next day, a date-released electronic message appeared
on her computer. Tal wrote eloquently of his love for Rayen
and hoped that she could forgive him for his selfishness and
for breaking his promise. Rayen understood. Deep down, she
knew Tal would never come down here. Through her tears,
she smiled at the thought of the man she loved, a man who
had but two passions – his wife and the universe outside his
back door.

8
Evacuation

TWO HOURS AFTER the news conference ended, every Martian had received an electronic message from the government, explaining the evacuation procedures and giving them their assigned location. Housing in the Underground was being constructed in proportion to the size of the population above, so that residents would not have to travel far to evacuate. As soon as they registered, their housing space was confirmed, eliminating the need to rush or stand in long lines.

The message also included a warning. It said that the elevators leading to the Underground would shut down and the elevator shafts would be sealed exactly one hour before impact. There would be no exceptions. The reason had to do with the atmosphere in the Underground. They could not risk the possibility that breathable air below ground would be sucked out as the Martian atmosphere reacted to contact with Koya.

As predicted, a majority of citizens registered to evacuate. But a significant number – thirty-one percent – chose to remain on the surface. Such was their right. Martians viewed personal choice as a cornerstone of their civilization and this included the right to decide when to die. Assisted suicide and the preferred method – by quick-acting self-medication – had been legal for hundreds of years. Reports were coming in of more and more self-medicated deaths. This included the death of Tal Anak and a number of prominent astronomers who had been tracking Koya for months and felt they somehow failed their people.

For the first time in history, the Administrative Council remained in continuous session. It was fortuitous that government managers had been trained in so many different duties because getting the Underground ready was not the work of specialists, but of generalists who could just as easily pick up a shovel and dig as type commands into a computer. Everyone was pitching in, doing whatever was necessary to complete construction of the evacuation centers.

Six days before impact, with Koya now bigger than a hand held up in front of it, construction on the evacuation shelters was nearing completion. Underground reservoirs were full, with enough water for two months. Food supplies were more than adequate and the entire agriculture system was available to add more food as needed. Factories that a month ago were building televisions and other consumer goods, had switched to a list of essential items needed for evacuees and rescue workers who would return to the surface to survey the damage.

On the surface, the stifling heat of the Martian summer had vanished and beautiful, cooler fall weather visited the northern hemisphere. In the south, spring was just beginning, but forecasts were optimistic that the south would not suffer the heat wave that afflicted the north for more than four months. Early rains had replenished many of the lakes, requiring less power to extract water from the ocean. Excess electrical capacity meant that more power could be diverted to the Underground. With a beautiful spring in the offing, one would never know that it would be the last season of its kind on Mars.

Nothing about Koya's course change had been released by Tal's team. As far as the government and the citizens were concerned, Koya would either miss or brush-by the planet. Learning of Tal's death, the team at the *Olympus Mons* observatory dedicated themselves to monitoring Koya's every move, each deciding not to evacuate. There was still a chance that Koya would wobble again and they wanted to witness that change. Besides, they said, if anyone had the power to move this rock from the beyond, it would be the late Dr. Tal Anak.

As to the media, the printing presses stopped as machinery was converted to produce paper supplies for the Underground. Television became the main source of information about the evacuation. The networks pooled their resources to present one around-the-clock news program broadcasting on all channels. Any media employee could evacuate, with volunteers remaining behind. The networks would remain on-the-air until the very end.

The public utilities, the suppliers of water and power, told their customers that they would also be open until the end, allowing citizens to stay at home in relatively normal conditions. Like the media, volunteers would staff the control rooms that managed the electrical grids and water systems. The fusion reactors supplying electricity were all in operation and were built so deeply below ground that only a direct hit by Koya could destroy them.

A walk through any settlement on Mars, now just five days before impact, would reveal little difference in the way citizens were conducting themselves. The bad news about Koya was taken in stride, as the ever-pragmatic Martians had always done during times of emergency.

Many homes were vacant – their owners now living in temporary quarters in the Underground. But those still on the surface mainly stuck to their regular routines. Some continued to go to work, although there was little left to do. Others decided to stay home or visit public centers with their families and friends. The parks and natural spaces were full of citizens enjoying a last bit of nature. Some packed camping gear and slept in the nature preserves, planning to remain there until the end. Oceanside resorts were booked solid as citizens soaked up the last bit of warm sunshine while walking on sandy beaches.

For humans, it would be difficult to understand the collective sense of calm and serenity of people who knew that they had very little time left. There was no panic or looting. There were no organized public gatherings, no outpourings of grief for others to witness. Those who believed in a deity had made their peace with their God, deciding that it was their Creator's will that Mars should end like this.

It wasn't that the Martians were automatons – beings without feelings or emotions. Quite the opposite. Every one of them, above or below ground, was suffering immense pain at the thought of losing family and friends, and at the destruction of their Martian community. But visible outpourings of grief were not in their nature. Most citizens simply settled into a form of meditation or personal introspection as they considered their lives.

The serenity shown by Martians came from a belief system that viewed the end of life as one part of a natural cycle that all living beings must follow. They were born. They lived. And when it was their time, they died. It was simple, understandable, and logical. Martians did not believe in a grand design in which they were central figures. All living things in the universe were the same, none better and none worse. The most that anyone could do was to live their life as best they could in service to others. At the end, that was their reward – a life well-lived.

Over the centuries, Martians tried many belief systems. Early on, many imagined that the universe was created by a higher power. These belief systems had a common theme – the promise of eternal existence – but only if the believer followed the teachings of the promoters of the faith. There were always strict rules. Failure to obey decrees laid down by those in charge would invariably lead to severe eternal penalties.

After a time, these organized belief systems faded away. Followers could not reconcile their innate need for scientific proof with a system of belief where the Creator God wished to remain hidden. And now, with the death and destruction that Koya promised, even the few who still clung to a belief in a Creator God had a difficult time reconciling the deaths of millions of their fellow citizens with any kind of grand design. That their lives could be snuffed out by something as unremarkable as an iron rock from space would not be consistent with a Creator God's plan for their lives.

But more than just abstract concepts of a Creator God, the ever-pragmatic Martians noticed something else about these belief systems. Their adherents seemed to have very strong views. And their views tended to polarize and alienate those who did not enthusiastically share them. From these uncomfortable and often intolerant interactions, some belief systems invariably led to strife, something the Martians found unacceptable.

In modern times, most Martians embraced a benign and tolerant philosophy called Ka-Atona. It was a rationally-based system that had one rule – only claims that could be proved were allowed to be called the truth. The grandest claims, therefore, required the highest level of proof.

While most Martians followed the teachings of Ka-Atona, it didn't mean that they were barred from believing in God. Each was free to believe as they wished. But the accepted view was that one's freedom to believe stopped at the end of one's nose. Proselytizing for one's own belief system was something that few would tolerate.

The result of adhering to the philosophy of Ka-Atona was a calmness that could be felt in the Martian community. Whether they evacuated, or chose to remain on the surface, Martians accepted what must be and readied themselves for the arrival of Koya.

9
Grannie and Kai

WITH PLANET-WIDE EVACUATION underway, Naira's daughter and her husband, Kaleo, were getting ready to move to the Underground with their young son, Kai. Dad's job was keeping the little guy, whose feet seemed to be in constant motion, from getting in the way of his mother as she packed for the evacuation. The rules were specific about what they could take with them. Only clothing, medicines, and one personal electronic device would be allowed. Everything else they would need after evacuating – food, water, and personal care products – would be provided. Space was very limited and each person had less than a cubic meter in which to store clothing and shoes. The instructions provided guidelines, but the real challenge in the Tuparnac household was Kai. He was constantly engaged in something and Tamara wanted to make sure she packed enough of his things to keep him occupied for long stretches in the crowded conditions below ground.

Kai had been excited about going to the Underground since he watched his Grannie on television, telling every-

one about Koya and the need to evacuate. That evening
over dinner, his mother and father rounded off some of the
rougher edges about why they had to evacuate, trying to make
the move to the Underground an adventure for Kai. Although
they had no idea how long they would remain in the Underground, they told Kai that the trip would be short – maybe
a few days – and then he could come home to build more
spaceships. Most of the ones he built and tried to launch by
various methods were still in the neighborhood, sitting on the
roofs of the neighbors' houses.

Yesterday, Kai's grandmother paid him a surprise visit,
coming up from Arens for a few hours to spend time with her
grandson before the family evacuated. She surprised him with
an offer to take him on a special tour of the Underground, to
the exact place where he would go in a few days. The Underground station was a five-minute walk and after an exciting
ride on a fast elevator, he was more than twenty kilometers
below the Martian surface, checking out the train station and
all of the activity as citizens arrived and were escorted to their
living quarters.

Naira and Kai visited some of the shops in the central
station. He got a new hat and a bag of his favorite candy –
little chewy shapes in bright colors. He saw the place where
he and his parents would live – but, only for a little while,
Grannie assured him. He inspected the playgrounds where
kids were already starting to gather. Kai spied some geometric blocks on the floor and immediately sat down and started
building things. While he played, Naira took a moment
to visit with some of the managers who had been working
around-the-clock to make everything ready. She thanked and
hugged each of them. Everyone assumed that Naira would
evacuate to be with her daughter and son-in-law, and of

course, with little Kai. But Naira deflected any questions about when she would evacuate.

After touring the living quarters, Kai and Naira walked to the cafeteria across the large central corridor. It was open and food was being served. The smell of baked goods was in the air and one of the staff brought Kai and Naira a plate of cookies as they sat down at a table. There was so much Naira wanted to say to her grandson, but he wouldn't understand. And besides, there was no time. She promised Tamara that she would have him back within an hour and Naira wasn't going to worry his mother by being late.

As he munched on a cookie, his grandmother sat watching him. If only his grandfather could be here to see him. Kai reminded her so much of Kalay – the same nose and forehead, the same intense concentration on everything he did. Her husband had been gone sixty years, killed in one of his own medical experiments gone terribly wrong. Kalay was a brilliant neurosurgeon who was working on a way to scan and store the thoughts and memories of an individual. He saw a number of uses for the technology – the restoration of lost intellect and memory due to injury and transference to a robotic body to replace an ailing one. He even imagined a virtual world, in which the collective knowledge of the entire race might be preserved, regardless of the environmental conditions on Mars.

Computer simulations showed promise, but Kalay needed a Martian subject to see if the scanning process would work. Unwilling to accept one of the many volunteers who stepped up, and against the advice of his colleagues, he placed himself on the scanning table and ordered the scan to begin. A faulty circuit in the scanner sent thousands of volts of electricity into his brain, killing him instantly. The project was immediately terminated, but Kalay had done breakthrough research in understanding how the Martian brain functions and how neurotransmitters could be mimicked by comparable code in a computer.

Naira waited until Kai was done with his cookie before asking him a question.

"Kai, do you understand why you and Mommy and Daddy are coming down here?" she asked.

"Uh huh," Kai replied, looking up at her.

"Do you really understand? Tell me," she asked gently.

"Well, the planet Koya is coming and it's going to bump into us," Kai said. "And you told everyone on TV to come down here to be safe."

"Kai, are you afraid?"

"No, Grannie, I'm not afraid. Are you?"

"No honey, I'm not afraid, either. Do you think you will like staying down here for a little while?" Naira was pleased that he understood what would happen, but not the part about the destruction that would come with Koya's arrival.

"Yes, 'cause we'll all be together, right Grannie?" Kai looked up at his grandmother, a big smile on his face.

"Yes, Kai, we will all be together," she said, choking back a sob. "But always remember Kai, that no matter where you are, your grandmother loves you very, very much."

"I love you too, Grannie," Kai replied, giving her that same huge grin that allowed him to win more discussions with his parents than lose. "Hey, can we ride the train again?"

"Of course we can ride the train," Naira said with a laugh. "Let's get on board so that you can get home to Mommy and Daddy."

With that, Kai jumped off of his chair and held out his hand for his grandmother. She reached for it and then swept him up in her arms, kissing him on his cheeks, while holding back the tears in her eyes. In a few minutes, he would be back home and she would be on her way back to the capital.

It would be the last time they would ever see each other.

10
Impact

SURFACE OF MARS – THE LAST DAY

AT EXACTLY ONE hour before Koya struck Mars, the elevators to the Underground were closed and sealed. On the surface, there were no desperate people left behind, banging on the doors to be let in. Everyone who wanted to evacuate had already done so. Those that did not stayed at home or took up positions outdoors to watch the impact.

Koya now filled half of the sky – almost close enough to touch. The deep red planet revealed all of its details – craggy iron mountains and valleys and the scars of billions of years of intergalactic travel as it bumped into other space junk on its way to an orbit around the Sun. As Koya entered the outermost edges of the Martian atmosphere, a fiery red ring formed around planet. At the speed they were both traveling, friction would light up the atmosphere long before impact.

The last remaining news program was carried live on all channels, with many of the best news anchors volunteering to stay at their posts. Dozens of scientists sat in bleacher seats on the set, allowing the news team to move about and get comments from each of them as everyone watched the monitors showing Koya. Fixed cameras located at various spots on the planet gave citizens a crystal-clear view of the churning and agitated Koya, as it moved closer and closer to Mars.

Viewers watching above and below-ground saw the television screen divided into parts. The top half of the screen showed a live image of Koya, closing in on Mars. The bottom half of the screen was divided in two. One half showed the news studio and the banter between the news anchors and their guests. The other half toggled between dozens of live locations across the surface of the planet. In the very top right corner, a digital clock was superimposed over the image of Koya, showing the time remaining until impact.

Attention was focused on one live report near the capital. A family with two young children sat on the grass in front of their house, staring straight up at the angry planet that was filling the sky. One of the kids, a pretty girl, probably not even old enough for school, sat cross-legged on the ground. As the camera slowly zoomed in on the little girl's face, she appeared so calm and serene that it seemed to have a soothing effect on those watching. Viewers weren't sure whether her parents told her about what was going to happen, but her eyes showed no fear of the terrible loss that this uninvited visitor was about to rain-down upon them. The reporter, his voice shaking in the background, signed off for the last time as the little girl's face stayed on the screen. After a few more moments, the camera switched back to the network, where the anchor team sat in tears.

Koya had one more surprise before it struck Mars. At fifty-seven minutes to impact, Koya shuddered when a cluster of six or seven geysers ejected white-hot steam from vents on the left side of the planet. A few seconds after the eruption started, these geysers of superheated water and magma began acting on Koya, moving it slowly at first, then more quickly to a new course away from Mars. As the geysers on Koya continued to blow, the speed of the angular change increased until Koya went from being directly overhead to appearing over the far right horizon.

Koya would not strike Mars head-on, but unfortunately, the eruptions on Koya came too late for a clean miss. Koya had returned to the course that astronomers had predicted when Tal spoke to Naira a month ago. But the destruction would be no less severe.

Friction building up in the Martian atmosphere sent a wave of super-heated air across the planet, raising surface temperatures past the boiling point of water. Within minutes, those on the surface were dying in agony, literally cooked inside their own bodies.

Then, with super-heated air enveloping the planet, Koya and Mars rubbed against each other, creating horrible, deep vibrations and shudders that increased in intensity on the surface. These low-frequency oscillations reduced every stone building to rubble, shaking even the biggest rocks until they were nothing more than hand-sized bits of stone. Martians were thrown high into the air and then dropped back to the surface. If the intense heat or the fall didn't kill them, then they were certainly killed as they were buried under the rubble that fell down on top of them.

The frictional force of the two planets rubbing together stopped Mars from spinning on its axis. The center of the planet took longer to stop, causing it to twist, creating the huge gashes that are still visible on the surface of the planet today. The full stop also caused the oceans to rise up and literally walk across the surface of Mars. As the two planets finally disconnected, Mars slowly began rotating again, this time in the opposite direction. The pent-up inertia in the oceans was released and the wall of water, two kilometers high, came crashing back down onto the planet, washing everything away.

The glancing strike, like two billiard balls artfully played off of each other, pushed Mars into a new orbit, twenty-two percent farther away from the Sun. The planet shifted on its axis, moving to twenty-eight degrees off center, an angle that would eventually create much more extreme seasonal variances between the northern and southern hemispheres. Koya's immense electromagnetic field effectively neutralized the weaker magnetic field of Mars, destroying the protective shield that kept solar and interstellar radiation from reaching the planet's surface. With nothing left to hold it, the Martian atmosphere drifted away from the planet, leaving behind just one percent of what was once a thick, carbon dioxide covering.

The impact with Mars knocked Koya out of its orbit around the Sun, sending it back into deep space. It has not been seen since, not by Martian astronomers nor those on Earth. But someday, Koya might be pulled into another solar system to deliver its own brand of destruction.

Seen from space, Mars was a hulk. Smoke and fine dust filled the atmosphere out to the limits of the planet's gravity, blocking out the Sun. In the weeks that followed, the planet continued to shudder and vibrate with aftershocks that sent what remained of the oceans in waves over the land. As the temperature dropped, the water that washed ashore was absorbed into the soil and froze, where it remains locked away today.

In the years that followed, the final act of this story was played out. With almost no atmosphere or magnetic field to protect it, Mars was bombarded by solar radiation – particles shot into space during solar flares. Even more devastating were the cosmic rays, including gamma radiation. These bursts were instant death to any living thing caught in their paths, down to the smallest, single-celled organisms that somehow managed to survive the impact. In less than a year, the surface of Mars was sterilized by radiation from space. Nothing would ever live on the surface again.

On Earth, in 1619, Galileo Galilei had been studying Mars for ten years. But his primitive telescope was too weak to witness the tragedy on Mars. Nowhere in his journals did he mention the Mars that looked very much like Earth. By the time other astronomers of the seventeenth century – Kepler, Huygens, and Cassini – aimed more powerful telescopes at Mars, its surface looked as it does today.

For the next four centuries, astronomers on Earth would conclude that Mars was a lifeless planet that may once have had water and may once have supported life. Koya's impact did such a thorough job of destroying the surface of Mars that what was left behind would leave no clue as to the richness of life the planet contained, or of the amazing civilization that once thrived there. And, it wouldn't be until the last quarter of the twentieth century when humans would finally be able to reach Mars to begin their incredible discoveries on a planet that is far more than it appears on the surface.

11
The Aftermath

MORE THAN ONE billion citizens evacuated to the Underground in the days before Koya struck. Of those, 462 million survived the impact. Most of the deaths in the Underground occurred on the side of the planet that made direct contact with Koya. Those tunnels collapsed under the tremendous pressure exerted on the Martian surface. Citizens died where they stood, killed instantly as the stacked tunnel system pancaked under the pressure. Spreading out in circles from the area of impact, more and more of the tunnel system survived, but shock waves radiating throughout the Underground killed many more who were struck by falling rocks or crushed under partial tunnel collapses. In some places, citizens were asphyxiated before rescuers could reach them.

One day after impact, rescue teams went to the surface to look for survivors. The first teams to arrive on the surface suffocated from a lack of atmosphere. Later teams carried breathable air, but the scene on the surface was beyond imagination. The once green and verdant surface of Mars was now a hellish place – bitterly cold and locked in darkness. Walking through the rubble was difficult. Even with powerful search lights, rescuers could see no more than a short distance, due to the fine dust that hung motionless in the air. Teams that fanned out from the entrances got lost in the darkness and never returned. With the planet's magnetic poles disrupted, the compasses they relied on for direction were useless.

Heavier rock, still floating at the fringes of Martian gravity, began falling back to the surface, killing anyone who stood where the rocks fell. The lighter materials – the grit and dust – seemed to just hang in the thin atmosphere, suspended with no wind to move it. It would take almost a decade before all of the dust and debris returned to the surface. When it did, everything was covered with a thick layer of dirt that eventually compacted and erased all evidence of the Martian civilization.

In the Underground, the citizens were in shock. Word quickly spread about the conditions on the surface and of the destruction and seared corpses that lie everywhere. Eight days after impact, they were told that they would never be able to return to the surface. The Underground was no longer a temporary home – it was where they would have to live. And, it was where they would all die.

But there would be time later to consider their long-term prospects. Right now, those who survived the impact with Koya were cold, hungry, and mostly in the dark. The first order of business was to get the power back on. Most of the planet's heavily-fortified power stations survived the impact. As crews repaired broken power lines, the lights and ventilation systems began working again. Pumps running the water cisterns fed clean water to more and more locations underground. Emergency medical centers quickly filled with patients who were treated by medical professionals who had evacuated.

After the lights and heat went on, agriculture specialists repaired the farm production facilities that fed the planet. Some of the plants had withered in the darkness and cold, but most of the crops returned to normal after some careful tending. While the population survived on packaged foods that were warehoused before the impact, the agricultural sector came back to life.

Six months after Koya struck, life in the Underground had returned to a state of new normalcy. It was clear that they would never return to the surface. But, a half-million years of evolution had burned the instinct to survive into their genetic makeup. No, they would not give up. They would not complain about their new world, hemmed-in by stone walls. What they would do is restart their civilization here, in the Underground. And while they were rebuilding, they would continue to advance – perhaps someday, even leave Mars for a place where they could live in the Sun again.

And slowly, they started over. This was Mars 2.0.

12
The New Mars

MARS — TEN YEARS AFTER KOYA

MARKING THE FIRST decade of living below the surface of Mars was cause for celebration. The resourceful Martians had restored a large portion of the life they knew on the surface. The planet's fusion-based electrical network provided heat and light. Filters and catalysts cleaned the air and changed its chemistry to something even more beneficial than the atmosphere they were used to on the surface. Food was abundant and the water cisterns contained more than enough to supply the half-billion citizens with drinking water.

A new generation of miners learned the ancient art and then set out across the planet to find the raw materials needed to keep the automated manufacturing centers operating, producing the same goods that were delivered to the surface a decade earlier. New housing stock replaced the large dormitory chambers used during the evacuation. Single family homes, modular in design, were assembled in rows, with streets and sidewalks that resembled those on the surface. Light that mimicked the Sun allowed trees to grow and parks across the Underground were planted with real grass.

Community areas were built where Martians could meet and talk. New shopping, entertainment, and recreation sectors were established and stores with familiar brand names reopened, offering the same goods and services that had been available on the surface.

And everywhere they went across Mars, the miners drilled up, opening more and more vertical shafts to the surface. These shafts were capped with thick borosilicate glass, faceted to refract the weak sunlight and aim it down into the tunnels. While not the same as standing on the surface, residents would often gather under these shafts to drink-in the sunlight that they missed so much.

Education and entertainment rivaled what Martians enjoyed on the surface. New computer technology provided everyone with access to the entire Martian library of educational and entertainment materials. Their two-dimensional televisions were replaced by new holographic devices, where everything could be seen in three dimensions.

The scientific community, accepting the reality of living underground, pressed on with its work. Mathematicians and physicists solved the last of the great mysteries of time, matter, and the universe. Although they had no means to get there, new telescopes were built to once again gaze at the solar system and beyond.

In the biological sciences, new research was needed as Martians came down with illnesses caused by things that had been dormant in the rock for billions of years. One of the new areas of specialty for doctors was the treatment of mental disorders, especially depression. While the Underground was their home, and though most survivors accepted that reality,

they certainly felt different about life. Brain chemistry was
kept in check with new medication to stave-off depression
and the stresses of living below-ground.

At the ten-year mark since Koya's arrival, life on Mars had
returned to normal. Until one day, it wasn't normal anymore.

A body was found in one of the unused tunnels. Another
was soon found. And, then another.

13
Extinction

MARS – 350 YEARS AFTER KOYA

A T THE TIME that humans were landing on the moon, Martian society was nearing extinction. There were fewer than 100,000 citizens remaining, with suicides and natural deaths far exceeding the birth rate. Demographers estimated that without a breakthrough of some kind, there would be no one left within fifty years.

On Earth, human evolution favored both intelligence and strength. Out of that early genetic stock, humans evolved to become strong and durable, able to live nearly everywhere on the planet. Human strength allowed civilizations to build before machines began doing the heavy work. Pyramids and other large structures were built by the sweat and toil of human muscle. Humans were tough and adaptable to extremes of temperature and weather conditions.

Mars was different. The small planet, with its low gravity and greenhouse-based climate, meant that Martians never had to adapt to severe environmental conditions. Evolution ignored physical development in favor of intellectual power. And so long as the planet cooperated, this lack of physical durability was not a problem. Until Koya arrived, Mars was a benign place to live. On the surface, the population thrived.

Koya changed everything. Those who evacuated thought that they would return to the surface. But the realization that the Underground would be their permanent home settled in the backs of their minds as a low, dull throb, sapping them of energy and enthusiasm. Living underground did not nurture them. Instead, it took, and took, and when they were worn out, it asked for even more – that is, if they wanted to stay alive.

And, what was the reward for staying alive in a place where swinging a pick had more value than the capacity to understand the laws of the physical universe or the metabolism of a healthy Martian? The reward was to merely push back the cold and dark for a time. And when there was light, what was there to see? Left, right, up, or down, endless rock stood in the way of sun and sky. All there was – indeed, all there would ever be – were long, dark tunnels that extended to the horizon. And once reaching the horizon, there were still more tunnels and more darkness ahead.

When historians studied pictures of Martians who lived on the surface, they noticed that a striking metamorphosis had taken place in the years since the evacuation. Underground, Martians had lost all of their pigmentation. Their skin was now a thin, semi-transparent covering over organs, vascular systems, and bones. Their eyes, once large and bright, weakened and clouded from the darkness and artificial light. And the cold and dampness – in spite of their best efforts to create a surface-like environment – were slowly wearing down their immune systems. They looked sick.

In fact, they were sick.

Not just physically sick, but the population was mentally and emotionally wrecked. Doctors were dispensing more and more medications to help them cope with depression and suicidal ideations. Lethargy lapped over many of them. They were too tired or depressed to do as much work today as they did yesterday or the day before. And as they slowed down, the quality of their society became more ragged. Economic production and innovation declined as Martians became incapable of making things – even growing the crops that were needed for their survival.

Mars had no real government on the surface and it was the same when they evacuated to the Underground. They reconstituted the planet's Administrative Council after all of its members died on the surface. But, the new Council still had very little power over the surviving population.

Before Koya, the Council rarely met. Now, the Council was in session daily to discuss options to save the population from extinction.

Extinction.

The word was used more frequently now. There was tacit acceptance that each of them was doomed to a slow and wasting death. More and more prescriptions for the approved suicide medication were written and the decline of the population picked up speed. Maybe the demographers were too optimistic. At the rate things were going, the population might give out much sooner than a half-century.

One member of the Martian community who refused to give into the malaise that smothered most of his fellow citizens was Kai Tuparnac. Kai was the little boy who ran through these corridors with his grandmother nearly four centuries ago. Kai was old now. But, he still maintained the vigor and enthusiasm that he had as a child. And Kai was not going to let his people die from apathy. Martians had solved many problems in their half-million years of existence. This one would be solved, too.

But, the answer wasn't on Mars. It was on the blue planet that he loved to gaze at through his telescope as a child.

Part II

14
The Vikings

JET PROPULSION LAB – PASADENA, CALIFORNIA

IN THE EARLY morning hours of July 20, 1976, the Jet Propulsion Lab campus was buzzing with activity. Brightly lit against the darkness of the San Gabriel Mountains to the north, the campus was jammed with scientists, engineers, dignitaries, and so many reporters and equipment that the von Kármán Auditorium had to be converted into a giant media center.

The first Viking lander was headed toward the surface of Mars. It was the biggest space story since man set foot on the moon. The fact that Viking 1 was landing on Mars, seven years to the day after Apollo 11's historic landing on the moon, just added to the mystique of NASA's ability to produce spectacular space successes and a sense of theater that made space exploration exciting.

Mission Control was a circular room with walls made of glass. Large television monitors hung from the ceiling, displaying the same information that was visible on the screens at the table in the center of the room. Seated in the dimly-lit room were technicians, flight engineers, and scientists. Their mission was to finish the eight-year, one-billion-dollar job of getting Viking to Mars, and then landing it successfully on the Martian surface.

So far this morning, the news coming from Mars was all good. At 01:51, George Sands, the "Voice of Viking," clicked open his microphone and told the waiting audience across the JPL campus, and around the world, that the Viking lander had separated from its orbiter.

We have separation. We have engineering data indicating separation.

Because of the distance between the two planets, almost 350 million kilometers, the radio signal coming from Viking took more than eighteen minutes to reach Mission Control. Whatever was happening – whether the mission was going to be a success or failure – everyone had to wait out those agonizing eighteen minutes for every update from Mars. One journalist likened it to listening to a football game on the radio and waiting eighteen minutes after a field goal snap to see if the kick was good.

With the separation phase completed, the most complex part of the mission was still ahead. The lander would have to pass through the Martian atmosphere on its way to a soft landing on the surface. A new announcer stepped-in to do the play-by-play as Sands returned to other mission duties. At 02:42, Albert Hibbs announced:

So far, everything that is supposed to have happened has happened and is right on schedule. We are rapidly approaching the surface of Mars.

The Viking lander was 11,000 kilometers from the surface and picking up speed. Friction from the Martian atmosphere heated the protective shield covering the lander, producing an increasingly-bright heat-glow. Although the Martian atmosphere is only about one percent as dense as Earth's, there were more than enough gas molecules to burn up the lander without its protective heat shield.

At 04:45, with Viking 1 less than ten minutes from the surface of Mars, Hibbs joked that Mission Control would talk the lander down to the surface. In truth, no one at JPL had control of the lander. Because of the time delay, Viking 1 was now completely dependent on its own programming to complete the complicated set of instructions to put the lander softly on the surface.

Ten minutes later, Hibbs returned to the microphone to announce that landing should have taken place.

Viking should be on the surface by now – one way or another.

There was a steady stream of data coming from Viking 1. That was a good thing because it meant that the lander was still in one piece. But Mission Control couldn't be sure for another eighteen minutes whether this data would be the first, or the last that Viking 1 would send from the surface of Mars.

Finally, more than three hours after separation from its orbiter, the Viking 1 lander reported that it had successfully touched-down on the surface of Mars. Hibbs announced:

Touchdown. We have touchdown!

The control room exploded with cheers and applause, with people all over the JPL complex yelling loudly enough to wake up the neighbors. For the first time, an unmanned American spacecraft made a successful landing on the surface of another planet.

News reports of the landing went out quickly over the wire services to newspapers and broadcast outlets across the world. Radio reporters called-in live reports to their stations. Television networks interrupted regular programming to report the story. But, for most Americans, the images from Mars would have to wait until that evening, when the networks would run their national news shows. John Chancellor would report for NBC. Harry Reasoner and Howard K. Smith anchored for ABC. And on CBS, Dan Rather was the announcer.

> *This is the CBS Evening News, with Dan Rather substituting for Walter Cronkite. Good evening. Mars – from the surface. Man's age-old dream of a close-up look at what it is like on another planet and of searching for life there, today became a reality. And, what a reality. Viking 1 soft-landed perfectly on the Martian surface and immediately began sending back photographs so spectacular, even project scientists were amazed. Terry Drinkwater reports...*

The world was getting its first look at the surface of Mars. By the next day, every newspaper featured pictures of the Martian surface on its front page. Many magazines devoted large sections of their next editions to the amazing photos that were being sent by the Viking 1 lander.

15
The Landing

MARS – NORTHERN HEMISPHERE – 20 JULY 1976

WHILE CONTROLLERS AT JPL waited out the agonizing eighteen-minute delay, events on Mars were happening fast. As the Viking 1 lander neared the surface, red dust swirled in small rivulets when three liquid-fueled rocket motors roared to life and began pushing against Martian gravity. The huge parachute that took away most of the lander's speed after entering the Martian atmosphere had detached and was drifting down and away, pushed by a light southwesterly breeze.

Each of Viking's three rockets funneled its energy through six small nozzles, reducing the amount of heat and dust that would be kicked up during landing. The innovative design would protect the soil under the lander, where Viking would search for evidence of Martian life.

Balancing the 600 kilogram lander against the pull of Martian gravity, Viking hovered a few meters above the surface. At this height, the onboard flight computer began dialing back the rockets. As the thrust tapered off, Viking slowly closed the remaining distance to the surface.

Slowly.

Slowly.

And touchdown.

When Viking's three lander legs nudged the Martian surface, the rocket motors shut off, sticking Viking to the planet. Shock absorbers in each leg allowed the craft to settle smoothly onto the surface. One of the three footpads stepped on a rock, causing Viking to tilt slightly. But it was no problem – the designers expected the surface to be uneven and built the landing gear to compensate.

It was a perfect landing – the kind any pilot would be proud to make. Only the pilots for this mission were more than 350 million kilometers away. And with the eighteen-minute delay between Viking and Mission Control, it was really Viking that did all the work.

The six-sided aluminum and titanium Viking lander was a marvel of 1970s technology. On the outside were appendages – a robotic arm with a shovel to gather soil for sampling, radio antennae, a parabolic radio dish, and two towers containing high-resolution facsimile cameras. Round tanks for the liquid hydrazine mono rocket fuel were strapped to either side of the body. An angular box sat over one of the two tanks. Inside were two SNAP 19 radioisotope generators. Each generator contained a small amount of radioactive plutonium. Its natural decay produced heat that was converted into electricity. Together, the generators produced seventy watts of electricity – enough to run all of the equipment on the Viking lander.

And Viking was packed with equipment – three biology labs, two spectrometers, and sensors to measure atmospheric pressure, surface temperature, and wind speed. Viking could even detect the slightest ground tremors with a three-axis seismometer attached to one of its landing legs.

Collecting the data was one engineering challenge. A lot of information was being generated, but the data pipeline between Earth and Mars was very narrow. Only so much information could be sent by Viking's radio transmitter at any one time.

Some way of storing the data waiting to be sent was also needed. Computer hard drives were still years away from being small enough to fit aboard a spacecraft. So, engineers designed an elegant eight-channel reel-to-reel tape machine to record and store the data. A special metallic tape was used, strong enough to prevent the tape from breaking as it recorded and played back over and over again.

Once the data was recorded, it could be transmitted during periods when the radio channel wasn't being used for scientific experiments. The Viking lander could talk directly with Earth or by up-link to its companion orbiter, which provided a faster data rate to Earth. The orbiter would then relay the information to one of NASA's tracking stations on Earth.

Like the tough Norsemen the craft was named after, this Viking was ready to go to work the moment it landed. Even before the rockets were cool, Viking was already working on a programmed sequence of tasks. But first, a few snapshots were taken to mark the occasion. The first picture of Mars was a high-resolution image – of its own foot. This was no accidental tourist shot of a Parisian sidewalk. It was intentional – a way for NASA to get a reference point for the scale of the rocks strewn around the lander. The image showed small rocks, mostly broken at angles. Many of the rocks were half-buried in a layer of red dirt.

The second picture was a panorama of the Martian land-scape. The image showed the Martian horizon gently rising to the right. In the foreground, the surface was littered with more rocks of different sizes. Sunlight overexposed the right side of the image, but it was still a breathtaking photo.

NASA chose the northern hemisphere for both Viking missions. This area of the planet once held a large ocean and the landscape was more cooperative for early Mars missions. Viking 1 landed in a flat area called *Chryse Planitia* – the Plains of Gold. And indeed, if Martian rocks could to be con-sidered gold, this place was aptly named.

But the Viking project was just beginning. Still inbound for Mars was Viking 2, an identical copy of Viking 1. Viking 2 would land in six weeks, giving scientists twice as much data to study.

16
Kai Watches

MARS – VIKING 1 LANDING SITE – 24 SEPTEMBER 1976

A S THE VIKING 1 lander continued sending photographs to Earth, the area chosen for its landing
seemed unremarkable, even for Mars. The flat,
almost featureless surface told very little about the geology
of the planet. The rocky surface had not worn with erosion –
the planet's atmosphere was too weak to round off the sharp
edges of the broken stones. For all anyone knew, these rocks
could have been here for a billion years or just a few hundred
years. Only the onboard laboratories would be able to provide
more information about the soil and rock composition of the
surface beneath the feet of Viking 1.

One photograph, taken six weeks after Viking 1 landed,
showed a modest pile of rocks a short distance from the
lander. Among the hundreds of photos already taken by the
lander, no one noticed that the pile of rocks was not present
when the camera snapped a picture of that same area the
day Viking 1 landed. Blame it on information overload or
the stresses of managing two Viking landers, but this visual
anomaly was never reported.

An amateur geologist could have deduced that this rock pile was not a natural occurrence. Someone had deliberately stacked the rocks to form a barrier. The builders of this rock wall wanted to watch Viking without being seen by the lander's cameras. For most of the day, the dim sunlight on the Martian surface covered the rock pile in changing shadows and Viking's cameras were not precise enough to make out any details in these shadows.

But its builders were there, watching Viking from behind the rock wall. They had been to the surface every day since Viking landed, constructing the wall when the lander's cameras were facing a different direction. Now, it was finished and they could observe the Viking lander without being seen, and while keeping as much radiation as possible from penetrating their surface suits.

For weeks, the Martians had been aware that Viking was coming. They had been tracking its inbound voyage and watched as the lander separated from the orbiter and descended toward the surface. They saw it gather speed, leaving a reddish streak behind as it entered the Martian atmosphere. And then, after ejecting its parachute, they witnessed the beautiful ballet of its soft landing on the surface.

One Martian in particular was interested in this spacecraft. It was Kai. And Kai had a plan to help save his people. It involved this spacecraft, so he needed to know as much about it as possible. That meant extended periods on the surface of Mars, a dangerous place where radiation exposure could be deadly. Still, it was a risk he was willing to take.

Each day, sitting behind the rock wall, Kai would watch everything the lander was doing. He would stay on the surface as long as he could – an hour or two at the most. Then, running short on breathable air and with the stinging effects of radiation on his skin, he would slowly withdraw and return to the Underground through a nearby elevator. Two video cameras and radio receiving equipment were stationed behind the rock partition. The video cameras would provide continuous observation of the lander. The radio equipment was there to listen to Viking's radio transmissions. If Kai's audacious plan was going to work, he had to know exactly when, and for how long, these radio transmissions were scheduled.

Today, as Kai watched Viking, his mind went back to a similar event five years earlier. A Russian spacecraft named Mars 3 was coming to his planet, the first lander to arrive from Earth. As with the Viking mission, it was Kai who was there to observe the landing. He traveled on the restored underground rail system to make the 1,200 kilometer ride from his home in the northern polar region to the southern hemisphere, a place Earth scientists called the Ptolemaeus Crater.

Kai arrived early and set up an observation position where he could watch the Russian landing, while minimizing his exposure to solar radiation. In his desire to remain hidden, Kai caught a break. A massive dust storm was blowing in the region where the Russian spacecraft was expected to land. The dust would make it almost impossible for Kai to be seen and would also attenuate some of the radiation Kai was absorbing by being on the surface.

But while the dust storm was good for Kai, it was very bad for the Mars 3 lander. The spacecraft would have to descend amidst the swirling winds and fine dust particles obscuring the surface. In addition to poor visibility, the storm grew angry, with lightning bursts from the accumulated static electricity that was building up. Just before the Mars 3 landed, a bolt of blue-green lightning struck less than a kilometer from the landing site.

As the storm raged, Kai scanned the skies, searching for the spacecraft. His support team, located directly below him in the Underground, told him by radio that the spacecraft should be visible at any time. As if on cue, Kai spotted the huge red and white parachute and the round, white metal craft that dangled below the chute.

As the spacecraft neared the ground, rockets attached to the parachute wires fired in bursts to slow the spacecraft down. About ten meters above the surface, the parachute disengaged and the Mars 3 lander dropped like a stone, striking the surface and bouncing several times before bobbing into an upright position. The Russians had a first – the first human spacecraft to successfully land on another planet.

Within seconds of coming to a stop, the Mars 3 lander literally sprang to life. Four white exterior panels popped back on heavy springs, revealing a smaller, white, egg-shaped craft inside. On one of the four panels, a silver metal box flopped out on another spring and landed flat on the Martian surface. This box contained instruments to sample the soil. But the Mars 3 lander had one more surprise – a little, motorized rover that rolled out of its own garage at the base of the craft. It moved on two alternating skis that pulled the craft forward, dragging a cable behind to keep it in contact with the lander. Two spring-loaded metal arms crossed the front of the rover. If it encountered a rock, the arms would stop the rover and adjust its course to go around the obstacle.

A few more minutes went by when four radio aerials popped up, immediately sending electronic signals skyward.

A metal pole rose a meter above the lander and a box with two glass lenses began whirring. This was the lander's television camera, preparing to send the first live television transmissions from the surface of Mars.

While this was going on, the dust storm was getting worse. Lightning bolts were striking the ground, getting closer and closer to the Mars 3 lander. The storm was moving directly over the spot the Russians picked for this landing.

In a flash, a bolt of lightning struck the Mars 3. The burst was so bright that Kai was temporarily blinded. His huge eyes were designed for low light, so this argon-fueled electrical burst created a painful aura in his eyes that lasted for several minutes. By the time he could see again, it was clear that the lightning bolt had done considerable damage to the spacecraft. The electricity contained in the lightning bolt easily passed through the metal surface of the Mars 3, into its interior, where it fried most of the equipment on board.

Smoke from Mars 3 got dark and thick as latent energy stored in the lander's batteries finished the job the lightning started. Within a minute, the spacecraft's white exterior was covered in black soot. With no more power coming from the lander, the little rover stopped in its tracks. The Mars 3 lander was dead.

On Earth, at the Baikonur Cosmodrome in Kazakhstan, everything about the Mars 3 landing seemed normal. Telemetry showed that the lander successfully entered the Martian atmosphere, deployed its parachute at the right time, and that its rockets slowed the lander to an acceptable speed for it to land. Signals received from Mars 3 told the Russians that it was alive and well on the surface. The rover was working. It was sending back data as it moved away from the lander.

The lander even began sending live television. This was what they had been waiting for – visual confirmation that Mars 3 was on the surface. The black and white television image tore and rolled and filled the screen with static. It was like trying to get a good picture on a television set that had rabbit ears back in the 1960s. Less than twenty seconds of video arrived before the camera went dark. In another minute, radio communication between the lander and its orbiter was cut off. While the Mars 3 orbiter overhead continued to work until the following summer, sending pictures of the planet from its elliptical orbit, the Mars 3 lander was never heard from again.

Kai's attention was pulled back to the present as he noticed the Viking's articulating arm reaching out to begin a soil sample experiment. *These humans are a busy people*, Kai thought. He liked them already. He watched as the robotic arm, an elegant bit of 1970s engineering, reached down to the surface to scoop-up some soil. Then the arm and its scooper returned to the lander body, where the soil was dropped into an opening, leading to small biochemical laboratories inside the lander.

The communicator inside his helmet was beeping. His support team was calling, telling him that it was time to go. He acknowledged their call, then carefully slipped out from behind the rock wall as Viking's cameras pointed away from his position. There was a light breeze blowing and the dusty footprints he left behind were quickly covered over.

A short distance away were the ruins of an elevator station, partially hidden by layers of rock and dust. But the vertical shaft that led to the Underground was still working. Kai activated the first electric seal, a thick slab of glass wrapped in a metal frame. It made a small whooshing sound as the atmospheric pressure changed inside the entry compartment. Kai climbed down the ladder to the first compartment, then hit a button to close the seal above.

When the door above closed, Kai could feel the welcoming atmosphere of the Underground below. He tapped another switch on the wall. This opened a second door located in the floor of the chamber. This one revealed a waiting elevator car that would take him to the Underground. When he climbed in and closed the door above, he was able to take off the helmet that kept him alive during his time on the surface.

There was a support team member waiting for Kai in the elevator. *She is very pretty,* Kai thought, as he kissed her. His wife, Mia, had been a member of his support team for every one of Kai's missions to the surface. They embraced for a moment before hitting the down button. Even though Kai wore a thick, protective suit, Mia still felt wonderful in his arms. He would have to say goodbye to her in a few days, but not just yet.

The elevator began its descent. In less than a minute, the car reached the level where the rest of the support team was waiting. The video cameras on the surface were working, sending live video to a monitoring station set near the elevator shaft. Although Viking 1 wasn't going anywhere, they wanted to monitor its condition and its activities.

The Martians were also listening to Viking, monitoring its radio transmissions, logging the times, durations, and the frequencies used to send data to Earth. This was a critical part of the mission because Kai intended to use the Viking's radio channel to set out on his mission.

A half-dozen technicians were waiting for Kai and Mia as the elevator doors opened. The medical team checked Kai's condition as they removed his surface suit. There were minor radiation burns on his arms and legs, but the injuries were treated with a salve that quickly cooled the sunburn pain he was starting to feel. He had scars from other radiation burns, so the ones he would get from today's visit to the surface wouldn't matter much.

A train was standing by on the track running north from the landing site. They climbed aboard for the twenty-minute ride to the northern settlement, where a majority of Martians resettled in the years since Koya. As the population declined, the Martians began shutting down unused tunnels and settlements, conserving power and the remaining water that was still frozen in the northern ice cap. Just three settlements remained – two in the north and one in the south – with about half of the survivors living in the northern settlement where Kai and Mia were headed.

Kai's day was over. He would shower and rest for a few hours. Later, he would go over the calculations used to draw-up his mission. This checking and rechecking of the data was something he would do up until the moment it was time to leave. He had only once chance to get there and everything had to be perfect if he was to survive.

17
Final Preparations

MARS — NORTHERN SETTLEMENT — 06 OCTOBER 1976

THIS MORNING'S MEETING of the Administrative Council was gaveled to order by Quanah Malik, the Council President. Quanah's grandfather was a member of the Council at the time of Koya. Karal Malik, Naira Tuparnac, and the nine other members of the Council were killed when Koya struck. Interestingly, there was a Tuparnac on *this* Council as well. Although he never had ambitions to be a politician, when asked to serve, Kai Tuparnac agreed, in honor of his grandmother.

That a Malik and a Tuparnac would eventually be on the same Council again was ironic, given the tempestuous relationship between their grandparents in the years before Koya arrived. But the truth was that Quanah and Kai were best friends. They attended medical school together, back in an era when universities still existed. Those institutions were gone, as were the public schools that provided the foundational education for generations of Martians. The school buildings were empty now. There were no children left.

Before the evacuation, the Council met infrequently. There wasn't much to do for a population that was essentially self-governing and a planet that was stable and prosperous. But here in the Underground, especially in the past five years, the Council was the scapegoat for everything that was going wrong. For the first time, Martians were showing visible anger. Somewhere in the deep recesses of their genetic map, primitive tendencies toward anger and violence were bubbling to the surface. Most Council meetings featured at least one angry outburst from an audience member, complaining about living conditions or the chronic shortages of food and everything else. The Council even had security personnel in the room after two members of the Council were physically assaulted several months ago.

Their anger was understandable – conditions in the Underground were awful. Most of the power plants were shut down for lack of fuel. The tunnels were dark and cold as the Martians huddled into just a few population centers. And even here, it always seemed chilly and damp. The agriculture system was failing as the crops died from lack of care. New strains of mold and fungus, growing on the wet walls of the tunnels, were killing the plants and sickening the population. Manufacturing slowed to a trickle as the robots that operated the machinery broke down and couldn't be repaired due to a lack of parts.

Doctors were treating the symptoms of the unhealthy living conditions by prescribing more and more psychiatric medications. But meds that controlled emotions also numbed the patients, making them less and less effective in their work.

The arrival of the two Viking landers brought the first rays of hope anyone felt in a very long time. And today's meeting would include a report from Kai on a mission that would begin in a few days to contact the people who sent these landers.

The door to the Council room banged open as Kai raced in and took his seat. He was late and apologized to the Council for his tardiness. Quanah smiled at his good friend who seemed a bit disheveled this morning. Kai and Mia were spending a lot of time together. That was understandable. In a few days, Kai would leave Mars. The chances of him returning weren't good. And no one in this room except Kai was willing to undergo the necessary procedure to make the trip to Earth. In Quanah's view, Kai could be as late as he wanted.

After a few opening remarks and reminders to the audience regarding acceptable decorum during the meeting, the council president asked Kai to summarize the project that was scheduled to begin in less than five days.

"Mr. President, we are ready to execute the plan," Kai said, as he pushed a button on a remote control. A holographic slide projector lit up as Kai explained what would happen.

The plan was complicated and dangerous. It involved interrupting the radio signal that Viking 1 used to communicate with Earth. Then, the Martians would replace that signal with their own signal in order to send a large digital file to Earth. This was not an electronic message in a bottle. The immense file they planned to send was Kai himself.

Five years earlier, after witnessing the Russian Mars 3 disaster, Kai returned home and spent the next several months locked in his private laboratory. He had retired from the practice of medicine and was devoting his senior years to the work his grandfather, Kalay, began while still on the surface. At the time, Kalay, who was a neurosurgeon, was looking for a way to extend the lives of the elderly and to restore brain function to those who had experienced serious brain injuries. The procedure involved using a powerful scanner to reach into the brain and pull out all of the synaptic processes and convert them into digital information. A person's intellect, memories, emotions, and the things that made each person unique, could be collected and stored. It was Kalay's hope that the person could remain in a sort of digital stasis until a suitable replacement body could be built by the automated machines of the day.

Kalay died when he tried the procedure on himself and the project was abandoned. But Kai believed that the technology had another use – a way of transporting someone from Mars to another planet by means of a directed radio signal. With the Viking landers sending data about Mars back to Earth, he saw no reason why that same radio signal couldn't be used to send him there as well.

The audaciousness of the plan was in assuming that humans would understand what they were receiving from Mars and would also have the technology to restore Kai to consciousness. It was a huge gamble. But given the death spiral that the Martian people were in, Kai believed that traveling to Earth was the only way he could save his people from extinction.

Kai concluded his presentation and took his seat. As he did, the Council rose and applauded him. The audience did the same, with the applause lasting for several minutes before Kai waved off the adulation and then excused himself from the meeting room.

Kai walked down the corridor to his home where Mia was waiting. As he walked, he noticed how quiet things had gotten. After the evacuation, this place was bustling. And for a time, it looked like Martian inventiveness would allow them to recreate the quality of life they enjoyed before Koya destroyed the surface.

But even the Martians, with all their knowledge and technology, couldn't change the fact that they were never built to live underground. Their society got another four centuries of life since Koya, but the end was near. Kai was the only hope that his people had. But Kai was also giving up everything to make the journey to Earth. Even if he survived, could he get them to help save his people?

Kai stood at the front door of his home for a moment, looking out at the empty sidewalks and the darkness of the tunnel that extended to the horizon. Inside the house was the one person he cared about, and by his own choice, he was about to say goodbye to her. He wondered how Mia could agree to his leaving. But then, he knew that Mia would do the same if it meant saving their people. And anyway, Kai was an optimist. He believed he would succeed and return to Mia.

Tomorrow, as they spent their last day together, he would make sure that she believed that, and that she would wait for him until he returned.

18
The Last Sunrise

MARS – NORTHERN SETTLEMENT – 09 OCTOBER 1976

KAI OPENED HIS eyes and smiled. He was in bed, lying on his side, facing the woman he loved his entire life. They often ended up in this position and he enjoyed watching her sleep – except for the times when she would be startled awake by his stare, thinking that he had died with his eyes wide open. Usually, this resulted in a round of playful tussling as she pretended to get mad at Kai for scaring her. But she did worry about how hard Kai pushed himself. He was past the 400-year mark – senior citizen status here in the Underground.

Before she woke, Kai wanted to drink-in this memory of his beautiful Mia. In less than two days, he would never again be where he was right now, holding her softly in his arms. As she slept, he thought back to that time so long ago, when his parents brought him here for what they called a short adventure in the Underground.

Kai and Mia were part of a rapidly-shrinking group of Martians who were old enough to have actually lived on the surface of Mars before Koya struck. They were the same age and their families shared the same evacuation shelter. Their families rode-out the horrible vibrations and the grinding sounds as the two worlds collided. Kai and Mia saw things that children should never see – the dead and the dying in tunnels choked with dust and smoke, and the cries for help that reverberated down the long corridors.

As life returned to a sense of new normalcy, Kai really noticed Mia for the first time. She was riding a teeter-totter with another girl in one of the play areas. When they talked about school, Kai found out that she was smart – a grade ahead of him in school, despite their identical ages. After sitting together in the sandbox for awhile, Kai gave Mia a toy spaceship he built from pieces and parts he collected from the cafeteria. She thanked him for the gift and gave him a little peck on the cheek. From that moment, Mia and Kai were inseparable.

Mia opened her eyes and saw that Kai was looking at her. He smiled brightly, a smile of hope. But despite her best effort, she could return only a weak smile to this man she loved. She pulled him in close to her and they quietly hugged. Kai could hear her crying softly.

The past two weeks had been draining for them. After Kai first told Mia about his plan, they entered a new phase in their lives, something divorce lawyers on Earth might call *irreconcilable differences*. There was no middle position. He wanted to go. She didn't. Kai would drop the subject for a time, but soon the discussion started up again. Mia could not accept the fact that this mission required Kai to lose his physical body. And if, or as Kai repeatedly corrected her, *when* he returned, he would still be a non-physical being. How could their marriage and their love continue, separated from each other by glass and metal and silicon?

What finally convinced Mia that Kai was right was the reality of their situation. Both were old and sick. Sooner than later, one or both of them would be dead from some kind of illness brought on by the unhealthy living conditions in the Underground. There was a death sentence waiting for everyone. The only question was when.

Mia finally agreed and told Kai that she loved him for the sacrifice he was making for her and for all of their people. But Kai needed a promise from Mia before he could make his journey to Earth. He needed to know that she would hang on, no matter how long it took him to get help and return. With that assurance, Kai could find the strength to return to her.

Kai and Mia got up, not speaking as they showered and dressed for the day. He had much to do before leaving for Earth in two days. But this morning, with the Sun rising in about an hour, they would put on protective suits and stand together on the surface of Mars. It would be the first time Mia had been there since she evacuated.

An elevator car near their home was waiting for them. They were escorted to the surface by a rescue team, who would remain below-ground while Mia and Kai walked on the surface. The ride took less than a minute. After clearing the first airlock and then the second, they climbed the ladder to the surface. The original elevator building had been destroyed in the impact and only some mosaic flooring material remained as evidence that a modern civilization once existed here.

With just a few minutes to go before sunrise, Mia and Kai walked toward the brightening horizon. The sky was still black, still filled with billions of stars. Kai pointed his finger at the sky.

"There it is," Kai said.

"Earth," Mia replied, the first word she had spoken this morning. "It seems so small and so far away."

"They sent two of their spacecraft here," Kai said, pointing to the Viking lander, which was barely visible in the opposite direction. "It's only fair that we reciprocate."

"And that is where you will be tomorrow," Mia said. A teacher of literature and semantics, Mia had little experience in the science of space travel. Her heart lived where the great Martian authors did, writing books and poetry about the power of love and the strength of bonds that existed between intelligent beings. She wondered if such emotions existed on Earth. And she feared that her husband would find a hostile reception waiting for him.

They stood silently for several minutes, watching the small orange dot peek above the horizon. The Sun was smaller than Mia remembered and the surface was much colder. She shivered from the cold or from the fear of what was going to happen to Kai.

"Mia?" Kai asked, turning her toward him. The helmets of their suits made it impossible to see anything but her eyes.

"Yes, Kai," Mia said, holding his hands through their suits.

"I love you," Kai said. "And you must believe me. I am coming back for you."

"And I love you, Kai," Mia said, looking deeply into his eyes. The Sun was rising now, casting a glare on the shield of his helmet. But his piercing black eyes drove through the brightness to remain in contact with hers.

"Will you wait for me?" Kai asked. "Will you hang on, no matter what?"

"Yes, Kai," Mia said, her voice cracking through the microphone that connected their two suits. She was crying.

"Please Mia, please be strong for me," Kai said. "It is all that will keep me going."

"I will, Kai. I will," Mia said as she squeezed his hands.

The radio in their helmets crackled. The rescue crew in the elevator told them that it was time to leave the surface. They stood for a few more minutes, watching as the dusty red surface began to glow from the light. This was the only Mars the humans knew. It would be Kai's job to convince them that there was another Mars and his people needed their help.

They watched for another minute before turning and walking back to the elevator. It was the last time either of them would ever set foot on the surface of Mars again.

For the remainder of the day, Kai and Mia would be together. Although few words passed between them, her acceptance of what Kai must do gave him comfort. As for Mia, his leaving would be devastating to her. But, she believed Kai would return. And she would wait, no matter how long it took.

Late this afternoon, they would say goodbye. It would be the most difficult thing either of them had ever done. After tearing himself away from Mia, Kai would be taken to the medical laboratory, where his grandfather Kalay's scanner had been reassembled, ready to change him into a mass of digital bits.

Last night, a team of engineers went to the surface to assemble the radio transmission equipment that would be used to send Kai to Earth. After overwhelming Viking's radio signal with their more powerful one, they would need at least twenty-eight minutes of uninterrupted radio contact in order to send Kai's complete set of files to Earth. Any gamma radiation bursts or solar flares that crossed through the radio signal could disrupt the transmission and kill him. It was just one more gamble in the riskiest thing he or any of his kind had ever done.

Once he arrived on Earth, Kai would have no awareness and no control over his environment. Only when the conditions were right would his programming allow his digitized body to be reassembled so that he could become the living Kai again. How long he would remain in stasis was unknown. But after watching Viking work for the past three months, he noticed that the people who sent this spacecraft to his planet were very attentive to what their two landers were doing on Mars. Kai was certain that it would be only a short time before he would reawaken and begin his mission.

Kai supposed that any people who could send a spacecraft to his planet must have at least considered the possibility that intelligent life might exist here. So, imprinting his own logic on the humans, they should not be surprised when he spoke to them through their electronic equipment. Perhaps it was a bit of hubris, but Kai was confident he could convince these humans that it was also in their interest to help him.

Kai's transmission to Earth was scheduled for tomorrow. It would be late Friday night on the western coast of the United States. Earth and Mars would be in the correct alignment to send Kai to Earth. After he was gone, all that Mia and everyone else could do was to wait.

19
Goldstone

BARSTOW, CALIFORNIA – 11 OCTOBER 1976

I T HAD BEEN almost three months since the Viking missions began. Six weeks after Viking 1 landed on Mars, it was joined by its twin, Viking 2. It also landed in the northern hemisphere, but NASA selected a spot on the opposite side of the planet. This gave NASA almost continuous contact with one of the two landers.

Viking 2 settled in a place called *Utopia Planitia*. Although a bit rockier than Viking 1's location, the photos from Viking 2 showed a similarly flat, featureless surface.

The two landers and their companion orbiters were working well, sending back the best information ever obtained from Mars. On the surface, the landers were revealing information about the chemical composition of the Martian soil and atmosphere. High above, the two Viking orbiters were making a photographic map of the entire Martian surface.

But by the time Viking 2 landed, Mars was yesterday's news. The large press contingent that came to witness the first

Viking landing didn't return for Viking 2. They had moved on to other stories. It was a busy year.

In 1976, inflation had already busted through the roof around the world and oil prices were about to skyrocket again. In China, 250,000 people were killed in an earthquake. Riots in Soweto Township marked the beginning of the end of Apartheid in South Africa. And in the United States, the 1976 presidential election was taking much of the media's attention.

The election would feature a quiet former governor from Georgia against a quiet sitting president who assumed the office when his boss resigned in 1974. The election would be close, but in the end, Jimmy Carter would defeat Gerald Ford to capture the White House. With all of the elections – local, state, and national – there was little time left to follow the antics of the two Viking brothers, who were still doing amazing work on Mars.

With the press gone, the Viking mission team had settled into a regular routine. Scientists with skin in the game – those who had championed the laboratories aboard the two landers – were still busy analyzing data coming in from their experiments. No one could know then, but the Viking landers and orbiters were so well-built that, instead of the estimated ninety days for each mission, both landers and orbiters would continue sending back photos and data about Mars into the early 1980s.

On the surface of Mars, the search for life was not encouraging. None of the soil sampled by the Viking landers revealed organic material – the stuff of life – in any quantity down to parts per billion. One researcher remarked that the Apollo astronauts found more organic material on the moon than the Viking landers were finding on Mars. It was becoming clear that Mars – or at least, the surface of Mars – was dead – continuously sterilized by radiation. Astrobiologists, an emerging branch of science, were hoping that life might exist deeper in the soil or below ground. But the Viking missions were designed to literally just scratch the surface of Mars. So far, the results were optimistically labeled as inconclusive.

Getting the data from Mars to Earth was a complex technical process. Two planets, each with their own orbits around the Sun and both spinning on their own axes, made it a challenge to keep radio contact with two small landers on the Martian surface. NASA had anticipated the challenges of radio communication from space when it built the Deep Space Network, or DSN. The network was a series of high-gain radio receiving antennas, positioned in such a way that one antenna was facing the Martian surface at any point during the Earth day. These large parabolic dishes – one at the Goldstone station, near Barstow, California, plus two others in Madrid and Sydney – were located in areas that would minimize interference in capturing the very faint radio signals from Mars. What made the DSN so important was that no matter what time of day or night, one of the big radio dishes would have a line-of-sight view of Mars, enabling almost continuous contact with the Viking missions.

It was late Friday night and Goldstone was on-line with Viking 1. Its twin, Viking 2, was on the opposite side of Mars, taking a nap until it would be visible to Earth again. Goldstone was getting a nice signal from Viking 1. Sunspot activity had been low and the signal quality had been good over the past few days.

Controlling the huge 70-meter antenna took a lot of skill. Because Earth and Mars were moving through three-dimensional space and both were turning on two dimensional axes, getting the math right was critical to keeping contact with the Viking missions. Finding the faint signals from Mars was as much an art as it was a science. Technicians had to constantly tweak the dish and keep radio receivers precisely tuned to the correct carrier frequencies of the landers and orbiters. It was a delicate dance in which the slightest misstep could result in NASA losing contact with an orbiter or lander.

One particularly good technician on duty tonight was Maggie Shields. The pretty 23-year-old, with undergraduate degrees in physics and math from UCLA, was working on her master's degree when she landed the job with NASA. Management liked Maggie and thought that she had a future in the space program. But management included someone who was particularly fond of the petite redhead. Her father, William Shields, was a deputy program manager for the Viking mission. Bill was an Air Force fighter ace during the Korean War, and then earned his doctorate degree in physics after returning to California.

Before sending in her resume, Maggie changed her last name to her mother's maiden name, just to be sure that she got the job on *her* merits, not her dad's. Within a week, Maggie had been invited to NASA for an interview. After the second level of interviews, Maggie received an offer to work on the Viking program. Before accepting, she disclosed that Bill Shields was her father, but didn't want that fact to influence management's decision. After a good laugh, the director assured Maggie that her presence could only improve the disposition of the hothead Bill Shields, who tossed curse words around like someone throwing rice at a wedding.

Maggie's first assignment was working at the Goldstone station in Barstow. It would be a juggling act. She had graduate classes at UCLA during the day and then a long drive to Barstow to work the graveyard shift. But she didn't mind. And, her dad was proud to see his daughter join the growing ranks of women who were coming into the space program in the late 1970s.

Tonight, Maggie would be handling the radio desk, making sure that Goldstone's radio receivers were getting a good signal from the transmitter aboard the Viking 1 lander. Radio was something of a specialty for Maggie. She got her amateur radio license when she was only nine. The worldwide amateur radio community was close-knit and most hams recognized her call sign when she CQ'd, mostly late at night. Female hams were rare and her father once told her that she would get marriage offers from every continent on the planet, including Antarctica. At the time, she didn't understand what he meant. Later, she found out that a female voice on shortwave was like honey to a bear. It didn't matter – she could deal with the occasional knuckleheads – but Maggie loved the chance to talk with hams all over the world.

Maggie expected a quiet Friday night at Goldstone. There were no experiments scheduled. She might even get some studying done. Her radio receivers were streaming a steady dribble of data from automatic sensors, mainly reporting weather and atmospheric conditions. Viking 1 was working well tonight.

The seismic sensor was working, too. Most scientists believed Mars had been dormant for a very long time. In fact, the seismic sensor was an afterthought – wired to one of the lander pads as a just-in-case kind of thing. But a series of blips coming from Viking's seismometer suggested that something was bumping around near the lander. The data appeared to be almost rhythmic – not in waves as Maggie had seen on seismometers recording earthquake activity in the Los Angeles basin. To her, the seismic data looked more like – well, like *feet* walking on the surface near the lander. One particular bump appeared louder than the rest, as if something heavy had been placed on the surface. Then, the seismic footsteps appeared to fade off into the distance. In a few minutes, they were gone.

Specialists started noticing the peculiar activity about two weeks ago, but chalked it up to ongoing problems they were having with the sensor itself. Maggie knew that, at her level in the pecking order, her interpretation of this data would likely be dismissed. So, she kept her theory to herself.

With a physics textbook in front of her radio console to keep her warm, she went back to reading, glancing up regularly at the radio signal meters. The VU meters measured the amplitude of the signal coming from Mars, the needles popping up and down as new data arrived. Each blip registered about sixty-percent on the meters, a good signal from such a small spacecraft. The blips were coming at about 70 beats per minute, absolutely nominal in all respects.

Maggie rested her chin on her hands, watching the predictable pattern of data being sent. She still couldn't quite grasp the fact that she was listening to a spacecraft sitting on the surface of another planet. What a rare chance to be part of something that she hoped to tell her grandchildren about. But, heck, by then, she might be speaking to them from Mars, at the speed the NASA space program was going.

Suddenly the speakers went silent. Maggie was jolted by the silence and quickly scanned the meters. Viking 1 was no longer sending a signal. She called out to another technician who was responsible for keeping the dish aimed correctly at Mars.

"Alan, do you have a lock on Viking 1?" she shouted to the technician, who was standing, talking to another team member. "Because I'm getting nothing here."

The tech immediately sat down at his station. He shouted back, "Yep. I have the carrier signal right in the cross-hairs." Viking had stopped transmitting and the problem was on the surface of Mars, not with their antenna.

"I need to call JPL," she said as she reached for the telephone. She was ready to spin the seventh number on the rotary phone when the transmission from Mars resumed. Data began flooding through her console again. The VU meters were pegged all the way to the right – well into the red. She turned up the speakers on her console to listen to the signal. The sound was a smooth whoosh of white noise; the kind she could hear when dialing her car radio between FM stations. The signal was so strong that it spilled out of the carrier frequency and into both sidebands. An oscilloscope displaying the radio's visual signature showed that the transmission filled the green phosphor screen from top to bottom. The transmission looked more binary than analog, something still unusual in 1976.

Maggie punched one of the timers on her console. She jumped up and ran over to the computer to make sure that it was recording data from her station. The IBM mainframe was working perfectly, with a fresh data tape installed just a few minutes before.

When she returned to her console, other members of the team had assembled around her to look at the data. No one had ever seen this kind of signal coming from Viking.

"What do you think it is, Maggie?" one of the technicians asked her.

"Well, it's not analog, that's for sure," Maggie said, sounding more knowledgeable about it than she probably ought to. She bent forward to get a closer look at the screen, an act which the fellows behind her thoroughly appreciated. "It almost looks like there's data inside this entire bandwidth here," she said, pointing at the oscilloscope. "Like digitized and compressed data."

When she turned around, she realized that she was talking gibberish to these technicians. These were guys who worked in AM radio or in early satellite programs like Telstar. None of them had any digital computer experience. While mainframe computers were being used to record the data from Mars, personal computers were still a decade away from showing up in people's homes.

Seeing the blank looks on their faces, Maggie decided to make a smooth course correction to get these guys away from her station so that she could study the anomaly herself.

"Or, it just might be a frozen switch. The ambient temperature at Viking 1 right now is minus eighty-four," she added.

The other technicians just shrugged and returned to their stations. Obviously, this woman knew what she was doing. Besides, her old man wore a suit at NASA, so they weren't going to question her – at least not to her face.

"Thanks guys. I think I'm just going to call it in to JPL," Maggie said, picking up the phone.

20
Kai's Arrival

PASADENA, CALIFORNIA – 11 OCTOBER 1976

A T THE JET Propulsion Lab, Mike Savin was a second stringer, pulling an overnight shift at Viking Mission Control. Not that he minded. Mike was thrilled to be here. A few days after graduating from Caltech, he received a call from the Viking project manager – from Jim Martin himself – inviting Mike to join the Viking team. Although the mission had already started, Mike was a quick study and caught up with the operational protocols.

As a kid, Mike was always interested in space. He read everything he could about space exploration and had an encyclopedic knowledge of every NASA space mission since Explorer 1 was launched in 1958. He even followed the Russian space program, when the Russians were in the mood to share information about what they were doing. While the moon missions were incredible, for Mike Savin, it was always about interplanetary travel. Viking was the first step in getting there. By the time he had completed his doctorate degree, the wheels were already in motion – first with the Russian lander and now with two Viking missions. This job at JPL was Mike's chance to get in on it – maybe become part of a manned mission to Mars that was sure to follow the success of the Apollo program.

Mission Control was quiet. Mike was one of a skeleton team on duty overnight. That was good. With little activity coming from Mars, Mike would have time to study the photographs and telemetry sent by the two Viking landers and the two orbiting satellites crisscrossing overhead. He might even get the chance to talk to the DSN team over in Barstow. Well, maybe one *particular* member of the team that he had been building the courage to call for over a week.

Mike was studying two photos taken by the Viking 1 lander. The photos were long shots of a part of the Martian horizon. He noticed something odd. The first photo showed a flat and uniformly rocky surface. This shot was taken the day Viking landed in July. But another photo of the same horizon, taken just two days ago, showed a mound of rocks that were not in the first picture. Back and forth, he swapped the pictures. How did that pile of rocks get there? Like most of the specialists working on the Viking program, he had no illusions about finding intelligent life on Mars. And yet, the evidence in the two photographs was irrefutable – the rocks were too many and too heavy to have blown there or been deposited by wind or water. It was very late Friday night and he wasn't going to bother the higher-ups, but he made a mental note to speak with other mission specialists when they came back to work next week.

Mike returned to his desk. It was time to man-up and call Maggie at the Goldstone station. But the stars must have been in alignment tonight because as he sat down, his telephone was ringing. And the object of his thoughts for the past few weeks was on the other end of the line.

"JPL, this is Mike Savin," Mike said, sounding as authoritative as he could.

"Hi Mike, this is Maggie Shields at Goldstone. I don't know if you remember me, but we met two weeks ago at that NASA conference," Maggie said, sounding nervous and speaking rapidly.

"Hi Maggie. Sure, I remember. How are you?" Mike knew he was talking because his mouth was moving, but he honestly couldn't remember any of what he had just said. Maggie Shields was the most beautiful girl he had ever seen. And, in the two weeks since that meeting, he couldn't get her out of his mind.

The two of them literally bumped into each other in the crowded foyer at the Kármán Auditorium. The meeting was called by NASA to bring everyone up-to-speed on the Viking program, and to show photos of the brand-new Space Shuttle that promised to revolutionize space travel. Probably half of the audience was there just to get a glimpse of the interior and exterior shots of the new spacecraft. Many of them would beg, plead, or cajole themselves into a spot in the shuttle astronaut program that was forming up. Mike intended to be one of those cajolers, but standing in the lobby, he was interrupted when a beautiful girl with curly red hair and green eyes accidentally bumped into him as the crowd compressed, waiting for the auditorium doors to open.

Mike stood a full foot taller than the petite Maggie Shields. But when he looked into her eyes, a strange phenomenon began. Poets have written about it for centuries. It's the one where a beautiful woman can literally slow down time as she completely takes over the mind of her subject. Mike stared at Maggie for what felt like minutes. It was Maggie who started the ball rolling.

"Hi, I'm Maggie," she said, extending her hand. Mike was still drinking in her face, her eyes, the little freckles on her nose, and the most breathtaking smile he had ever seen.

"Um, hello. I'm Mike." *Wow, that was clever,* he thought, taking her hand. *Try to think of some catchy words, dummy, before she gets away.*

The auditorium doors opened and people began filing in. Neither of them moved from their spots, their handshake in limbo as they stared at each other. The crowd had to move around this island of two, standing at the entrance.

"I think we're in the way," Maggie said, her smile growing more impish now. Her mind had also gone into vapor-lock and one-syllable words were all that she could manage.

"Maybe we should go in," Mike replied. "Hey, do you want to sit together? I really don't know anyone here."

"Neither do I," Maggie said. That was a bald-faced lie. Her father was in the foyer and rapidly moving toward the two of them. Her eyes cut away from Mike for a second to gauge her father's reaction. From where she stood, Maggie couldn't tell whether he approved of this guy who towered over his daughter.

"Hi Dad," Maggie said, as Bill Shields stepped up, lightly bumping into Mike's shoulder. Mike's head pivoted to the left to see – not Maggie's dad, but his advisor – Dr. William Shields.

"Uh, Dr. Shields, Good Morning," Mike said grinning nervously. He was still holding onto Maggie's hand. When he tried to release from their handshake to shake her father's hand, Maggie wouldn't let go. She giggled as he struggled to deal with two members of the family, doing his best to maintain his composure.

"I see that you've met my daughter, Dr. Savin," Bill replied, still maintaining his stoic composure. *Mike and Maggie. A match made in heaven,* Bill thought, although he wasn't going to reveal his cards at this juncture.

"Your daughter? Maggie? Maggie Shields?" Mike asked. She hadn't told him her last name.

"Dr. Mike Savin, Daddy?" Maggie quickly returned. Mike hadn't revealed his last name, either. Her face darkened a bit, but not in a way Mike would detect. But her father could see bad weather approaching.

"Ah, yeah. Mike is – check that – Mike *was* one of my students. He finished his doctorate in June and joined us right after the launch." Bill was trying to figure a way out of this little storm that was brewing between him and his daughter. "You might remember that I talked about his dissertation, you know, the work he was doing with subatomic particles?"

"Oh, I remember your mentioning Dr. Savin's dissertation, Daddy." Maggie still called him that. It was a tough habit to break for two people who were so close, but managed to annoy each other so much.

"Yes, well, maybe we should go inside? Maggie, your mom sends her love. See you next weekend?" he said, with his voice ending on a vocal up-tick, hoping the storm had passed.

"Mike, would you save me a seat? I need to talk with Dr. Shields for a moment." Her tone got serious, but she did manage to fire off a quick smile at Mike.

"Oh. Yeah. Sure. I'll see you inside, Maggie. See you later, Dr. Shields," Mike said as he hustled toward the auditorium doors. *My advisor's daughter,* Mike thought. What were the chances? He smiled as he headed toward the front of the auditorium. He had an in with Maggie and was damned glad about it.

Maggie waited until Mike was well inside before she turned back to her father.

"Dr. Savin? Dr. Michael Savin?" Maggie asked. "The guy you've been telling me about for, what, the last four years? The *Maggie why-can't-you-find-a-guy-like-Mike-Savin,* Mike Savin? I was expecting a guy with Buddy Holly glasses and a propeller hat. This guy must have a Rolodex full of girl-friends."

"Don't sell yourself short, honey," Bill replied. "There was a spark there. I saw it in your eyes from across the room." He bent down and kissed his daughter on the cheek. "Now forgive your old man and go sit with Mike. I love you."

She couldn't stay mad at her father. From the minute she first crawled up on his lap as he talked to his buddies on his ham radio, her daddy was Maggie's first love. And that was the problem. Every guy she met fell short of her father. It was an ongoing problem for Maggie – the endless series of half-stepping nitwits she had dated. But Mike? Well, maybe her father was right. She walked into the auditorium, looking for Mike. The tall guy was standing, waving at her. Of course he would be in the front – to get the best view. That's the place she would have picked.

After the conference, Mike and Maggie met for coffee at a little place in Pasadena. Maggie had a class and Mike had one, too. Only, in his case, he was *teaching* the class. In addition to his gig at JPL, Mike had landed an assistant professorship position at Caltech. His new office was only a few steps away from the classrooms where he sat as a graduate student.

Over coffee, they asked about each other, nervous and overcompensating for the feelings each of them was trying to hold back. Mike learned about graduate school and Maggie's plan to get her doctorate. Incredibly, it would be in physics, too.

But time was short and they had to leave.

"I like your shoes," Mike said as they stood up to leave.

"I like yours, too." Both were wearing original Anna Kalsø Earth Shoes. But the tips of the high-in-front-low-in-back shoes barely showed beneath the wide bell-bottom jeans she was wearing. Mike had been admiring those jeans since they walked into the coffee shop together. There was no denying it. He was nuts about this girl.

"Can I call you?" Mike asked.

"That would be great." She reached up on her tiptoes and gave him the slightest peck on the cheek. Mike was devastated.

"See 'ya," Maggie said, as she walked away with Mike enjoying every step on her way back to her Datsun. She waved as she left. He grinned and waved back.

∞

"Mike? Mike! Are you still there?" Maggie's voice on the telephone jarred him back to the present.

"Oh. Sorry, Maggie. I was just thinking...well...actually, I was thinking about you," Mike said. That was a bold move and he waited for Maggie's reaction.

"So, were you planning to call?" Maggie asked. "Or, were you going to wait until we had a crisis to talk again?"

"No, I was going to call – what do you mean, crisis?"

"Well, it's not an emergency or anything, but I wanted to let you know that we're getting some real strange data from Viking 1."

"How long has it been going on?" Mike asked, still thinking of her question about Mike calling her. *Score!*

"Over twenty minutes. We've got a recorder on it, but it doesn't look like normal data from the lander. It's not telemetry. Not analog. Not a sine wave. On the scope, it looks like a packed square wave from 18 Hz out to over 30 кHz. The orbiter's transmitter is pegged at 110 percent and the signal is bleeding into the sidebands. I'm worried we might lose the lander's transmitter if this thing keeps going."

"So, it's coming from the lander?" Mike asked.

"Yes, we're direct with the lander right now. The orbiter doesn't clear the horizon for another twenty minutes," Maggie said, as she tweaked the monitor to get a better look at the signal picture. "It looks like..."

Mike waited, but Maggie stopped talking. "Maggie, are you still there?"

"Well. There you go. Now it's gone. Back to the normal 70 BPM data signal. Modulation at sixty-percent, exactly as before."

"What do you think it was?" Mike asked. He would not let this opportunity get away from him. If he had to drive to Barstow tonight, he was going to use this excuse to see Maggie again.

"Maybe a frozen actuator or even a gamma burst," Maggie replied. "Whatever it was, it's gone now. Everything is nominal, again."

"Maggie, that run of data tapes won't get to JPL until Monday afternoon. Could you pull that tape?" Mike asked, sounding more in charge than he should have. "I could drive out and pick it up tonight."

"Or, you could wait until tomorrow and meet me for brunch. The Jazz House in Malibu? Some live jazz? I'll bring the tape with me," Maggie answered. She had this scheme planned for the moment she set the hook. Now, it was time to reel him in.

"That sounds great. Around eleven?"

"Perfect. See you then."

"Hey, Maggie? I'm really glad you called."

"Me, too. See you soon."

The phone clicked off and Mike slouched back in his chair. He pumped both arms in the air, although no one noticed. He doubted he would get any real work done for the rest of the night.

21
Malibu

WITH HIS VOLKSWAGEN aimed toward Malibu, Mike prepared for what was possibly the most important day of his life. Everything else – the job at JPL and his new teaching gig at Caltech – faded in importance as his mind filled with images of Maggie.

Mike experienced little glimmers of this kind of feeling before – a few brief crushes in high school and college. But the feelings eventually passed. Maybe it was his youth, or the goals he had set for himself, but no one ever affected him like Maggie did since they met two weeks ago.

It was ironic. Here he was, a guy trained in the scientific method – theory, observation, measurement, and testing. Yet, Mike had come to the conclusion that he was in love without any of these things. He didn't even know Maggie. Hell, he didn't even know that her father was his advisor. But, the moment their eyes met, a spark jumped between them that shorted-out any objective analysis of the moment. *They're called feelings*, he reminded himself – thoughts that come from another part of the brain. They weren't formed in the analytical part of Mike's brain, the place where he lived most of the time. He liked being in this new place. It made him feel free and alive.

His mind drifted back to the good fortune that brought him to this moment. *How does a poor, working class kid from Detroit manage to get here anyway?* It wasn't money. He had none. There were no political strings or influence in his family. His dad tightened bolts on an auto assembly line. And it wasn't luck that got him here, either. Mike didn't believe in luck. He was here because of all of the work and sacrifices his parents and grandparents made to give him the opportunities that were now being placed in front of him.

Although it didn't sound Russian, the name Savin was solidly Slavic and Mike was proud of his heritage. He could trace his family back seven generations, back to a group of Savins who were farmers in Czarist Russia. But all of that ended more than a generation ago. In 1917, Russia was in the midst of revolution. Because the Savin family owned their land, they were members of a group accused of exploiting the working class. But the Savins didn't exploit anyone. They did all the work themselves, or hired others and paid them fairly. The Savin farm had not one *kholop* – unpaid laborers, slaves really, who worked for many landowners. After the Soviet revolution, these workers took control of the large farms.

Mike's father, Viktor, was born in 1916, a year before the Bolshevik revolution. As the Bolsheviks consolidated their power, families like the Savins, who were loyal to the deposed Czar, were rounded up. Some were sent to gulags. Other were

summarily shot. With the First World War raging across
Europe, every border with Russia was closed to keep out refugees trying to flee the revolution. With no overland routes to
get the whole Savin family out of Russia, Mike's grandparents
decided to get their children out first. They bribed a friend
in the customs office to stow their three children – ages six,
four, and thirteen-month-old Viktor – as well as an eighteen-
year-old governess, aboard a Norwegian steamship bound for
Canada.

The ship set sail from St. Petersburg without incident, but
the young governess, whose family had been in the employ
of the Savins since she was an infant herself, had to be put off
in Stockholm when she was diagnosed with typhoid fever.
The family learned that she was shipped back to Russia on a
stretcher. Later, she was sent to a gulag, where she was never
heard from again. The three Savin children were now alone,
heading west aboard a cold, creaking steamer and facing a
grueling winter voyage across the Baltic Sea, into the Atlantic,
and then on to North America.

But they weren't alone for long. Other Russian stowaways
were onboard and the sympathetic ship captain invited all of
them to come out of the hold and join the crew in the heated
part of the ship. They were given cots, blankets, and food.
Most importantly, they were out of the frigid hold of the ship
and kept warm and dry as the small ship plowed through the
choppy, snowy Atlantic.

Thirteen days later, the ship steamed down the St. Law-
rence Seaway and tied up in Montreal. As the kids disem-
barked, family members already in Canada were waiting for
them on the dock. Viktor and his sisters were put aboard a
train for Windsor and the children moved in with an aunt
and uncle, who arrived from Russia a year earlier with their

four children. The Savin kids were warmly welcomed into the family and into the larger Russian community that settled in Windsor and Detroit.

Letters to the kids arrived from Russia almost daily for a while. Their aunt and uncle would gather the children around the kitchen table to read the words their parents wrote. They wrote of the things that were happening in Russia, but Viktor's aunt and uncle knew that it was much worse than they were letting on. In every letter, their parents pledged their love and devotion to their children and promised that they would get out of Russia as soon as possible.

After a time, the letters became less frequent and the kids sensed that some parts were not being read to them. By 1919, the letters stopped. In 1921, they got word that the Savin family estate outside of St. Petersburg had been seized by the Bolsheviks and turned into a collective farm. But there was still no word about Viktor's parents. Despite efforts by family on both sides of the Atlantic, his parents were never heard from again.

By the start of the 1930s, Canada and the United States were in a depression. Viktor quit school in the tenth grade to help support his adopted family. He set pins for tips at a Windsor bowling alley. He hawked the *Detroit News* and *Windsor Star* along the rough waterfront to tough-looking guys who sometimes paid and sometimes didn't. When Viktor was approached by a small-time gangster and asked if he wanted to make some extra money running numbers, his uncle pulled some strings at the longshoreman's union and got Viktor a job as a laborer, unloading coke that supplied the steel mills lining the Detroit river. With the money he made, Viktor paid back his aunt and uncle for the cost of caring for

him and his two sisters. He put the rest of his earnings in a
bank account.

Viktor was twenty-four when Germany invaded Poland in
1939. The United Kingdom was calling on its Commonwealth
partners to send troops after declaring war on Germany.
Like a lot of young men of his generation, Viktor signed up,
joining a new regiment that was forming in Windsor. He was
sent to Halifax for training and three months later, Viktor
was on another cold ship, this time eastbound for England.
Twenty-one years earlier, war and revolution were the reasons
Viktor left Europe. Now, another war was taking him back.

Although he hoped to get back to Russia, it was not to be.
His regiment was attached to the British Eighth Army and
Viktor was wounded in Sicily. He was eventually sent back to
Canada for convalescence.

When World War II ended in 1945, the twenty-nine-year-
old Viktor Savin was unemployed. Factory jobs were tough
to find, especially with all the veterans coming home. But
Viktor eventually got a job as a laborer at Ford Motor Company's River Rouge steel plant in Detroit. He met his future
wife, Nika, at a Russian Orthodox church festival in Detroit.
They were married in 1945 and moved to the U.S. side of the
Peace Bridge in 1946. The family eventually settled in a small,
two-story home in Dearborn, where Viktor got a new job
with Ford, assembling cars in the booming post-war years.

Mike was born in 1950, the third of three children. He
attended public schools in Dearborn, which had a diverse
cultural mix of Eastern Europeans, Italians, Jews, and Afri-
can-Americans. Although he spoke English at school, the
family still spoke Russian at home. For the rest of their lives,
Nika and Viktor spoke mainly Russian. Mike was usually
asked to translate when his parents visited a doctor or needed

some other kind of professional service. But in their neighborhood, where everyone spoke Russian or Polish or Slovak,
not having a working knowledge of English was never an
issue. Even on Sundays at the Russian Orthodox church, Mass
was in Russian, as were Mike's Sunday School lessons after-
ward.

In high school, Mike excelled, but he especially loved
math and the sciences. He wasn't much of an athlete and had
the reputation of being quiet and bookish. Today, he might
be called a nerd. To the utter consternation of his father, Mike
studied German in high school. To be fair, language choices
were limited in the public schools. The only other offerings,
French and Spanish, didn't suit his goal of becoming a scientist. Many of the best books on physics were written by
German physicists. It was a good reason to study the language, but his father still got scratchy every time he saw one
of Mike's German textbooks.

By the time he graduated from high school, Mike had his
pick of colleges, nearly all of the costs paid by scholarships.
It was a good thing, too, because his family couldn't afford to
send him to college. And so, in an egregious act of disloyalty
to his Michigan family, Mike Savin chose Ohio State, that
school down in Columbus. Every late November, he would be
reminded of his choice when Michigan played Ohio State in
the biggest grudge match in college football.

Mike graduated with degrees in physics and mathematics
and was accepted into graduate school at Caltech, where he
would earn his master's and doctorate degrees in physics. So,
in July of 1972, with Nixon and McGovern signs popping up
on front lawns all over Dearborn, Mike packed up his sec-
ond-hand VW Beetle, kissed Viktor and Nika goodbye, and
set out for California.

It was the first time Mike had ever been out of the
Midwest and he had plenty of time to take in the sights along
I-70. He stopped in Indianapolis to see the Brickyard, where
Mark Donohue won the Indy 500 a few weeks earlier. He
rode to the top of the St. Louis Arch, and then marveled at
the endless Prairie land and the distant Rocky Mountains that
stretched out in front of him. In Utah, he turned south into
Arizona, where he stood on the rim of the Grand Canyon. He
stopped in Phoenix for a few days to visit a college classmate
who also headed west after graduation. Leaving Phoenix, he
drove west on I-10. Two weeks after leaving Michigan, Mike
arrived in Los Angeles.

Graduate school at Caltech was brutal and competitive.
Everyone was just as smart, or maybe smarter than Mike.
But he was learning from some of the best minds in physics
and the competition only sharpened his determination. He
was befriended by a number of faculty members, who saw
real potential for Mike as a physicist. One professor, a brilliant ex-fighter pilot named Dr. William Shields, became not
only his school advisor, but next to his father, Bill Shields was
the biggest influence in his life. Dr. Shields was a self-made
man, working his way through undergraduate and graduate programs while serving in the military. He liked Mike's
working-class ethics and his desire to make it on his merits.
He was tougher on Mike than he was on his other students,
but no matter how much work he gave him, Mike came back
for more. There would be no stopping this kid from making a
name for himself in the world of science.

Graduate school went by quickly. He wrote his doctoral
dissertation on subatomic particles, elusive bits of matter that
can be observed for only a fraction of a second. Mike was
entering the profession at a time when physicists were starting

to unlock the secrets of these particles that make up the particles that make up matter.

In mid-May 1976, Mike's dissertation was signed-off by
his advisor, with only a few minor editorial suggestions. A
week later, his doctoral committee approved the document in
a meeting that lasted less than an hour. Outside the conference room, he was congratulated by members of the committee and welcomed as a fellow colleague. Bill Shields was the
first to shake his hand, the first to call him Dr. Savin, and the
first to buy him a beer at a nearby campus watering hole to
celebrate his achievement.

In June, with most of the Savin family in town for the
graduation, Mike stood up and took his place in the single-file
line walking toward the Romanesque columns of Beckman
Hall. His maroon doctoral robe, adorned with three black
stripes on each arm, flapped in the brisk breeze as he moved
up the line. When he reached the stage, Caltech President Dr.
Harold Brown handed him his degree and shook his hand
warmly as he congratulated Mike on his accomplishment. In
another year, Brown would leave Caltech to become Secretary
of Defense in the Carter administration. John Knowles, then
president of the Rockefeller Foundation, gave the commence-
ment speech. Like every other graduate that day, Mike tried
to pay attention to the speech. But knowing that his family –
his father, mother, two sisters, and about twenty other Savin
family members – were sitting to his left, smiling and waving
at him, made it very difficult for him to pay attention.

After the ceremony on the grass mall, Mike's family and
friends would eat and drink at Pyotr Romanov's, considered
the best Russian restaurant in Los Angeles. But since just
about everything being said that night was in Russian, Mike
spent most of his time translating for his non-Russian-speak-

ing guests as the congratulatory speeches and the off-color jokes flowed along with the chilled vodka.

After graduation, a new teaching job at Caltech was waiting for him – the reward for graduating at the top of his class. Later that summer, Mike would get the chance to be part of the space program, landing a part-time job at the Jet Propulsion Lab. Two NASA spacecraft had just arrived on Mars. Mike Savin, the poor kid from an ethnic Detroit family, had joined the ranks of some of the best minds in science.

Lost in thought about his family and his life, the drive to Malibu was over before he knew it. As he pulled into the parking lot at the Jazz House, he noticed that Maggie's Datsun was already there. His car radio was tuned to KNX-AM and the song that was playing as he parked was Bachman-Turner Overdrive's *You Ain't Seen Nothin' Yet*. He stared out at the Pacific Ocean for a moment, shook off his nerves, and walked into the restaurant.

22
First Date

I T TOOK A few seconds for Mike's eyes to adjust to the dark restaurant. The windows overlooking the bright Pacific were covered with sunscreens, but the water was still a deep blue, unbelievable to a kid who grew up around the Great Lakes. Mike scanned the room and saw Maggie sitting at a window table. She was staring at the ocean, sipping a glass of orange juice with a straw.

Maggie turned just as Mike reached the table. Their eyes met and that same electricity jolted him again, from his brain down to his toes. Maggie stood up, smiling brightly, and moved forward to give him a light hug and kiss on his cheek. Her curly red hair flowed down over her bare shoulders. She was wearing a green print sun dress with little spaghetti straps. On her feet, she was wearing tan sandals and her toes were painted a pretty shade of coral. Nothing about her escaped his attention.

"Hi. Have you been waiting long?" Mike asked, holding onto this beautiful woman for a few more seconds.

"No, just a few minutes," Maggie said softly, still looking up at him. They finally released and sat down. "I ordered some juice for you, but maybe you'd like something stronger?" Maggie asked. They were still at that time in their lives where neither knew the protocol for ordering wine or having a cocktail.

"No, this is great. Thank you," Mike replied, turning for a moment toward the stage, where a trio played an Oscar Peterson classic. Turning back, he noticed Maggie staring at him, the smile still on her face.

"Have you been here before?" Mike asked, looking around the room.

"Oh yeah. This is one of my favorite places. I was raised on jazz. My dad has quite a collection and this place features a lot of local jazz talent," Maggie said, sipping her orange juice. "Have you been out here to the beach?"

"Only a few times," Mike said. He paused for a moment. "Breathtaking."

"The Pacific? Oh yeah."

"Actually, I was referring to you," Mike said. He had seen enough Humphrey Bogart films to know how it should be done.

"Oh, thank you," Maggie said as she blushed. It had taken her hours to get ready and if this outfit didn't knock this big guy over, then nothing would.

The waiter came by. Maggie ordered and then Mike did, but later, he wouldn't remember what. He had been looking at Maggie since he sat down, his eyes moving away from time to time so he didn't come off looking like a psychopath or something. So far, he thought he was doing a decent job, showing the right amount of attention and cool.

There were a few seconds of uncomfortable silence as the two of them sized up the situation. Mike was the first to jump into the pool.

"You know, in a way, I feel like I already know you," he said. "Your dad brags about you all the time."

"He's always talking about you, too," Maggie said. "I've heard your name since you started at Caltech."

"Why don't we start at the beginning," Mike said. "Tell me about Maggie Shields." With that Mike shut up and leaned forward.

Wow, nice start, Maggie thought. *A guy who listens.* She had read about this sub-species of the human male, but she had never actually met one in the wild. And here he was – a guy way out of her league – actually interested in her, as a person. Was it sincere or just an act? It wouldn't take long to find out. She would know after a few sentences, if he started checking his watch or shoveling food into his mouth.

For the next few minutes, as the jazz drifted around them, Maggie talked while Mike listened. She told him about her early years, growing up in Santa Monica – high school, sports, and electronics. Then, her undergraduate studies at UCLA. Just like Mike, she had a double major in physics and math. Now she was in her first year of graduate school, hoping someday to teach physics at the college level.

As she talked, Mike asked questions – another hallmark of a good listener. When she answered, he tilted his head to the right, the same quirky kind of gesture Maggie used when she was listening intently. He was sincere. He wanted to know about her – the *real* Maggie Shields.

With their breakfast getting cold in front of them, Mike entered the conversation a little at a time. It was a subtle shift, but he never dominated. The back-and-forth was not something that Maggie expected from a man. Maybe the world was changing?

At the same time, Mike was getting a good idea of the scope and depth of this woman. She was as brilliant and kind as she was beautiful. His eyes were transfixed on her face, drinking in every nuance in the way she talked, the way her eyes and nose crinkled when she laughed and the same adorable little tilt of her head when she was asked a question.

"You said that you wanted to teach when you're done with school," Mike said. "Do you plan to stay here, in California?"

Maggie thought about the question. There was a reason why he asked. Would she stick around after school? Maggie wanted to assure him that she did, but she didn't want to come across as desperate. She wasn't going to be just another phone number in his Rolodex.

"Maybe," she said. "I'm looking at some post-doc opportunities. They're planning some awesome things at CERN in Switzerland in the next decade or two," Maggie said, taking little bites of her breakfast. The jazz trio was on break and it was just the ocean waves and the murmur from other tables in the background.

"What about the new shuttle program?" Mike asked. "Did you like what you saw at the seminar?"

"Me, an astronaut?" Maggie laughed. *Of course I've been thinking about it.* "There aren't many women in the space program."

"That's changing," Mike said. "You have what it takes. Besides, it's a chance to go into space."

"Is that what you want to do?"

Mike waited for a moment before replying. "Maybe. But, I really love teaching. Then, two weeks ago…" Mike said, looking away, drifting out to sea for a moment. He returned his eyes to Maggie and decided to let his heart, not his brain, take it from here.

"Maggie, I want to ask you something. No, wait, never mind."

"No, please, go on." Maggie's stomach was churning.

"God, this is going to sound so corny," Mike said, reaching across the table to hold her hand. "Okay. Do you believe in love at first sight?" There, he said it. He pulled the pin on the grenade. Now, he had to wait to find out what kind of damage he caused.

Maggie looked into Mike's eyes, her beautiful face still wearing a smile. So far, so good.

"Yes. I do *now*," Maggie replied as her hand squeezed his. It was the same spark she felt when they shook hands at the seminar – a transmission of energy that communicated the realization that she had been waiting all of her life for this moment, and for this man.

"Maggie, I haven't been able to get you out of my mind since we met two weeks ago," Mike said.

"I know. Me, too. My dad said he saw it in my eyes from across the room."

"You know that I think of your dad like he was a second father?" Mike said, trying to gauge the strength of their father-daughter relationship.

"He talks about you like the son he never had," Maggie said. "Listen, I've heard the name Mike Savin for so long that I already had a mental picture of you before I met you."

"And did it match the chucklehead that walked over to your table this morning?"

"Well, not quite," Maggie laughed. "I pictured a guy with thick glasses and a pocket-penholder," she giggled. "And one of these." She reached into her purse, pulling out a little slide rule. The era of calculators was just beginning. "Do you have one of these, Dr. Savin?"

Mike laughed. "Of course I do," he said, taking an identical slide rule out of his back pocket and putting it on the table. The little white German-made device had its own plastic sheath, like a comb protector. "But I left my thick glasses in the car."

Both of them laughed. It was a good time for a break. Mike made the overture. "Maggie, do you want to walk on the beach for a little while?"

"I would love it," Maggie said. Mike flagged the waiter, while Maggie excused herself. He waited outside at a railing, looking across the perfectly blue Pacific. Maggie walked up beside him, putting her arm through his.

"C'mon, Dr. Savin," Maggie said. "Let us study the gravitational and lunar forces that cause this saline liquid to behave the way it does."

She was already barefoot – her sandals in her other hand. Mike removed his Topsiders. He was glad he didn't wear those nerdy socks he set out for this morning's date with Maggie.

For the next hour, they held hands as they walked on the beach. A Yellow Lab ran up and they bent down to pet her. Their reward was a hearty shake of seawater that sprayed their clothing. The owner ran up and apologized, but they all had a good laugh as the Lab took off for the waves again.

Along the way, they played twenty questions. Kids? Yes and Yes. Pets? He liked dogs. She liked dogs and cats. Mike would have to work on the cat thing. Smoking? No and no. Substances? No and no. Religion? She was a retired Episcopalian and he was an atheist. Would that be a problem for Maggie? Nope.

What about Mike's parents, Viktor and Nika? Would they like her? Absolutely. They would be nuts about her. Siblings? Maggie was an only child. Mike had two older sisters, both physicians, still working in Michigan.

And what about Maggie's mom? Mike had a pretty good feel for her old man, but knew little about her mom.

"Her name is Betty. Elizabeth, really," Maggie said. "She's a nurse at Santa Monica Lutheran. She is also my best friend. So, it's Bill and Betty."

"And Maggie and Mike," he quickly countered.

Maggie looked up at him, grinning. "Or, Mike and Maggie."

"I like it the first way," Mike said.

"Hey, does anyone call you Mikey?" Maggie asked.

Mike looked at her and laughed. "In my old neighborhood in Detroit, everyone had an *ee* at the end of their name," he said. "I was Mikey. My mom used to shout it from the front porch when dinner was ready – like 'yo *Mikeyeeee*.'"

"Okay, Mikey. Or, maybe Michael, if you piss me off," Maggie said.

"Mikhail, actually – it's Russian."

"*Izvinite. Moya oshibka,*" Maggie replied. "Sorry, my mistake."

"*A! Ty govorish po russki?*" Mike was absolutely flabbergasted. He had no idea Maggie could speak Russian.

"*Nemnogo,*" Maggie replied. "*Budete li vy uchit' menya po-russki?*"

"Will I teach you Russian?" Mike replied. "*Bezuslovno!*"

"*Khorosho,*" Maggie said. Mike had a feeling he was being sandbagged. Her pronunciation was a little too good for someone who said she only knew a little bit of Russian.

Walking back to the parking lot, both of them were quiet. When they got to her car, she opened the door and then turned back to face Mike. For a few moments, they said nothing, just holding hands and looking at each other. It was Maggie who spoke first.

"Oh. Standby. Incoming message to the Enterprise," Maggie said. "It's from Bill and Betty Shields." She put her hand up to her ear, the way Uhura did on *Star Trek*.

"Relay the message, Lt. Uhura," Mike said, hamming it up, just like Capt. James Tiberius Kirk would, sitting in his swivel chair on the bridge of the Enterprise.

"Dinner. Tomorrow afternoon. Shields residence," Maggie said. "Here are the coordinates." She gave Mike a piece of note paper with little hearts in the corner. It had her home address and phone number.

"Lieutenant, advise Starfleet that I will be changing course for Santa Monica tomorrow," Mike said. "Hey, what should I bring?" Mike was well-trained in the Slavic tradition of never visiting someone's house without bringing alcohol, food, and more alcohol.

"Nothing," Maggie replied. "Just that adorable smile." She reached up on her tiptoes to kiss him. Mike put his arms around her and kissed her deeply. She returned the embrace. He was so happy he could almost cry. He put her head against his chest and hugged her.

"Your heart is beating so fast," Maggie said, pulling back to look up at Mike.

"Maggie? Maggie, I love you," Mike said.

"I love you, Mikey," Maggie said as they kissed a second time, her hand caressing his face. Maggie smiled at him for a moment before getting into her car.

"*Proshchay do zavtra*," Maggie said before backing out of the parking space.

"Goodbye, until tomorrow," he repeated, smiling as she drove away.

Later that night, Mike would get very little work done at JPL. He couldn't take his mind off of the beautiful woman he held in his arms a few hours ago. He was in love. And he learned something today. The heart can sometimes find the truth without the scientific method. After seeing her just twice, Mike was certain that Maggie was the woman he had been looking for his entire life.

Mike walked over to a shelf where he pulled down the Yellow Pages. He leafed through the big book to the letter *J* in the directory. He noticed that there were a number of fine stores in Santa Monica. Certainly, one would have what he was looking for. He would leave early for the Shields house, giving himself plenty of time to find the right one.

23
Betty and Bill

O N SUNDAY, MIKE drove to Santa Monica to have dinner with Maggie and her parents. He loved Maggie and her father and was hoping her mother would be as welcoming. Mothers can be tricky, requiring the right mix of respect, deference, and confidence. That meant that the man standing in front of Betty needed to represent the sum of all of her dreams for her daughter. It could also mean, depending on the mother, that he represented a potential threat to her relationship with her daughter. There was no way to know which mother he would find until he got there.

And, there was something else about this dinner. Maggie's dad had been his teacher, his advisor, and his closest friend. At JPL, he was Mike's boss. They'd spent hours together, talking about physics, life, and philosophy. Mike was as close to Bill as a friend could get. But today might change everything. Maggie was the center of Bill's world and like her mom, Mike had to carefully measure the impact he would have on Bill's relationship with his daughter.

He pulled into their driveway, a beautiful California Bungalow, built at a time when an average family could still buy a home in Santa Monica. The house had the well-manicured look of an Air Force officer's house, but with flowers everywhere – no doubt Betty's ongoing contribution. He knew this because someone was constantly replacing the one plant in Bill's office at Caltech. Sooner than later, every plant that arrived wilted, died, and was replaced.

He rang the doorbell and looked himself over. He frowned at what he was wearing – the same tired graduate school clothes he owned for years. He only had three pairs of shoes, and Maggie had already seen his Earth shoes and the old Topsiders he wore yesterday. All he had left was an old pair of tennis shoes. He picked the Earth shoes, hoping no one would look any farther south than his face while they ate dinner.

Mike had his hands full when he knocked on the door. He had a bottle of *Stolichnaya* vodka in one hand and bottles of white and red wine in the other. He wasn't sure if Betty drank, but Bill certainly did. The two of them spent many an hour at Pasadena watering holes, bending a few and solving the world's problems.

Mike's knock on the door riled the dog inside and he heard a *woof-woof-woof* getting louder. Maggie opened the door, her face beaming. She kissed him lightly, and welcomed him into the house. Maggie's parents were standing behind her and saw the kiss. He handed the bottles to Maggie and then got down on his knees to pet and nuzzle the golden retriever. The dog was doing a combination of tweeting and barking at the same time, a yellow tennis ball in his mouth. Mike bent lower to let the dog sniff his hair and lick his forehead.

"Gus! Oops! Sorry about that," Betty said, as she tried to pull the dog away. "We got Gus for protection, but he prefers to be the official greeter instead. Hi, I'm Betty." Maggie's mom extended her hand and looked into his eyes. "I am so glad to meet you."

"It is very nice to meet you, Mrs. Shields," Mike said. It was old-school, but he wanted to get an early read on this woman.

"It's Betty from now on," she said, her eyes still locked on him with a huge grin.

Maggie's dad stepped forward after the dog and the women had done their work. He extended his hand. "Hello, Mike. Great to see you. Do you have the day off?"

"I do. It's great to see you, sir," Mike replied. They were both academic equals now, a point that Bill had repeatedly reminded him of. But Mike still couldn't make the leap from Dr. Shields or Professor Shields to plain-old Bill.

"Cut the crap. It's just Bill from now on," he said, slapping his hand on Mike's shoulder. "Hey, thanks for the booze. C'mon in."

Bill walked next to Mike, his hand still on Mike's shoulder, while the two girls fell in line behind. Mike couldn't see if they were looking at each other, but they were and it was all good. Gus had already returned into the family room and took over a sizable portion of the couch. A football game was on. The Rams were still in Los Angeles, and in 1976, they would win their conference and make an appearance in the playoffs.

"Maggie, why don't you show Mike the rest of the house?" Betty said as she took Mike's jacket. She was doing Italian this afternoon and whatever it was, the smell was fabulous. "Mike, would you like something to drink? We're also going to have wine with dinner."

"Keep out the *Stoli*, too," Bill said as he stood and watched the football game.

"Nothing right now, thanks," Mike said, "but I'll have some wine with dinner."

Maggie took his hand and gave him a quick tour of the house. The floors and the trim were old-growth oak and the walls were a creamy white, finished in lath and plaster, a lost art in a time when houses were made with drywall.

They walked upstairs and the beveled glass windows along the stairway produced rainbows of light as the Sun crossed through them. They stopped for a moment to see Betty and Bill's bedroom and then went down the hall to Maggie's room.

The walls in her bedroom were covered with pictures of the moon and the planets. Model airplanes and rockets hung by wires from the ceiling. There were very few girly things lying around. Before Mike arrived, Maggie tossed all of her stuffed animals into a storage area beneath the window seat. The data tape from the Viking mission was there, too. She would come up and get it for Mike before he went home. Her desk was covered in textbooks and a bookcase had some of the best physics and math textbooks in the business – a number of them written in Russian.

Stuck to the edge of her dresser mirror was a pencil drawing. It was the face of a guy with heavy black glasses, a beanie with a propeller on his head, and a buck-toothed grin. He looked a lot like Alfred E. Newman.

"So, this is your image of Mike Savin?" Mike said, turning to the girl standing behind him with one finger pressed to her lips and her head pointing down.

"Not an accurate representation, is it?" she asked playfully.

"No, my buck-teeth are a little larger, I think," Mike said, enjoying this devilish side of her personality. "You know you have something on your blouse."

"I do?" she asked, as he pointed toward her top. As she looked down, he gently bumped her nose.

Maggie stepped closer and kissed him. Her hand was sliding down the front of his shirt. When it reached an area south of his belt, Mike had to stop her. "We better get back," he said. "I wouldn't want Betty to see me in this condition." Maggie gave him another kiss, this time with some tongue. She was a temptress and he loved every bit of her teasing.

As they walked downstairs, Mike noticed that Maggie was wearing those amazing jeans again. She also wore her own Earth shoes and a tight little blouse, tied off at the waist. He had a little trouble walking down the steps, but got everything under control before they reached the kitchen.

"You have a beautiful home, Betty," Mike said, as Betty prepared the serving plates for dinner.

"Thank you, Mike," Betty said as she looked up from the counter and smiled at him. "We just love it."

Bill was sitting at a counter stool, watching Betty appreciatively. They decided early in their marriage that things were better at mealtime when he watched instead of helped. In front of him was a half-empty tumbler of the *Stoli* Mike brought. Mike took the bottle and topped-off Bill's glass.

"*Blagodarnost' za vodki,*" Bill said as he hoisted the vodka for another sip.

"*Dobro pozhalovat,*" Mike replied. "Where did you learn to speak Russian?"

"In the Air Force," Bill said. "In Korea, I had to dance with some of your comrades over MiG Alley."

"Russian pilots?" Mike asked, pretending not to know that Russians flew in the cockpits of those MiG-15s during the Korean War.

"Well, they certainly cussed at me in Russian," Bill said. "That's how I learned all the swear words."

Mike walked into the family room, looking at a wall of photos. There were lots of pictures of Maggie, from baby photos to her wearing her cap and gown at UCLA. In each of them, those beautiful eyes shown back at him. This was a happy girl, comfortable with who she was, and with parents that loved her.

There were also a number of black and white pictures of Bill wearing an Air Force uniform. Several showed Bill standing by an F-86 fighter. One had Bill pointing at several ragged holes in the fuselage.

"Those came from a 23 millimeter canon on a MiG-15," Bill said. "He was trying to shoot down an Air Force B-29. I wouldn't let him."

"What happened?"

"Nothing," Bill said. "The Superfortresses all returned. But my guy ended up in the weeds."

"Were you hurt?" Mike asked.

"Naw, just a hydraulic leak," Bill said. "No problems."

"He barely got back himself," Betty said, correcting her husband. "Didn't you land at Kimpo Air Base without landing gear?"

"Yeah, I bent the plane a little," Bill said sheepishly. "But they fixed it up. Hey, I got five kills with that plane."

"You were an ace?" Mike asked.

"Yep. One of twenty-five in the Fourth Fighter-Interceptor Wing."

Another set of photos showed Bill standing in front of different jets. Some of the planes Mike recognized. One photo had Bill standing with some other pilots, all wearing high-altitude pressure suits.

"Is that Chuck Yeager?" Mike asked, looking closer at a group of pilots standing in front of an X-15 experimental jet.

"Yep. And there's Slick Goodlin, and Cooper, Slayton, and Grissom. You know, that's where we got the name Gus for the dog. Yeah, we all did some flying out at Muroc. Well, now, it's Edwards," Bill said, handing a tumbler of vodka to Mike. Mike took it and tapped Bill's glass before downing half. He could have put the whole thing away, but didn't want to show off.

Maggie was in the kitchen with her mom. Like Mike, Maggie worried about how Betty was going to feel with a new man in her daughter's life. She and her mom had their ups and downs over the years. The problem was Betty's job as a nurse. The emotional costs of dealing with patients sometimes came home with her. But she and her mom got over that hump as Betty learned to separate her work and home life. And things were improving for Betty. A new position in nursing management took her off the floor, putting more distance between her and the daily heartbreaks that doctors and nurses have to endure.

Over a dinner of lasagna and Italian wine, the four of them talked and laughed. Betty and Bill told Mike their life stories. They met in high school, here in Santa Monica, and married right after graduation. Bill joined the Air Force and went to flight school. When the Korean War broke out, he was sent to Korea. Betty stayed here. She went to nursing school and joined the staff at Santa Monica Lutheran Hospital, which later became part of the UCLA Medical System.

When it was Maggie's turn, she talked about life as a kid, growing up in the quiet beach town that was now a bustling commercial and residential community. She was a tomboy and liked baseball and electronics. She told Mike about her amateur radio experience and all of the boyfriends she accumulated around the world.

When it was his turn, Mike talked about his father's journey from Russia to North America and then back to Europe during World War II. He introduced them, at least by story, to his Mom, Nika, the quiet seamstress who worked in their basement, sewing clothes for everyone from bricklayers to bankers. She made most of the wedding dresses for the young brides in a community where buying a dress from a bridal shop wasn't an option.

Going around the table, it seemed as if the four of them had been a family forever. Betty's early flutters were gone and she was seeing the four of them doing this weekly. Betty also understood what her daughter saw in this man. She especially enjoyed the way they held hands under the table. It explained why Mike ate most of his dinner using just his left hand.

After dinner, the four went out on the patio for a final round of drinks. It was the last act of the day for Bill and Betty. Bill was sold. Betty was, too. And Maggie was glowing – as happy as they had ever seen her.

It was time to give the kids some space. Whatever happened after today was Maggie's decision. And Mike's.

"Oh, hey, you and Mike should head down to the Pier this evening," Betty said. "They're running a Bogart movie."

"Of all the gin joints, in all the towns…" Bill said, doing a fair impression of Bogart drowning his sorrows in the film classic *Casablanca*.

"Do you like Humphrey Bogart, Betty?" Mike asked. Bogart was Mike's favorite actor and he had seen nearly all of his films.

"As a matter of fact, I actually met him," she giggled. "Oh, he was gorgeous. He was doing a U.S.O. visit in Hollywood. It was 1943. I was thirteen and my mother took me to see him."

"Was Lauren with him?" Bill asked.

"No, but oh, she is so beautiful," Betty answered.

Mike had a bit of trivia he thought he would never use. "You know, I have actually been to the house where Bogey and Bacall got married."

"You're kidding?" Betty said.

"No, really. My parents came down to Columbus to see me when I was at Ohio State. They were huge Bogart fans – couldn't understand much of what he said, but man, did my mother love him. Anyway, we drove up I-71 to a place called Malabar Farm. They were married in the front foyer of the main house. Their honeymoon night was spent, uh, upstairs. Well, anyway, my mom and dad got to see…" Mike stopped. Everyone was laughing.

"Maybe a little too much detail there?" Mike said.

Maggie stood up and then Mike did. He thanked Betty and Bill for a wonderful afternoon. Betty gave him a huge hug and kissed him on the cheek. Bill was smiling from ear to ear. "See you around campus, Dr. Savin," Bill said as he gripped Mike's hand.

Mike and Maggie went out the front door and walked down the tree-lined sidewalk toward the ocean. By now, holding hands was routine, only this time, Maggie interlocked her fingers in his, an especially nice gesture.

"Your mom is fantastic," Mike said. "And your dad, well…"

"You wowed them, if that was your intention," Maggie said. "Did you have any trouble finding the house?" Maggie asked, changing the subject for awhile. No pushing allowed, she remembered her mother telling her about men.

"No trouble, but I did have to make one stop," he said vaguely.

"Where?" Maggie asked.

"Look! The Pacific. It is so beautiful." Mike ducked the question, leaving a puzzled look on Maggie's face.

They walked around the Santa Monica Pier for about thirty minutes and then found an outdoor coffee shop that was still open. The waves were crashing in as the tide was rising. So was the lump in Mike's throat as he waited for the right moment. They hadn't said much in the last few minutes, like trying to keep the lid on a boiling pot.

"Maggie?" Mike asked.

"Yes?"

"What you said yesterday. Do you still feel that way?"

"Yes. Do you?"

Mike stood up, reached in his jacket pocket for something and then got down on one knee in front of her. It was a velvet ring box, which he opened to reveal a beautiful diamond ring.

"Will you marry me?"

24
The Wedding

THE NEXT EIGHT months of Mike's life were a blur. Maggie accepted his proposal, bursting into a combination of tears and laughter at the same time. From the moment they met until she accepted his proposal, it had taken a little more than two weeks.

There was a lot to do to prepare for the wedding, especially since both Maggie and Mike worked and had classes. Her dad pulled some strings and got her transferred to the Viking Mission team in Pasadena, saving her the long commute to Barstow. On some days, Maggie and Mike worked the same shift, but as nuts as they were about each other, they kept their time at work as low-key as possible. After all, they were babysitting two amazing spacecraft on Mars and they needed to do their jobs.

The wedding was set for June. Maggie finished her master's degree in physics and was accepted at Caltech to begin her doctoral studies. By the time of their wedding, the Viking landers had been on the surface of Mars for almost a year and most of its mission objectives had been met. As the project moved from discovery to maintenance, NASA began reducing the size of the project team. Second-level staff members like Mike and Maggie were let go. But Mike was glad to have the time to devote to his teaching responsibilities at Caltech. And when she could break away from her doctoral work, he had more time to spend with Maggie.

In the spring of 1977, with the weather warming in Michigan, Maggie and Mike flew to Detroit to meet Mike's parents. Viktor and Nika fell hard for this American girl who spoke Russian. Maggie had been a little unsteady with the language, so she and Mike spoke Russian when they were together in California. By the time they got to Detroit, Maggie was able to keep up with Viktor and Nika. It was a form of respect and bonding that few other women could pull off. Mike's two sisters were there to meet Maggie and, like her, they stayed in their parents' preferred language. In the Slavic tradition of wrapping a baby tightly in swaddling, the Savin family wrapped themselves around Maggie. By the time they boarded their flight for Los Angeles, she had two families to love.

In June, Maggie and Mike were married at her parents' church in Santa Monica. Maggie wore a dazzling white wedding dress that Nika made in the months since they announced their engagement. Dozens of Savin family members flew in from Detroit, Windsor, Cleveland, and Pittsburgh. They were joined in Los Angeles by hundreds of friends, faculty, and members of the NASA and JPL families. The wedding reception was huge – more than four hundred in attendance.

The next day, the newlyweds boarded a plane for Hawaii. For two weeks, they barely left each other's embrace. If Mike thought he loved Maggie when they first walked together on the beach in Malibu, it was nothing compared to how his love would grow in the years ahead. For Maggie, Mike was everything she ever imagined a husband could be. Together, they began a loving partnership that would last for the rest of their lives.

Part III

25
Retirement

SANTA MONICA, CALIFORNIA – PRESENT DAY

A LIGHT PACIFIC breeze drifted through the house as Mike sipped coffee and studied the photographs that covered the breakfast table. Lying near his feet, a six-year-old golden retriever named Sasha was in the middle of a vivid dog dream. His muffled barks and jerky paw movements suggested to Mike that he was on the beach, maybe jumping to catch a Frisbee or diving head-first into the surf with a bunch of his dog friends.

Forty years had passed since Mike and Maggie met, fell in love, and married. They taught together at Caltech for thirty-five of those years, helping to prepare thousands of physicists to go out and study the universe. They were celebrities on and off-campus, with regular appearances on television science programs. When they weren't teaching, they were in their lab, working on projects and co-writing papers that were published in science journals around the world.

Five years ago, when Mike turned sixty, they decided to retire from teaching. Rumors about the Savins leaving Caltech had been circulating for some time and the administration did everything it could to keep them on the faculty. They were offered reduced teaching loads and even team-teaching. But all good teachers eventually wear out from the stresses of the job. It was time to go.

After retiring, they sampled some of the traditional activities that one might do when no longer punching a clock. They joined a golf club. Maggie wasn't bad, but Mike sucked and after repeatedly holding up the course while looking for lost golf balls in the weeds, other club members politely suggested that he consider something other than golf. Maybe an art class.

They gave up on golf and signed up for an art class at the senior center. But after their protractors and rulers were confiscated again and again, the instructor politely suggested that they consider another hobby. Perhaps golf might be better.

Finally, in one last-ditch effort to salvage a carefree retirement, they became mall walkers. That idea lasted eight-and-a-half minutes when Maggie pulled Mike out of the line of walkers and pushed him up against a storefront.

"We are so done with this," Maggie said. "C'mon, slick. We have work to do at home."

Within an hour, they were back home, working at the large table they shared in the study. The whiteboards that lined the walls overflowed with new equations. They were physicists and even though they weren't teaching anymore, there was still a lot of work to do.

This was Bill and Betty's house, the California Bungalow that Mike admired when he first came here for dinner, forty years ago. The house was built in 1925. Bill and Betty purchased it when Bill returned from Korea in 1952. Back then, this house cost them the princely sum of $21,000. Over the years, with the help of a few honest contractors and Bill's own fastidious attention to its maintenance, the house was considered one the best remaining examples of the style in Santa Monica.

∞

It was almost twenty years ago, in 1997, when Mike got the phone call. He could still remember the police officer's voice. Speaking in calm and measured sentences, she said that Maggie's parents had been critically injured in a car accident. A delivery truck ran a red light and smashed into their car. Rescue workers had to cut the twisted metal away to reach them. They were taken to the UCLA Medical Center, where they were treated by the same doctors and nurses that Betty had worked with for years.

Standing outside her classroom door, Mike watched Maggie lecture to a packed auditorium. She was especially animated that morning, her curly red hair tossing back and forth as she rushed from one chalkboard to another. Hands popped up with questions and the classroom crackled with the kind of electricity that is generated when students and their teacher are tuned to the same frequency.

Maggie must have said something funny because the class erupted into laughter. Noticing that Mike was watching her at the classroom door, Maggie smiled and gave him one of those little folded-hand waves. Mike returned the gesture. But he wasn't wearing that famous grin – the one that could cure a rainy day for Maggie. Her face darkened and she excused herself to speak to him. When she walked out of the classroom, Mike stood there, trying to find the words.

"Honey, is everything okay?" Maggie asked.

"Maggie, it's your mom and dad," Mike said. "We have to go."

By the time they got to the hospital, her parents were dead. A physician met them as they rushed in, explaining that Betty and Bill suffered massive trauma from the impact. Maggie wanted to see them, but the doctor shook his head. Mike held her for the longest time as she grappled with the reality of losing both of her parents in an instant. Outside the crowded emergency room, doctors and nurses arrived in twos and threes, expressing their condolences to Maggie and Mike on their loss.

The funeral was immense. Family and friends packed the church in Santa Monica and the overflow spilled out onto the sidewalks. So many came to mourn – Bill's Air Force friends, colleagues from Caltech, NASA, and JPL, and from the UCLA Medical Center, where Betty worked for nearly thirty years. At the cemetery, an honor detail presented the colors to Maggie before their bodies were interred.

After a few months of grieving, it was time to close Bill and Betty's estate. Their wills were simple – everything went to Maggie, including this house in Santa Monica. Living near the Caltech campus, they considered selling it. It was worth a fortune in the booming California real estate market of the late 1990s, especially considering its location – just blocks from the beach.

But Maggie wanted to come back here. This was where she grew up, went to high school, and lived during her undergraduate days at UCLA. As a kid, she remembered the house filled with pilots, engineers, and doctors. Her world was formed around stories of aviation, space flight, and science. All seven of the original NASA astronauts were here for cookouts when the space program was still in its infancy. And the little girl who might have gone in a different direction, joined the guys and became a physicist. There were good memories here, Maggie said, and with Mike, there would be many more ahead.

⚭

That was twenty years ago – just halfway through a marriage that none of their friends could match in either longevity or devotion. It was funny, really. As a physicist, Mike was supposed to know a thing or two about the concept of time. Even so, Mike still couldn't understand how quickly the years went by. It all began with that crazy radio signal from Mars. Now decades later, that same radio transmission, recorded on a metal reel when Maggie pulled an overnight shift at the Goldstone receiving station, was back again, right on the kitchen table in front of him.

Directly above the kitchen was Maggie's old bedroom. Two weeks ago, they had a water leak that dripped down into the kitchen – just about where Mike was sitting.

They called a plumber whose website promised speedy service. Just like the site said, he showed up – two days later. The leak wasn't in the bathroom, but in the wall, near the window seat where Maggie used to stash her secret treasures. But in a curious departure from the quality construction of the rest of the house, the carpenters left a six-inch gap between the wall and one side of the storage area. Over the years, a number of Maggie's things fell into that gap. One of those things that disappeared into that dark space was now sitting at the edge of the kitchen table.

∞

"Dr. Savin, I found this in the wall," the plumber announced, handing the bag to Mike. Inside was the silver metal data tape, recorded in October, 1976. Also inside was this typewritten memo:

```
To: Memo to File
From: M. Shields
Date: 11 October 1976 10:02 GMT

This data reel contains anomalous
data received from the Viking 1 land-
er. The signal duration was 00:28:31.
The profile appears to be encoded dig-
ital data. No similar data anomalies
recorded during remainder of shift.

Contacted JPL Pasadena and spoke to M.
Savin. Per his instructions, tape will
be transferred by hand delivery. Cleared
to deviate from normal data trans-
fer protocol per R. Strauss at JPL.

M. Shields
```

That afternoon, while the plumber worked upstairs, Maggie and Mike sat on the back porch with the data tape on a small table between them. Mike didn't know the full story of how the data tape got lost, so Maggie needed to fill in a few gaps.

"After talking to you from Goldstone that night, I cooked up a little plan," Maggie said.

"The brunch invitation at the Jazz House?" Mike asked. "You were supposed to bring the tape."

"Yes, but accidentally-on-purpose, I forgot to bring it," Maggie said. "The next part of the plan was to get you to come here to meet my mom."

"Sunday dinner the next day."

"That's right," Maggie said. "I stashed all my girly stuff in that window seat. The tape was sitting on top. It must have rolled off the stuffed animals and into that space in the wall."

"We forgot about it that Sunday," Mike said. "It had something to do with a little ceremony we had on the Pier."

"When you asked me to marry you and you gave me this ring," Maggie said.

"You know, Rick Strauss never asked me about that tape," Mike said, referring to the *R. Strauss* in Maggie's memo.

"Well, now you know the full story," Maggie said, squeezing his hand. "Glad you married me?"

"No complaints," Mike said, turning away to hide his smile. Marrying Maggie was the thing he was proudest of in a life full of achievements. "What about you, kiddo?"

"Yeah, well, except maybe in the sack," Maggie said.

"You've been faking?" Mike asked. "All these years?"

"Sorry," Maggie said. "I should have told you."

"Well, when that chump upstairs leaves, I'm gonna show you some moves," Mike said. "I've been reading on the outside."

Mr. Promptness popped his head outside and told them he was finished. He must have heard that last part of the conversation because he wasn't smiling. Maybe chump was the wrong word to use for this guy. And after he saw the bill, Mike felt that *he* was the chump for calling this guy in the first place.

But at least the leak was fixed. The next day, one of Bill's old contractor friends was coming to fix the old-style lath and plaster walls that were water-damaged. Drywall would have been cheaper, but Maggie and Mike continued the tradition of keeping the house maintained with the same materials used when it was built.

That was two weeks ago. This morning, the tape and about a dozen black-and-white photos were spread across the kitchen table. Mike was studying the photos with a magnifying glass when the front door jangled open.

Sasha woke up and ran to the door. He practically knocked Maggie over with his swinging tail as she petted the big golden. As was his duty, Mike got up and opened the back slider. When one of them came home, it was Sasha's habit of bolting for the back yard and then running at full speed in and out of the house. Their veterinarian called the condition the "feel-goods" and said that there was nothing they could do about it. Mike just stood back as Sasha raced in and out of the house, *woofing* with a tennis ball in his mouth.

The cause for this celebration was Maggie's morning jog. At 62, she still looked fantastic, with that lean, muscular frame that runners develop from years of pounding the pavement. A month ago, she finished a half-marathon with a respectable time. One of these days, Mike promised himself, he would start getting in shape with that step-and-move-your-arms machine Maggie bought him last Christmas. It was stuffed somewhere in the garage.

"How was your run, slim?" Mike asked, as Maggie came around the table and hugged his neck. *How could a woman so sweaty smell so good?* Mike thought.

"Great," Maggie said as she pulled up a chair next to him. "That Realtor caught up with me again. She was wearing a pair of neon yellow running shoes."

"A little bulky to take up running at her age."

"She's something else. Her mysterious buyers have increased their unofficial offer. At least, that's what I think she said."

"You think she said?"

"Yeah, she was breathing so hard she couldn't speak very well," Maggie said. "She stayed up with me for about two minutes."

It wasn't exactly stalking, but for more than a year, a Realtor had been accidentally bumping into Mike or Maggie when one of them was out and about. She had a client interested in the house. They politely said *no*, but she was persistent. Each time she spotted one of them, she had a new offer, a little higher than the last.

"So, what was today's offer?" Mike asked.

"Three-point-two," Maggie said. "All cash."

Three million, two hundred thousand dollars. Houses in this condition were scarce in Santa Monica and there were always buyers looking for houses like this near the beach.

"So, do you want to make a cool three million?" Mike asked.

"Don't forget the point-two," Maggie said. "Two hundred thousand ain't exactly walking-around money."

"So?"

"Nope, no deal," Maggie said. "You?"

"No, and hey, if she shows up at the pool when you're doing laps, let me know," Mike said. "I'd like to get a look at her wearing one of those spandex thingies."

"You know damn well that the junior college girl's swim team works out when I do," Maggie said, smacking Mike on the shoulder.

"Ouch," Mike said. "So don't call me. I'll stick with women's beach volleyball."

Another smack.

"Maggie, look at this," Mike said, pointing at the photos. "This first picture was taken about a week after Viking 1 landed at the *Chryse Planitia* site."

"I remember these pictures."

"And this next one was taken about a week later. The rest of these were taken in about ten-day intervals. The last one here was shot in early October of '76."

Maggie looked at each photo and then zoomed into several with the magnifying glass Mike had on the table. She saw it almost immediately.

The first photo showed a flat expanse of Martian surface to the east of the Viking 1 landing site. Aside from some loose rock over a surface of what looked like sedimentary material, there was nothing remarkable about the photo. But in the second photo, a few of the rocks had been moved. They were in a line. Each picture that followed showed the rock line getting taller and longer. By the last photo, taken a few days before Maggie recorded the anomalous radio transmission, the rock wall was nearly two meters tall and four meters wide. It curved slightly away from the lander, making it impossible for Viking's cameras to detect shadows from behind the rock wall.

"This was no accident," Maggie said. "Someone made this."

"Watch this," Mike said. He scooped up the photos into a stack. Then, holding the left side, he flipped through the photos rapidly. Like an arcade movie from the 1890s, the stone wall came to life, growing and expanding as Mike flipped the photos.

"This would be the perfect place to sit and study the Viking lander," Maggie said. "And we never spotted it back then."

"Information overload," Mike said. In 1976, JPL was managing two Viking landers on the surface and two orbiters circling overhead. All four were sending photos and data back to Earth.

"So now we have evidence of some sort of activity on the surface of Mars," Mike said. "That's news."

"And we have the Viking data that we can finally study after forty years."

"All due to an itty-bitty water leak."

"That cost us two grand."

"Next time, I won't call the guy a chump when he's standing right behind us," Mike said.

26
The Warning

AFTER LUNCH, MAGGIE and Mike went to work in the study. In addition to their own research as physicists, they were reviewing editors at *Science* magazine. Maggie was working on an article about gravitational waves that was scheduled to be published in a few months. Mike settled down in front of his computer. It was time to find out, once and for all, what was on that tape that Maggie recorded in 1976. But getting the data into a form that he could study was almost as challenging as getting the signal from Mars.

The problem was copying the tape onto something that a modern computer could read. There were very few working mainframe computers from the 1970s that could read the data. He found two local companies that still had the equipment. How they made any money, he wasn't sure, but they seemed confident that copying the data tape to a hard drive would not be a problem. At the first place, Mike's tape fried the guy's mainframe computer. He could still hear the man crying as Mike got back in his car.

The second place, in a rundown part of Los Angeles, was owned by an old fart who still wore a vintage IBM white lab coat as he fiddled with the switches and knobs on his beloved mainframe computers. His office, and the fact that he was an exact copy of Dr. Emmett Brown from *Back to the Future*, made the trip worthwhile.

Unfortunately, Dr. Brown couldn't copy the tape, either. When Mike suggested that a flux capacitor might help, the owner suggested that Mike do something with the tape that was physically impossible. Strike two.

Next, Mike called Steve Gabriel, an old friend from Caltech. Steve was a computer science professor who made it big in the private sector. Steve lived in suburban Washington D.C. and specialized in cryptanalysis – finding ways to make data more secure, or looking for ways to break open someone else's data. While he didn't talk much about his clients, Mike knew that Steve's skills were in demand at places like the NSA and the Department of Defense.

After Mike explained what he was trying to do, Steve suggested that Mike overnight the tape to him in Falls Church. The next day, Mike got a phone call. The caller ID said 000-000-0000. And while Mike never answered blocked or masked calls, in this case, he thought it might be Steve calling with questions about the data tape.

"Hello?"

"Hey Mike, it's Steve."

"Hey Steve. Are you on a secure line? The caller ID was masked."

"Yes. We are."

"Did you get the tape?"

"I did indeed," Steve said. There was a pause for a moment before Steve spoke again. "So tell me? Are you now a computer scientist as well as a world-class physicist?"

"I don't understand."

"Aw, c'mon, Mikey," Steve said. "You're talking with the other half of the famous drinking duo of Gabriel and Savin. You told me that this data tape was some lame-ass telemetry from the Viking 1 mission back in '76."

"That's what it is, Steve," Mike said. "I recorded it during an overnight shift at JPL in October, 1976." Mike was keeping Maggie out of this in case there was some kind of blow-back from NASA or JPL. "Why? What did you find?"

The phone went quiet for a moment.

"Sorry, Mike," Steve said, his voice sounding like it was being scrambled, "but this is definitely not telemetry from the Viking 1 lander."

"It's not? Well, then, what is it?"

There was another pause on Steve's end of the line. Mike could hear other people talking as Steve tried to muffle the sound.

Steve lowered his voice, almost to a whisper. "What you have is stuff I have never seen before."

Steve confirmed that the files on the Viking tape were, in fact, digital, as Maggie surmised when she looked at the signal waveform back in 1976. It was what Steve said next that pushed Mike back in his chair.

"Mike, are you guys working on some sort of quantum computing project?"

Quantum computing was the next big thing in computer science. Instead of binary code – a series of ones and zeros that were the foundation of programming since the beginning of the computer age – quantum computing involved mysterious bits of subatomic matter called *qubits*. Depending on their electrical charge and the temperature in which they lived, these little bits could move data much faster than binary code.

"You know I can't do stuff like that," Mike said. "I'm a physicist, remember?"

"Qubits *are* physics, my friend," Steve said. "And you're married to another physicist who is prettier and much smarter than you are."

"So what does that have to do with the data tape I sent you?" Mike asked.

"Well, the only way this much data could have been compressed and sent was by using some kind of quantum computer."

"What are you talking about?" Mike asked. "That stuff came from the Viking 1 lander on Mars forty years ago."

"Whenever it arrived and wherever it's from, that's what it is," Steve said. "You read my paper on quantum computing in *Nature* last year. Well, what you have is way beyond anything we're working on right now."

"So what are you telling me?"

"One of two things. One, you are a much better computer scientist than I gave you credit for."

"Or?"

"Or, the sender of this data is way smarter than anyone on this planet."

"But, the Viking landers reported no indications of life," Mike said.

"Fine. But even if that's true," Steve said, "the Viking twins sure weren't looking for someone or something that could do this."

First, it was the photos with the changing surface near the Viking lander. Now, his friend was telling him that the signal sent could not have been programmed by NASA engineers. And even today, forty years later, the information was beyond a guy like Steve, who was the best in the business. Mike had the scientific discovery of a lifetime. That is, if Steve was going to return the tape.

"So, what are you going to do?" Mike asked.

"Me? Nothing. You asked me to transfer the tape. That's what I did," Steve said. "It's on its way back to you. The tracking code should be coming by text in the next few seconds."

Mike's phone dinged as the SMS message appeared on his screen. It was a FedEx tracking code.

"You mean that you're not going to tell anyone about this?" Mike asked.

"You know that's not how we do things," Steve said. "If you made a discovery, then publish. That's how Nobel Prizes are won."

"You know, all I wanted to do was look at some Viking data and then chase Maggie around the house."

"Well, you're in fat city, now."

"What do you mean?"

"Look, you and Maggie are sitting on a billion dollars' worth of new technology," Steve said, "not to mention that you might have made the greatest discovery of the century, maybe in human history. I have just one bit of advice for you."

"What's that, Steve?"

"Well, if you do find something, you need to be very careful."

"What do you mean?"

"Everyone's listening to everything right now," Steve said. "The whole world is spooked."

"At what?"

"Shit's happening everywhere," Steve said. "The world is moving into another crisis era."

"Where are you?"

"I'm in Brussels," Steve said. Brussels is the location of NATO. The Russians were misbehaving again and the Chinese were throwing their weight around in the South China Sea. The tension in the air was almost palpable.

"Can you tell me what's going on?"

"I wish I could," Steve said. "I have to run. Good luck with the files."

"How much do I owe you?" Mike asked.

"Nothing. We never had this conversation," Steve said. "And Mike?"

"Yes."

"I meant what I said. You and Maggie need to be careful."

The phone clicked and then clicked again as Steve's phone disconnected. Mike looked at the call history on his phone. It showed that he received no calls in the last hour.

27
Decoding the Tape

YESTERDAY'S CONVERSATION WITH Steve was still playing in Mike's head as he opened the FedEx box that arrived this morning. Inside was the original data tape from 1976. It was sealed in a green plastic bag. The box also contained a solid-state hard drive – the kind that fits inside a standard computer case. Steve somehow transferred the data from the old tape to the new hard drive that Mike would install in the computer sitting in front of him.

Then, if all went according to plan, he would open the files and study the data that Maggie recorded in 1976.

Steve attached a note to the hard drive telling Mike that the data was compressed at a ten-to-one ratio. With the four-terabyte hard drive nearly full, he would need at least forty terabytes of storage to accommodate the data from Viking. That was way more data than the Viking 1 lander could send in its five-year lifetime, let alone in the twenty-eight minutes that Maggie recorded.

Data storage wasn't going to be a problem. A few months ago, Mike built a Network Attached Storage (NAS) server. He was planning to digitize all of their old movies, his cherished *Three Stooges* and *Star Trek* collections, and the hundreds of vinyl record albums he and Maggie owned before CDs came along. The NAS rig had more than a hundred terabytes of storage. After looking at the Viking 1 data, Mike planned to reuse the storage to watch Curly get smacked by Moe a few thousand times.

It took Mike ten minutes to open the computer case and install Steve's new hard drive. Next, he connected the NAS server to the computer. When Mike hit the power button on the computer, everything came to life. Whatever was on the hard drive would have plenty of room to stretch out in the new storage space.

When the computer finished its startup process, Mike clicked open the file manager. The hard drive Steve Gabriel sent had just two files. One was immense – almost four terabytes in size – with a file name containing a long mix of letters, numbers, and symbols. The second file was just a few megabytes in size. It didn't look like an executable file – the kind that you can just click and make something happen. He had other ways to open the file, but sometimes, the simplest approach is the best. So, with everything working on the computer, he double-clicked the small file with his mouse to see what would happen.

The double-click must have done the trick because the computer spooled up and went to work. An activity program running on the screen showed the computer's six-core motherboard processing a flood of instructions. The drive lights on the NAS were flashing, indicating that data was being written to the new space. It was almost like the small file was scouting the computer before deciding where to unpack the large file.

He clicked over to the NAS and saw it quickly filling with new files, each with sequential file names. The file manager listed over a thousand, then 2,000 files copied. In another minute, there were over 10,000 files and the unpacking had consumed half of the storage system. Finally, the number of files slowed and then stopped at around 18,000 files. Fifty-two terabytes were needed to unpack just one file.

Whatever was going on, the programming was extremely sophisticated. The activity monitor showed the computer processors were running at nearly full speed, but just below a level that would fry them. The fans and the liquid cooling system Mike installed in his hand-built computer were working well – the computer seemed to have no trouble handling the workload. It almost seemed as if the startup file had some sort of intelligence – shepherding the computer to work at its fullest capacity, but not so hard that its components might fail while unpacking the very large file.

The computer's activity monitor slowed down and then went quiet. Mike watched to see what would happen next. Three minutes after the rest period, things started happening again. Only this time, the process was going in reverse. The thousands of files on the NAS were going away. They were being added to a new file that had been created. This file had a very short file name – KAI.exe.

Completely immersed in the almost artificial intelligence behavior of his computer, Mike hadn't noticed Sasha in the room. That was odd for a dog who usually arrived to great fanfare with tinging collar sounds, sniffs and snorts, and a well-placed sneeze in Mike's lap, as he asked for an ear-rub. Instead, Sasha walked in silently and sat staring at the computer. His ears were up and his head tilted slightly as if he was tuned into what was going on inside the computer.

"Chto sluchilos, Sasha?" Mike asked the dog in Russian. Maggie and Mike spoke so much Russian at home that the dog had become bilingual. Sasha didn't respond, so Mike asked him what was wrong – this time, in English.

Again, no response.

Mike put his hand on Sasha's head to pet him, but the dog remained fixated on the NAS storage rack. Looking at Sasha caused him to miss about thirty seconds of activity on the computer. And evidently, a lot had happened in that short period of time.

When he looked up at the screen, the file manager showed that there was just one file left on the NAS. It was the KAI.exe file. *Okay, so the files have unpacked and created this mother of a file,* Mike thought. But before he could click on it to see what would happen next, the new file also vanished.

There was a fifty terabyte file somewhere inside his computer. But Mike couldn't find it. He ran some maintenance routines and looked at computer log files to see what happened just before the new file disappeared. Every log file was blank. It's as if the unpacking program covered its tracks after doing its job.

Steve's hard drive was empty, as was the NAS drive system. As far as the computer was concerned, no activity had occurred in the last hour.

"What the hell?" Mike said.

Maggie looked up over her readers at Mike. The two of them had been together for nearly an hour-and-a-half, an unusually long time for them to sit in silence.

"How are you doing over there?" Maggie asked.

"This is some weird shit," Mike said, shaking his head.

"Can you define weird?" Maggie asked. "Because I know weird when I'm looking at it." She giggled, trying to get a response.

Mike gave her a semi-sneer and then smiled. In all of their years together, he couldn't recall a harsh word or argument they had ever had. No one believed him when he told that story, but it was true. Even in his frustration with the computer, he wasn't going to get mad at his lovely wife sitting across from him in their study.

Mike gave Maggie an executive summary of what had been going on for the past ninety minutes or so. As far as the computer was concerned, there were no longer any files from the Viking mission.

"So, what do you think?" Maggie asked. "Do we still have the Viking data?"

"I don't know," Mike said, rubbing his eyes.

"Why don't you take a nap?" Maggie said. "I'll wake you up for dinner."

"What's on the menu tonight?" Mike asked.

"Your favorite," Maggie said.

"Pizza?"

"Oh, and you were so close. Actually, we're having quinoa with cucumbers, peppers, and *lots* of other good vegetables."

"That stuff tastes like a front lawn," Mike said as he headed out the back door for the hammock.

After dinner, Maggie and Mike settled in for a movie, but the news was more interesting. In Asia, North Korea was threatening the United States again. In central Europe, Russian-backed Ukrainian rebels captured another city in the eastern part of the country. And in the South China Sea, a U.S. Navy guided missile cruiser was bumped twice by a Chinese naval vessel while operating in international waters.

Two Chinese fighters circled above, and then were met by eight F/A-18s from the USS Reagan, which was operating off the coast of Japan. The face-off didn't go any farther, but it was the closest the two countries had come to a shootout since the Chinese knocked a U.S. reconnaissance aircraft out of the sky and forced it to land in China in 2001.

Maybe Steve was right, Mike thought. *The air did feel charged with static electricity – like something was about to happen.*

By 9:00 p.m., they were ready to turn in. The computer stayed on in the study. Although it was politically correct to turn off devices like computers to save power, Mike was old-school, preferring to leave them on most of the time. As the lights in the house went down, the amount of electricity being consumed by the computer started going up. Mike couldn't hear the computer from their bedroom, but it was working hard. The computer monitor blinked on and then off. The little green light for the computer's camera turned on.

Whatever was inside the computer could now see outside.

28
Kai Awakes

KAI OPENED HIS eyes and blinked. As his vision came into focus, he found himself standing in an immense room that had no walls or ceiling. There was a soft, uniform glow about the place, but he could find no source for the illumination. He turned slowly, completing a full circle. The room seemed to go on forever in all directions. It was the same looking up and looking down, although when he stomped his foot, he seemed to be standing on solid ground.

Was he alive or dead? Kai couldn't be sure. His mind felt small, even primitive. He looked down at his body. It was covered in a simple fabric tunic. Even his feet had shoes made from the same material. Bashfully, he looked down through the neck hole to see if he was all there. Yes, everything was where it was supposed to be. When he released the fabric, it gently returned to its former shape around his neck. He stretched it again and it reformed again. If he was dead, this miracle fabric garment was what they gave you in the afterlife.

Kai raised his arms, putting his hands in front of his face. He could see them clearly, the loose sleeves of his tunic giving way to expose his arms. He was wearing the silver-white rhodium wedding band that Mia gave him. But who was Mia? He could remember her name, but nothing else about her. Kai slid the ring off his finger, but it slipped from his grasp. Instead of falling, the ring wobbled a few times and then settled into a place right in front of him. He studied the effect for a few seconds before taking the ring and putting it back on his finger. Gravity? There was something about gravity, but he couldn't remember.

Kai saw that when he moved his hands, a trailing set of ghost images remained for an instant before fading away. Holding his hands directly in front of him, he moved them back and forth and watched this effect. It was as if this new space gave way to his physical presence, and then filled-in the empty space he left behind.

In fact, Kai was deep inside the large NAS storage space that Mike built. When Mike clicked on that small file, what he did was begin the process that reassembled Kai, one file at time, from the thousands of files that were sent to Earth. Kai's assembly into a whole being was the first step, but there was a lot more to do before he would be ready to carry out his mission. In order to protect him from hurting himself, Kai's mind would awaken in carefully programmed stages, one set of capabilities building on the next, to a point where Kai's intellect, memories, and emotions would be fully restored.

The first part of Kai's restoration was to create an awareness of self and place. He understood that he was alive because his programming told him that he was alive. And it told him that he was safe, even if he didn't know exactly where he was. That wasn't an omission on the part of the program.

His father's original programming assumed that Martians who went through the transference would be on Mars. But changing the program for Kai's mission to Earth meant that they couldn't be sure where he would be after getting here. So, a starter program was added to wake Kai. If the program found that the environment was safe for Kai, then he would be restored. As to exactly where Kai was, that would have to wait until he had full use of his intellect.

But right now, Kai's mind was still working at a child's level. And like a child, he examined his new world through his senses. He could see, but there was very little to look at. Touch was next. He rubbed his hands together, feeling the warmth of the friction being made. He interlocked his fingers and stretched his arms out in front of him. But something was missing. He remembered that doing something like this on Mars would hurt his arthritic joints. Now, he felt no pain. He contorted his hands, twisting his fingers until he felt a sharp jolt. Yes, that hurt. He *could* feel pain. And, although he wouldn't learn this for a day or so, Kai would be unable to do anything that could damage him physically or emotionally. The reason was simple – there was no one here to fix him if he did.

So, he could see and touch his new world. What about smell and taste? He inhaled and exhaled through his nose. He could breathe, but when he exhaled, he couldn't feel breath. He had a heartbeat and found that curious, but wasn't quite sure why it was curious that he would have a heart with no air to breathe. His nose worked, but the aromas were new. He picked up a whiff of electricity – bits of ozone that formed as electricity passed through oxygen. He could smell other things – small notes of gold and copper and materials made with iron. He picked up strong aromas of hydrocarbons.

These were coming from the plastics that made up a large part of his environment. But right around him, what he smelled was silicon. He remembered something about silicon. Maybe in a different time and place.

Even Kai's sense of taste worked, although the tastes he was picking up on his tongue weren't as pleasant as the food he loved sharing with Mia. There was that name again! He still could not make the connection but the emotions connected to her name were getting stronger.

As he moved through his senses, it was the last one that intrigued him the most. He could hear. The computer's microphone picked up sounds around him. *But the old way of hearing – sound waves against my ear drums – shouldn't work in a computer environment,* he thought.

In fact, Kai's sense of hearing was a combination of the computer's technology plus a minor bit of telepathic magic programmed to replace the hearing parts of his brain. What he was hearing were sound waves converted into digital bits, plus a dash of telepathy, the kind of thought processes that start before a word or sentence is spoken. Telepathy was not an innate skill for Kai, any more than it is for humans, so his programmers did the best they could to give him a chance to listen to human communication.

Concentrating on the sounds, Kai determined that there were two voices nearby, each with a different pitch and timbre. But, there was something else making sounds. The voices were interrupted from time to time by these loud plosives. Wasn't there something about humans and smaller animals who shared the same living space? Maybe. And if vocal abilities were a desirable trait in these creatures, this one was evidently prized by its human companions.

With all of his senses working, it was time for Kai to move around a bit. He tried to walk. Unsure at first, he moved his feet, taking one step and then another. He repeated this process until he got used to walking. There was an occasional stumble, but his legs and swinging arms felt loose and natural. He was walking, but without any physical markers, he wasn't sure how far he traveled.

Something from behind startled him. When he looked over his shoulder, he saw those same ghosting images, images of his whole person trailing behind and then fading away. When he stopped, the ghost images closed ranks behind him and disappeared. If he was going to live here, he would have to get used to these eerie shadows that followed him everywhere.

So, two hours into his new life as a non-physical being, what did Kai know about himself? He knew that he was alive and safe, living in some sort of silicon-based world. He was intact and had all of the senses that he had on Mars. He wasn't afraid, but he was cautious. That was good. Irrational fear was of no value to him. But, caution could protect him from harm.

As these thoughts coalesced in his mind, Kai felt a sudden fatigue overwhelming him. He didn't want to sleep. There was so much more to learn. But his programming was in control. And, right now, it needed him to sleep in order to complete the most complex tasks – the assembly and sorting of billions of neural bits of information that made up his intellect and memories. These were the most difficult things to get right and his programming would check and recheck its work before allowing Kai to reawaken.

Despite his efforts to stay awake, his programming did its job. Kai was put into a long, deep sleep.

29
Orientation

MORE THAN A day after going into a forced sleep period, Kai woke again. The twenty-nine hours he spent asleep would be the last time he would be unconscious for such an extended period of time. From now on, rest periods would be shorter and come when they were needed. These light, semi-conscious events would give his management programming time to keep him repaired and in good health.

Kai's mind was fully restored. He had all of his intellect, memories, and experiences. He remembered everything with crystal clarity, something that was becoming harder to do when he lived on Mars. Physically, he felt wonderful – better than he had felt in centuries. Gone were the old-age aches and pains. Getting old would no longer be a problem for Kai and so long as he had a place like this, he could live indefinitely. That wasn't his goal in coming here, but this feeling of youthful vitality and the almost limitless space of his new home on Earth were consolations for the risks he took in coming to Earth.

Kai's new world was the spacious NAS hard drive system. It was empty now, but in the days ahead, he would fill this place with files and images from all over the world. A big part of his early education would have to do with language – learning to speak and write some of the 6,000 languages spoken by the human race. His mission team on Mars determined that, at minimum, he would have to achieve native fluency in English, Mandarin Chinese, Japanese, Russian, French, German, and Spanish. After that, he could explore other languages if he wanted, but these core languages would allow him to speak to the governments that had space programs large enough to help his people.

As Kai moved around his physical space, he eventually found walls. This was a finite space. But along the walls, Kai noticed apertures – round openings that appeared to lead to other places. The apertures were really just copper wire connections between the NAS system and Mike's computer. But because he was now made of electrons, they looked like long, wide corridors through which he could easily travel. Moving was effortless. Within a few minutes of waking, he discovered that he did not have to physically walk anywhere. He needed only to think where he wanted to go and he could move instantly from one place to another.

Kai went through one of the apertures, a large one that led to the computer's main hard drive. This space was filled with millions of clusters of data, some large, some small. They were orderly – stacked above and below and in aisles as far as he could see. He could reach any level of the files by just willing himself upward, forward, or back. In this neat, warehouse-looking space, small gaps would appear from time to time. These gaps were filled with files that moved slightly into position or with new files that had just arrived. Aisle after aisle, this storage space contained the sum of information that a person named Mike Savin had collected on his computer.

Although Kai understood computer science as well as anyone on his planet, he had never seen a visual representation of files stored and collated from *inside* of a computer. Kai reached out to touch some of the data clusters, but they only moved out of his way and then resumed their original positions when he withdrew his hand. These computer files were different from the kind used on Mars, but not so much that he wouldn't be able to eventually understand the semantics being used.

Attached to each file was a numeric representation that appeared to be a date stamp of some kind. Each file had one of these stamps with eight numbers, followed by four more. The first set was the date that the file was placed here. The second set appeared to be a time code. Kai knew that an Earth day was twenty-four hours, nearly the same as on Mars.

Kai found files with dates as early as 1986. He remembered that he was sent here in Earth year 1976. That would mean that he was asleep for ten years. But as he moved through the rows of data, he found later dates. Here was one from 2005. Another was from 2010. That would be thirty-four years. He increased his pace as he realized that he had been asleep for a very long time.

Here is a file from 2015! No, wait, this one is from 2016. Forty years! I have been asleep for forty years!

Kai withdrew from the hard drive and returned to his own storage space. He stood shaking, anger welling-up inside of him. He had been in some kind of suspended animation for forty years. Was that intentional? The Martians thought that humans could understand the digitized information that they sent over the Viking radio signal. But if humans were only *now* capable of working at a level where some sort of communication with his planet would be possible, then his mission was a failure.

How could my people be expected to wait forty years for me to communicate with them? Mia! Is Mia still alive?

He punched one hand into the other until he started feeling pain. His programming stopped the action before he could do any harm. After a few moments, Kai calmed down.

Maybe it's not too late. Maybe they have already been in touch with my people. There is a world out there, full of information. I need to go and find out what has happened since I arrived. Yes, my mission can still work!

It was time to learn about Earth and its people.

30
World Tour

KAI LEFT THE Savin house in Santa Monica and spent the next two days exploring the cyberworld. With more than two billion computers, the Earth was a very big place. Even traveling as fast as he did – about half of light speed – he would never be able to look at every possible place where help could be found for his people.

But Kai had a road map. He would concentrate his search in countries that had space programs. Russia and the United States had extensive files on their space programs. China's files were newer, but it appeared intent on reaching the moon, and perhaps, Mars. Japan, India, and the Europeans also had active space programs. While there seemed to be cooperation, humans didn't have a single space program. That meant that Kai would have to approach each country separately in order to get help in building a spacecraft that could return to Mars and communicate with those of his people who were still alive.

Kai had no trouble moving in and out of even the most secure computers. Cybersecurity can only protect against things it knows to look for. But the restored Kai was different from any other computer file on this planet. None of the security systems built to guard national secrets was a barrier to Kai.

After two days in cyberspace, Kai returned to the Savin house. If he owned a passport, it would have been full of country stamps from around the world. His tour was the equivalent of a master's degree in Earth studies. But Kai wasn't happy. The hope he felt before he set out to learn about this new world had changed to a grim realism that it would be unlikely that humans would cooperate in organizing a mission to Mars.

The cost required for such a mission certainly would be an issue. But other challenges would be based on what humans called *national interests*. A worldwide consortium might be possible, but given their preference for arguing instead of cooperating, such a mission would take years to complete.

Working with just one country would be faster, but others might object and view the quantum leap in knowledge as a threat. Kai's presence could even cause a war, something he would never allow.

Instead of his original plan to reach out to humans as one group, Kai would have to think smaller. That meant starting with the owners of this computer. He already knew Mike and Maggie from their computer files. Yes, he would start with them and hope that they could open doors to those in power.

It was time to reveal his presence. But, Kai's first encounter wouldn't be with a human. He made so much telepathic noise on his return to Mike's computer, that Sasha was alerted to something going on. The dog trotted into the study to investigate.

The computer camera was on and Kai could see into the study. The face that popped up on the desk in front of the camera startled him. This wasn't a human. He had a long nose with a black button on the end. He was sniffing the computer screen, leaving nose marks. Reddish-gold hair covered his head and face. And, he had floppy ears that seemed to go up and down whenever Kai did something inside the computer.

This creature was called a dog in the English language. And from what he could tell, this dog was very curious about what was going on inside this computer.

Kai had seen enough photos to know that humans expressed happiness by showing their teeth with their lips parted – something they called a smile. Evidently, dogs did the same thing, because this guy seemed to have a big smile, with lots of pointed white teeth showing. And what was with that long, pink tongue hanging out of his mouth?

Kai and Sasha engaged in a sort of staring contest for a few minutes as Kai considered his next move. He was hoping to talk to Mike Savin, the official administrator of this computer.

But from small beginnings come great things, so what better way to save his people than to have his first conversation with a golden retriever?

"Hello, Sasha," Kai said telepathically. The dog's ears lifted up and his head tilted slightly as he listened to the disconnected voice coming from the computer directly into his brain.

"Hello, Sasha," Kai said again. "It is a pleasure to meet you. You are a dog – a golden retriever, I believe?" The dog snapped his mouth shut, appearing to understand what Kai was saying. Kai decided to try something.

"Sasha, are you a good boy?" He heard the humans use that expression and it seemed to engage the dog.

The dog's tail wagged so hard that his backside swayed and bumped into the desk chair. The dog's smile got even bigger and Sasha was panting and bobbing his head up and down at the mysterious voice that was coming from the computer screen.

During Kai's visit to Mike's hard drive, he noted that Mike and Maggie were fluent in several languages. Many of the files were written in Russian. Others were written in German. Kai wondered if the dog understood these languages as well.

"Vwee khoroshaya sobaka?" Kai asked.

Evidently, he was good boy in Russian too, because Sasha jumped up and put his front paws on the desk. Sasha didn't know who this guy was, but he sure was digging the voice from behind the curtain.

Kai was picking up happy vibes from the dog. How these animals processed information would be an interesting study for a later time, but for now, it was clear that dogs, or at least this particular dog, had telepathic abilities.

"Sasha. Will you sit down for me?" Kai asked.

The dog stayed where he was, looking into the computer screen. *He understands words, but maybe not sentences,* Kai thought. *Let's make it simpler.*

"Sasha, sit."

The dog pulled himself off the desk, taking several files and stacks of paper with him. That would be an inexplicable mess that Mike would have to deal with. But at least Kai knew that Sasha understood short, telepathic phrases and words.

"Sasha, up."

The dog popped back up on the desk. Again, he sniffed the computer monitor. A big slurp from his tongue put a wet streak across the center of the screen. Mike would notice that, but there was no way he could get Sasha to clean up after himself.

Kai decided to take the next step. If his telepathic connection with Sasha was strong enough, maybe he could connect directly with this dog. Kai could see through the computer, but how much better would it be if he could visit the rest of this house through Sasha's eyes?

Kai concentrated on the telepathic connection with Sasha. The dog remained motionless, locked into Kai's signal. The connection opened wider in Kai's mind and he was now outside of the computer, seeing the room through the dog's eyes. He gently nudged Sasha to turn his head to the right, which he did, revealing more of the study. The walls were covered with whiteboards, all filled with equations and notes. The symbols were alien, but he knew mathematics and physics when he saw them. Yes, he could understand these equations! He even found several errors that he would correct, if the humans would accept his help.

Kai tired quickly from the telepathic connection with Sasha. He disconnected and pulled back into the computer. His head ached from the exercise. It was a pain warning. He was alerted that he would go into a rest period. There was no arguing the point – he had no choice in the matter. But he did learn that he could travel short distances with the telepathic power he now had. He had just one more mission with Sasha that he would need to try after his sleep period.

Kai woke to the sounds of human voices. A lamp on the desk flicked on. Kai noticed the computer's clock was 18:06 –

six minutes after six in the evening. A male human appeared at the desk. It was Mike Savin. At first, Kai could see only a side view. But after a little activity, Mike turned his attention to the computer. He looked into the monitor and typed some information on the keyboard. As Mike waited for whatever program he was using to open, he noticed the nose prints and the huge slobber marks across the computer screen. And as he moved in to examine the smear, he also noticed that the green camera light on the monitor was on.

He pulled back from the computer, alarmed as if he was being spied on.

"Why is the camera on?" Mike asked, looking directly into the lens.

So this was Mike Savin, the man who brought him here. Kai smiled at Mike's appearance. He looked a lot better than the photo of him at the California DMV. Mike was very much like Kai pictured a human would be. His hair was a mix of gray and brown, quite thin on top. He had the facial hair that Kai noticed many human males wore, only his was trimmed and short. On his nose, he wore some kind of mechanical device with glass lenses – half-circles surrounded by a dark frame. He appeared to do most of his looking at the computer through these lenses.

Sensing that Mike was getting frustrated with the camera light, Kai turned it off. That changed Mike's disposition toward his computer, although he still seemed puzzled by the reason the light was on in the first place. Evidently on Earth, humans did not like to be watched and the light on the computer monitor was one way to indicate when the computer camera was turned on.

A woman came into the camera's view. She had long, auburn-red hair that cascaded over her shoulders in curls. This was Maggie Savin. He recognized her from the thousands of photographs Mike stored on his computer. Most of the photos were of her. Evidently, Mike didn't like having his picture taken.

Kai watched as Maggie walked up behind Mike and put her arms around his neck.

"What's going on in here, Dr. Savin?" Maggie asked, as she kissed him on the cheek. Then, she did something Kai thought was odd. She nibbled on one of his earlobes, which seemed to have some effect on Mike's pulse.

"Not much, Dr. Savin," Mike replied. "But this computer is still a little hinkey. I'm going to have to do some maintenance tomorrow."

"If you used a Mac, this wouldn't be happening," she said, kissing him again.

"Different strokes for different folks," Mike answered.

"Well, maybe I can show you a different kind of stroke," Maggie giggled, still noshing on Mike's ear. Maggie left the room and Kai watched as Mike got up quickly and followed. He could hear some talking and laughing. Then, the sound faded and things got quiet. It would be the last Kai would see of Mike or Maggie Savin this evening.

31
Sleepwalking

THE SAVIN HOUSE was quiet. The humans were entering their own sleep periods. It was during their period of inactivity that Kai planned to try his next telepathic experiment. His mission tonight was much bolder than the connection he had earlier with Sasha. Tonight, he intended to explore the Savin house.

There was risk involved. By leaving the protection of the computer, Kai wasn't sure if he could retain enough energy to get back. But his curiosity about these humans was overwhelming. He had to know more about his hosts. He was the first of his kind to see humans up-close. Not content to be an observer, he was going further – attempting to walk among them, even if it meant being carried by another living being. Kai was in uncharted territory, but with the forty-year delay stuck in his mind, he had to take bigger risks to complete his mission.

Kai already knew a lot about Mike and Maggie. Government records and their computer files gave him a pretty complete picture of who they were. He learned about their early years, their education, and the work they did on the Viking space mission. They were physicists like Kai, and teachers like Mia. It was almost as if destiny brought him to these two people.

Martians already knew from monitoring Earth communications that humans still did not know whether life existed on other planets. They knew nothing about Mars before Koya destroyed the surface. And even after forty years of missions to Mars, they hadn't detected life in the Underground.

They were reaching farther and farther out into the universe with orbiting telescopes. But despite claims of UFOs and other alien sightings, there had been no contact with living beings from other planets. It was the same on Mars, until astronomers detected light and then electronic emissions from Earth within the past two centuries. That made Kai's presence in the Savin house one of the biggest events in both planets' histories. Kai understood the implications of revealing himself to these two humans. But from what he could tell, they were at the top of the charts, both intellectually and in their respect for life. They were, like him, scientists in search of the truth. Who better to reveal himself to than Mike and Maggie Savin?

After resting for a few hours, it was time to talk to Sasha again. He scanned the house for the dog's strong telepathic beacon. There. He found him. He called softly to Sasha. The dog's head popped up in Mike and Maggie's bedroom.

A minute after calling his name, Kai could hear Sasha's collar jangling as he approached the study. Like the last time they met, Sasha jumped up on the desk and looked into the camera. Their second telepathic connection was easier than the first and Kai crossed over. He could see the outside of the computer and the rest of the dark room through Sasha's eyes.

Kai asked Sasha to take him on a tour of the house. They visited the kitchen, where Sasha took the opportunity to slurp some water from his bowl. Then Kai saw the dining and living rooms and a hallway leading upstairs. This was something Mars never had – houses with more than one story. The mostly silica-based stone wasn't strong enough to allow taller buildings, something that plagued the population before Koya changed everything.

"Sasha, let's go see Mike and Maggie," Kai said. The dog just stopped and turned his head from side to side. His panting made the visual image a little bumpy, but Kai got used to the dog's way of seeing things. Kai needed to use different words to visit the second level of the house.

"Sasha, let's go above." *No response. Wrong words.*

"Sasha, let's go upstairs." *Correct words and response.*

Sasha climbed the stairs. They were entering another hallway with rooms attached by open doorways. By his own choice, Sasha chose Maggie and Mike's bedroom and Kai found himself facing a bed with two sleeping humans, covered with blankets.

"Go see Mike," Kai told Sasha. The dog walked over to Mike's side of the bed, where he was sleeping on his side, away from Sasha. The dog stood by Mike for several minutes, but Mike didn't move. Concerned about how long he could keep up this telepathic connection, he gave Sasha another command.

"Go see Maggie."

Sasha walked over to Maggie's side of the bed. She was lying on her side, facing the dog. Sasha moved in closer, staring at Maggie and sniffing her face.

Maggie opened her eyes and saw Sasha's nose on the bed, staring at her. She smiled at the dog and reached out to pet his head.

"Hey, Sasha, how you doing?" Maggie asked. The dog didn't respond. He just stared at Maggie, his eyes fixed on her. Maggie sat up, startled at the dog's behavior.

"Sasha, are you alright?"

Kai was tiring fast and losing control of the telepathic connection with Sasha. He broke the connection and was pulled immediately back into Mike's computer. He felt dizzy. Kai's management programming stepped in, putting him immediately to sleep.

Upstairs, with the connection with Kai broken, Sasha snapped back to normal.

"What's the matter, Maggie?" Mike asked, lifting himself up, still half-asleep.

"It's Sasha. He's acting strange," she said as she flipped on the nightstand lamp. By the time Mike lifted his head, Sasha was just sitting there, his wagging tail brushing the carpet behind him and panting with a dog smile on his face.

"I think the fella needs to go outside," Mike said, putting on his slippers and walking downstairs with the dog.

While Mike and Sasha were outside, Maggie couldn't shake the feeling that there was something wrong. Maybe it was her own telepathic powers being awakened, but whatever just happened with Sasha was not normal.

Mike returned to the room and stumbled back into bed. He nuzzled up next to Maggie, mumbled a few incoherent words about Sasha doing his duty, and then fell asleep.

She wouldn't trouble Mike with what she saw, but it would take her an hour to get back to sleep. Tomorrow, they would talk.

32
Kai and Mike

TODAY WAS FRIDAY, the unofficial start of the Memorial Day weekend. Maggie and two high school friends were driving up to Santa Barbara for a spa weekend. Mike wasn't sure why women did that sort of thing. But whatever the reasons, Maggie always came back looking prettier and more invigorated.

He had the place to himself. The Dodgers and Tigers had two-game stands and the Indy 500 was running on Sunday. Mike would watch all the action in the study, while taking whatever time was needed to find the missing Viking data that was hiding somewhere on his computer.

Mike was up before sunrise, washing the nifty set of wheels that the girls would take to Santa Barbara. Parked nose-out in the driveway was a Sea Mist Green and White 1955 Chevy Bel Air Coupe. Mike's father-in-law bought the car new for a tad over $2,000 and the odometer had only 23,000 miles on it. Last year, Mike did a frame-up restoration and the sixty-year-old Chevy was now in showroom condition. Several of the big auto auction houses asked if the car was for sale, but like the house and garage that stored this prize, the '55 Bel Air was staying in the family.

After prepping the car, Mike made breakfast while Maggie finished packing. Sasha was in the kitchen. He knew a human breakfast when he smelled it and this one had an especially-prized commodity – bacon. In his mind, Sasha was extremely reasonable as far as humans and their food were concerned. Take a breakfast like this morning's, for example. Sasha would allow them a generous amount of time – let's say seven to ten minutes – to eat breakfast. Then, he would stand and begin the long-stare.

If the long-stare failed to get him what was rightfully his, he would begin his vocal exercises. Sasha would warm up with short whines, followed by a set of deep and soulful wailing sounds. Usually this was enough to break the crusty exteriors of these humans and move the plates to the counter for scraping his portion into his bowl. But, if necessary, he was prepared to serve up a series of *woofs* and then official barks until he got what he deserved.

Maggie walked into the kitchen. She wore white shorts with sandals and a pastel sleeveless top. It was the perfect outfit for a drive along the Pacific coast. Mike poured her a mug of coffee and set it down on the table in front of her.

"Good morning!" Mike sang out. No response.

"It's spa day!" Mike repeated the three-note fanfare as Maggie stared down at her coffee.

"Hey, are you okay?" Mike asked.

"Mikey, do you remember anything about last night?" Maggie asked, still staring into the coffee. "I mean, about Sasha?"

"Only that he woke *you* up to go outside," Mike said. "I figured my training with him was starting to pay off." Mike winked at her, but she didn't notice.

Finally, Maggie looked up at Mike. "No. The way he acted."

"What do you mean?"

"You didn't see him?" Maggie asked. "He just stood there like a statue, staring at me with spooky eyes. Even in the dark, I could see his eyes. They were different." Maggie shivered a bit.

"You mean like dog-possessed kind of eyes?"

"Yes, that's exactly what I mean," Maggie returned, looking at Mike with a serious expression.

Mike got up for a moment to take the pans off the stove and serve up the eggs and bacon. He watched as she began eating slowly, her head still down.

"Okay, I got a vibe," Maggie said, finally looking up at Mike. "It wasn't rational or scientific, but there was this sense of power that I was getting from Sasha. And there were the images."

"What sort of images?" Mike asked.

"A collage. Explosions. Rocks and dust. Tunnels or caves. And, the people..." Maggie trailed off.

"What kind of people?" Mike asked, holding her hand.

"Small. Frail. Maybe even sick. Bodies with large heads. Not like us, but like us, too," Maggie said. She rubbed her eyes with both hands, as if she was trying to erase the images.

"Hey, maybe you should stay home this weekend?"

Maggie shook off the images and looked up at Mike.

"No," she said, smiling at Mike. "It was just a nightmare."

Maggie's mood brightened during the rest of breakfast. She peaked outside to see the '55 Bel Air sparkling in the morning light. Except for modern tires, the coupe looked exactly like it did when it drove off the assembly line. As a kid, Mike loved the '55, but since dad worked at Ford, buying a GM product was a no-no.

Maggie looked at her watch. It was time to go. She had to pick up her friends soon, so Mike was spared the excruciating details about all of the spa treatments the women would enjoy this weekend. And of course, there were the restaurants, the pool, and the bar. These semi-annual events were part of the amazingly-close relationship of these three friends that went back to their middle school years.

"Hey, I have to go," she said. She got up quickly and then came around to Mike's side of the table. She hugged his neck and kissed him a dozen times on both cheeks. A few more kisses and he might try to persuade her to stay for a while longer.

"What do you have planned for the weekend, slick?" Maggie asked as Mike walked with her to the car.

"You know, guy stuff," Mike said. "Baseball, pizza, baseball, and, did I mention pizza?"

"I guess the casseroles in the freezer won't be used this weekend."

"Only if the pizza delivery guys go on strike," Mike said. "Now, keep it close to the speed limit, okay? This thing handles like a Conestoga wagon."

"Under ninety, the entire way, I promise," Maggie said, hugging Mike and planting a big kiss on him. Maggie got in and fired up the 265 cubic-inch V-8 engine. The twin exhausts made a low rumbling sound – loud enough to sound cool, but not so loud that they couldn't enjoy the car radio. Although Bill would have objected, Mike made one other minor change to the Chevy – a killer audio system that could connect to

Maggie's mobile phone. She and her friends would be grooving to hits from the 50s, 60s, and 70s all the way to Santa Barbara.

With the song *Be My Baby* by the Ronettes pumping from the speakers, Maggie pulled the Chevy out of the driveway. She blew some air kisses at Mike before chirping the back tires as she headed north. He could still hear the music a block from the house.

When Mike returned to the kitchen to clean up the dishes, he noticed that Sasha's bowl was still filled with the eggs and bacon he scraped from their plates.

"Yo, Sasha. You got bacon and eggs up in here."

The dog didn't respond.

"Sasha?"

Mike walked into the study, where Sasha was sitting near the desk, staring at the computer monitor. He didn't notice Mike come in. Mike slipped past the dog and sat down at the desk.

"So, what's your story this morning?" Mike asked, patting the dog's head. The physical contact must have broken Sasha's concentration because he looked up at Mike. Then, his nose picked up breakfast fragrances and he ran for the kitchen.

Mike laughed as Sasha spun out a little as he left the room. He would be seeing that kind of action on the Brickyard in Indianapolis tomorrow. Then he noticed the files and papers scattered on the floor around his desk.

"Hey, did you do this?" Mike shouted as he scooped up the files. Sasha wasn't a jumper, so his presence on the desk was strange. Sasha trotted back into the study, snorting and licking his lips. He seemed satisfied with the home-cooked meal and nuzzled his head onto Mike's lap for some pets.

"Young man, if you're going to share my desk, you have to learn to put your files away," Mike said as Sasha stared at him blankly.

"Okay, then. What do you say we get to work?"

Mike tapped the spacebar on the keyboard to wake up the computer monitor. He used the computer only lightly since Monday. Kai was there, waiting on the other side of the computer glass. He was as ready to make his first contact with a human. Kai overheard the conversation in the kitchen about his telepathic visit to their bedroom last night. Scaring one of his hosts was not the best way to make a good first impression. The hill he had to climb to win this guy over got a little steeper since last night. Using Sasha for surveillance was something he would not do again.

As he tapped on the spacebar, Mike noticed that the camera light was on, but the computer screen was not. No, wait. The screen was on, but it was black. A simple white cursor blinked in the upper left corner. It reminded him of the early days of computing, when everything was done with text commands on a blank screen.

Mike tried the keyboard. He typed a few early DOS commands to see if the computer was still working at some level. He tried "C:\" and there was no response. He typed "DIR" to see if he could find the computer's file directory. Again, no response. One last oldie but goodie was "CHKDSK," which could sometimes repair a wonky hard drive. No response.

"Well, my friend," Mike said, looking down at the dog, "it looks like this thing is toast." He tapped on the spacebar and moved his mouse around a few more times as he reached under the desk to hit the power button. Rebooting the computer would be one of his final options before opening up the case and doing some high-tech work under the hood.

He was ready to punch the power button when his peripheral vision noticed motion on the screen. White letters were going across the screen at high speed. At first, the letters and numbers were gibberish. Then, the return key was hit twice and a complete sentence followed.

"Hello, Mike. My name is Kai."

Mike stared back at the computer. *Well then,* Mike thought, *it looks like I got me a hacker.*

Now he was sure this computer had to go. But before pulling the plug, he decided to pull the chain of the jerk who broke into his computer.

"Who is this?" Mike wrote. A response came up instantly.

"My name is Kai."

"Hello, Kai," Mike typed. "Can you tell me where you are."

"Well, right now, I'm in Santa Monica. But I am actually from Mars."

That was clever. The hacker knew where Mike's computer was. He was probably watching Mike with the camera on the computer monitor.

"Let's try this again," Mike typed. "Where are you?"

"Why don't you check?" came the response.

The text box was scaled down to a smaller black rectangle. The Windows 10 desktop was now visible so that Mike could access other programs. He clicked on Firefox and the web browser opened right up.

Mike's plan was to stall this punk until he could log into some experimental web programming that a colleague at Caltech had developed. This program provided geolocation and IP address information, but did a much better job of pinpointing the exact location of the computer being used. If he could get the address, he could call the cops and report the hacker.

"My name is Kai Tuparnac. I am a visitor from Atona, the planet you call Mars."

"And, how did you get here, Kai Tupernik?" Mike typed.

"The spelling is T-u-p-a-r-n-a-c," Kai typed. "I arrived here when your wife recorded my radio transmission from Mars in October, 1976."

"What the f…" Mike hit the backspace key to remove the last sentence. "Explain."

"On October 11, 1976, your wife recorded a radio transmission sent from Mars to the NASA Goldstone station in Barstow," Kai typed. "I was in the compressed file that Maggie recorded that night. You brought me back to life when you decompressed the two files that were stored on that tape."

This guy knew everything – things no one beside Maggie would know. If this was a hacker, he was very, very good.

The web tracker program popped up with a location for the hacker. It showed that he was *here*, in the house. *That's spooky*, Mike thought. He got up from the desk, grabbed an old baseball bat from behind the door, and checked the house.

He was alone. Mike returned to the computer and started typing again.

"You said that I restored you," Mike typed. "How did I do that?"

Kai's responses to Mike's questions were instantaneous. A hacker would need more time to make up this stuff. His answers were coming up even before Mike finished his questions.

Kai wrote several paragraphs, beginning with the encrypted radio transmission from forty years ago. He knew the radio frequency and the type of signal modulation used by the Viking lander to talk with Goldstone, where Maggie was working the late night shift in October, 1976.

Then, Kai walked through the steps Mike took on Monday to install the hard drive from Steve Gabriel and begin the startup program. Kai described the unpacking of the 18,000 files and then the disappearance of all of them.

"Isn't that why you are working on your computer this morning," Kai typed, "to find those missing files?"

"I don't believe you," Mike typed. He was bluffing. So far, this guy was spot-on with his information. No one could pull a con like this.

"Let me show you some of the code that was used to wake me up," Kai typed.

A new window opened on the screen and began rolling with line after line of computer code. The letters and symbols were not a language Mike had seen before. As he scrolled down through the code, Kai studied Mike's face through the camera. Mike did not seem visibly shaken by the prospect of an extraterrestrial. There was still anger, but that was fading. He was behaving like a scientist. Query and response. Kai would be doing the same thing, if the situation was reversed.

"Can you see me, Kai?" Mike wrote.

"Yes."

"What am I doing right now?" Mike typed. He was holding up his left hand.

"You are showing me your left hand. On finger four, you are wearing a wedding ring."

"Why did you call it finger four?" Mike wrote out of pure curiosity.

"I am a growing fan of the piano," Kai wrote. "Pianists count the thumb as finger one. So, your ring finger would be number four."

"Wow, that was clever," Mike wrote somewhat sarcastically. "By the way Kai, what color is my ring?"

"The color is silver, but the ring actually has two metals – cobalt and silver."

Amazing. No one looking through a computer camera could deduce the metal varieties of his ring. But Kai was right. The ring was cobalt with a thin band of silver in the center.

"I see that you already met my dog. What is *her* name?" Mike asked. If the hacker was foreign, he might have trouble with personal pronouns.

"The dog is a male named is Sasha. *"On nakhoditsya pod stolom,"* Kai replied.

"Did you just tell me that my dog is on the *roof*?" Mike asked.

"No, Mike," Kai typed. "In Russian, I said that your dog is under the desk."

"Vy obshchalis' s moyey sobakoy?" Mike asked.

"Have I communicated with your dog?" Kai replied. "Yes. Twice," Kai typed. "Yesterday, Sasha jumped on the desk and scattered some of your files. He licked the screen right there when we talked yesterday." A white circle formed around the smear mark still on the screen.

"And did you frighten my wife last night?" There was no reply.

"Okay, chump, let me repeat the question. Did you scare my wife last night?"

Mike had his hand on the power cable connected to the NAS where Kai was located. Kai saw where his hand was placed and knew that he had only a few seconds to provide an acceptable answer or everything was lost. One thing was certain – Kai would not survive if this man felt that his wife was being threatened.

"Yes. I am sorry. It was not my intention to frighten her."

"So, you have telepathic powers?" Mike asked, releasing his hand from the cable leading to the storage unit.

"Not on Mars, but I was programmed with limited telepathic powers to help me in this new environment."

"Can you read my thoughts?" Mike asked.

"No." Kai answered. "But you know that I am not a hacker."

"Why would you say that?"

"Because your computer is not connected to the Internet," Kai typed.

He was right. About a minute into their discussion, Mike kicked the network cable out of its socket. If this was a hacker, he should have been cut off. Instead, the typist continued to provide accurate information as Mike asked for it. The only place Kai – or whatever this was – could be, was *inside* Mike's computer.

Mike didn't believe in the supernatural. But, he also knew that a hacker couldn't provide the answers he was getting from the computer. And, there was one more fact that Mike could not ignore. No one – not at NASA or JPL or even a friend – knew the details of that night in October, 1976, when Mike was on the phone with Maggie as she recorded the radio transmission from Mars. The chain of custody of that data went from Maggie to Mike, and then into this house, where it remained hidden for four decades.

"Why did you come here?" Mike asked.

"I volunteered," Kai began. "The surface of Mars was destroyed in 1619 by a rogue planet named Koya. The impact killed millions of my people and forced the survivors to move underground. I was just a boy then." The writing on the screen stopped. A minute passed. Then another.

"Are you still there, Kai?" Mike typed.

"Forgive the delay," Kai continued. He was having a difficult time writing about the event, especially the loss of his
grandmother.

"When I left for Earth, there were only about a hundred
thousand citizens still living on Mars," Kai wrote, "But everyone was sick. We were dying."

"How did you manage to use the Viking's radio signal?"
Mike wrote. "We never even considered that someone from
another planet could arrive here by electronic means."

Kai typed another few paragraphs, describing his grandfather's work in developing a transference process to move Martians out of their sick bodies into an electronic world until
they could be fitted with some kind of natural-feeling physical
bodies. He also told Mike that his grandfather died during the
experiment and that Kai was the first Martian to successfully
complete the transference process.

"As for getting to Earth," Kai said, "that was easy. We interrupted Viking's radio signal with Earth. You were using the
Goldstone station to receive the signal."

"That's in West Franistan, correct?"

"There is no place called West Franistan," Kai answered.
"The Goldstone station is in Barstow, California." A satellite
map popped up on the screen with a red circle around the
Goldstone facility. "As I said, we took over Viking's radio
frequency so that I could be sent as compressed digital data to
Earth."

"How long were you in transit?" Mike continued the
cross-examination.

"Twenty-eight Earth minutes," Kai replied. That was
correct.

"What happened then?" Mike asked.

"I woke up last week," Kai typed. "I spent the past few days learning where I am – and *when* I am."

"Do you know how long you were in stasis?" Mike asked.

"Call it stasis or being asleep, but I have been suspended between life and death for forty years," Kai typed. "May I ask you a question, Mike?"

"Of course."

"Why did it take so long for you to restore me after I arrived here?"

That question hurt. Mike wrote about the night he and Maggie were on duty when Kai came to Earth. He explained that, in 1976, humans didn't have the technology to decode Kai's digital signal. Even today, he wrote, it had been very difficult just to copy Kai's files and open them.

And to add insult to injury, Mike told Kai that the tape with his signal had gone missing for forty years.

There was no response from the computer for about a minute. Kai was trying to grasp how such a minor thing could determine the success of his mission.

"I understand," Kai said.

"Kai, I am sorry," Mike said. "Maybe if you had called ahead or made a reservation?"

It was a bad joke, but it still got a laugh from Kai, who never figured that two young people falling in love would interrupt his mission. But the facts were the facts and Kai would have to make the best of his situation. Besides, Kai knew firsthand about the power of love. It was the reason he was here.

"I have something to show you," Mike said as he opened a manila envelope on his desk. He pulled out the photos taken by Viking of its landing site.

"Did you do this?" Mike asked, as he showed Kai the time-lapsed photographs, revealing the assembly of the rock wall not far from the Viking lander.

"No," Kai said. "I am too old to be *schlepping* rocks." The Yiddish word got a laugh from Mike, which Kai could see through the computer camera. He was winning Mike over.

"Did you see Viking land?" Mike asked.

"Yes. I watched it land. And, I saw the Russian Mars 3 land five years earlier."

"Wasn't the Mars 3 lander destroyed?"

"It was. From a lightning strike during a dust storm," Kai replied.

That checked. Colleagues inside the Russian space program told Mike that they lost contact with Mars 3 almost immediately after it landed. They suspected that it exploded or was fried by electrical energy from the dust storm.

But no one could know that – unless they were on Mars at the time, Mike thought.

"Have you left the computer since you arrived?" Mike asked.

"I have been around your planet many times since arriving."

"Well then, can you tell me the score of the Dodgers game?"

"If you connect the computer to the Internet, then I can."

Mike was still holding the blue network cable that connected the computer to his cable modem. He plugged the network cable into its wall plug. A second or two elapsed.

"The game begins at 4:10 p.m. That's Pacific Time."

Mike looked up at the clock. It was coming up on noon in Los Angeles. The Dodgers were playing the Mets in New York. With the time difference, Kai's report was correct. The game would begin in about an hour – at 4:10 p.m. That checked. Kai was the real deal. Mike was about to ask more questions when his cellphone rang. It was Maggie.

"Hey, sweetie. How's your chick weekend going?" Mike asked.

"It's going great," Maggie said. "We had a fabulous ride up and got honks from good looking guys in pickup trucks."

"So, what are you doing?"

"We're sitting at the bar having Bloody Marys."

"It's a little early, isn't it?" Mike asked, looking at the green light on the computer. Kai was quiet during this interlude.

"Well, it's noon somewhere," Maggie said, sounding a little tipsy. "No wait, it's noon *here*." Mike could hear Maggie's friends laughing in the background. "What 'cha doing, Mikey?"

Just how does one tell his wife that he's having a conversation with a Martian?

"Ah, I'm in the study with Sasha." That part was true. "Not much going on." That part was not.

"Okay, honey. I'll call you later tonight," Maggie said.

"Sounds great. Hey, Maggie?" Mike asked.

"What?"

"When was the last time I told you I love you?"

"This morning," she giggled.

"Well, it's still true. See you Sunday."

"Bye, Mikey."

Mike and Kai talked for a few more minutes, but Kai said he needed to sleep. He explained his mandatory sleep programming. Mike was tired, too. He suggested that they talk later.

There was just one last thing Mike needed to do.

"Kai? You said that you can get into any computer. Is that correct?" Mike typed.

"Yes. They cannot see me."

"Are you honest, Kai?"

"I am not familiar with that term."

"Never mind. Would you go to any bank that you want and transfer $10 million into my checking account?" Mike asked.

"No, Mike. I will not."

Mike grinned into the camera. "Congratulations, Kai. You passed. Welcome to Earth. Tonight, let's get you a voice. No more of this typing business."

"Thank you. My fingers are getting tired," Kai said. The computer screen resumed its normal appearance and the camera light turned off.

33
Realization

MIKE WALKED OUT of the study with Sasha trotting at his side. He stopped at the door and looked back at the computer. The screen was dark and there were no blinking lights on the computer box. The weight of the moment was pressing down on him. He was wobbly. Mike shuffled to the family room and sat down in his old, overstuffed chair – the place he came to read and think.

There were competing voices in his head. In fact, a debate was going on.

You've discovered life from another planet.

No, you didn't. None of this is real.

It is real. He knows everything.

You're a scientist. No, wait, you're a gullible scientist.

But, I worked the plan. The scientific method. There is no other answer.

Back and forth, the conversation continued as Mike's mind reeled. All he could do was sit and stare at the wall. Then, the debate faded and Mike was left with his own thoughts.

If this was a hacker, I did everything I could to trip him up. But there is no way that the text on my screen was coming from anywhere else but my computer.

It did seem impossible, but there was so much in favor of all of this being real. Mike was slowly getting control of his thoughts – putting some order to the facts he had.

The only way for Kai – or whoever he is – to know what happened forty years ago was if he was on Mars at the time. The only way! There was no other rational explanation for what Kai knew about the mission.

Mike exhaled and took a step back. If he was in a courtroom, he would have lots of solid evidence to back up what Kai said.

I have physical evidence. The photographs. The surface near the Viking lander had been altered. Unless a planetary geologist can tell me how a rock wall could naturally form in less than three months, then it had to have been made by someone on Mars.

And, the radio signal. Maggie recorded twenty-eight minutes of digital data of a kind never seen before or since from Mars. And, it came from a spacecraft made in 1976, with a computer that had just six kilobytes of memory. Viking didn't even have the ability to send that kind of signal. It had to have been sent by another transmitter on Mars.

Then, don't forget the data itself. More than fifty tera-bytes of data! It was way beyond binary code. It was so complex that it took an expert like Steve Gabriel just to copy it. And even he didn't understand the complexity of the data.

One last piece of physical evidence came to light since the tape was found. After the water leak was repaired, Maggie cleaned out the old stuff in the window seat. She found a personal journal she kept at the time. Maggie had made an entry on the night the radio transmission came from Mars.

```
Oct. 11, 1976

Very curious data from Viking 1 tonight.

Seismic Activity - The V1 seismometer re-
corded 4-6 nm beats at 3.5 Hz. Periodici-
ty is at 2.1-2.6 bps. This pattern could
not be seismic activity, background noise
from the lander deck, or wind resonance.
No one here would ever believe me, but I
think the pattern looks like footsteps
moving toward and away from the lander.

Signal Anomaly - At 37:58 minutes af-
ter seismic activity concluded, Vi-
king began sending digital signal con-
tent on the 381 MHz direct frequency.
Signal bleed into both sidebands. Data
transfer was at 2.45x nominal rate.
I recorded 28:32 of data, which will
be given to a JPL rep this weekend.

P.S. That JPL rep is Mike Savin. I sug-
gested brunch tomorrow at the Jazz
House. He said yes! Can't wait!!!!
```

After he read the journal entry, Mike paused and enjoyed the moment. Maggie had written little hearts all over the journal page.

The voice in his head – the one telling him that all of this was fake – was starting to fade. The physical evidence was convincing him.

But does all of that equate to a life form? Maybe. Whatever was replying to my typed queries replied in real time – even though my computer was disconnected from the Internet. And, Kai's responses matched things that only Maggie and I knew about the Viking mission that October night.

Finally, the doubting voice was gone. Based on the physical evidence, Mike believed that the entity in his computer was real. It might be lying about what it was and what it wanted, but it was real.

So what's next? There was Steve Gabriel's warning that serious things were happening in the world. Kai's presence would only complicate the situation. Then, there was Maggie's safety to think about. And, Kai's, too. He's safe in my computer, but with Steve's comments about computer privacy, would Kai be at risk from others?

I'm not a diplomat, but I do know something about history. My dad's journey from Russia and the Cold War taught me how we humans waste time, talent, and resources on stuff that helps no one.

What if the United States had a rocket on the pad, ready to go to Mars? Would we share with Russia and China? If not, how would they react? Would they send spacecraft to Mars to get a Martian or two of their own? Or, would they try to sabotage the mission? Maybe kidnap Kai?

The stakes are high. Kai represents a leap of centuries in human development. Just in my area, Kai could provide breakthroughs in physics that any country would want. He could give us a jump-start on technology that would make us more powerful. Would other nations stand around and allow that to happen? No way!

What about religion? What would Kai's presence mean to organized religion? Would Kai validate the existence of God? What if Martians had different religious beliefs, or had shown that God doesn't exist? Would Kai's presence tear down thousands of years of religious tradition? How would billions of followers who devoted their lives to their faiths deal with a change of this magnitude? I don't know.

For sure, Kai's presence would mean a new definition of life. Kai is alive, but he doesn't have a physical body. We would have to change the definition of life to add more weight to intellect in the abstract. Would something without a body that has independent and rational thought be considered a life form? Animals have rights. And maybe when quantum computers start thinking on their own, they'll have rights, too.

Mike's head was throbbing. He needed some air and to do something normal with an already-defined living being. Sasha sat at his feet, panting for attention. Mike hadn't patted his head or rubbed his belly all day. His living, thinking friend needed him and Mike needed Sasha.

"C'mon boy, let's go outside," Mike said, as he reached for a beer in the refrigerator. The dog sprinted into the backyard, while Mike stood on the porch and tossed the Frisbee to the far end of the yard. Sasha got there in time to turn around and leap up, catching it in mid-air. He brought the Frisbee back for another throw – again and again.

Life. Death. Heaven. Hell. None of these things matter to Sasha. He lives in the now, enjoying each moment of life. When his time comes, he'll go, and there will be no complaints, no prayers for mercy for unknown sins committed. Sasha lives for today. Tomorrow, Scripture tells us, will take care of itself.

Although he grew up in the Russian Orthodox church, by the time he reached college age, Mike no longer believed in God. During his career as a physicist, he found no reason to change that view.

Certainly, humans weren't created in the likeness of God – not the way we behave toward each other. And where is God anyway? Different religions, different rules. God is a shy guy who seems content to allow humans to make up all kinds of rules in His name. A lot of terrible things have been done by the religious faithful who justified their acts with a belief that what they did would please God.

Setting aside the what-ifs for a moment, the fact, Mikhail Savin, is that you have a visitor from another planet living in your house! Of course, his arrival isn't how we expected, not after decades of science fiction books and movies. Kai's arrival certainly puts an end to the notion that when extraterrestrials arrive, they'll show up in majestic spaceships, festooned with lights

*and powerful ray guns that can instantly microwave the
world into submission.*

*No, this guy hitched a ride. On a radio signal! I know
the kind of bad stuff that zips back and forth across the
universe. Any one of those bits of cosmic radiation could
have intersected with Kai's radio signal and sliced him
apart. He took a huge risk coming here. His people must
be desperate.*

*And what about those Martians, hunkered down in
caves below the surface? What can we do to help them?
Kai thought that there might be a hundred thousand
Martians still trapped underground. Do they want to
come here? Hell, we don't even have a manned launch
vehicle right now.*

Mike looked at his watch. It was close to 7:00 p.m. and the
sky was getting dark. He looked up at the sky.

Things were going to get a lot more interesting now
that Kai is here. Since Aristotle proposed that the Earth was
the center of the universe – with the Sun, the stars, and the
planets revolving around it – people have been chipping away
at the concept of a human-centric universe. Even the Vatican
has an observatory and is looking for life on other planets.

Now it is proved – we are not alone.

Mike went back inside. Sasha was hungry. He was, too.
Mike filled the dog's bowl and then went to the refrigerator.
There was pizza there, each slice neatly sealed in aluminum
foil. Mike tapped the oven button and slid several slices
inside. While the pizza warmed, he cracked open another
beer and reached for an astronomy magazine. He got two
paragraphs into an article and then laughed aloud, tossing

the magazine into the air. *Forget the damn magazine! All the answers to my questions about the universe are right there, in the next room.*

Sasha ate his dinner and then stood by, in case Mike needed any help finishing the pizza. When they were done sharing Mike's dinner, Mike slid into a horizontal position on the couch. He was exhausted and his mind was blank. He covered his eyes with his arm and immediately fell asleep.

It was 9:15 p.m. when Mike woke up. The house was dark. He reached down and felt Sasha, who was lying next to the couch, snoring. Evidently, Kai didn't use Sasha to surveil the house again.

Mike got up and walked into the study. He sat at the desk and clicked on the desk lamp. He plugged in a headset and checked to see if the audio was set up properly on his computer. Talking to Kai would be much better than typing. After all, humans have come a long way since Joshua asked Matthew Broderick, "Shall-we-play-a-game?" in the movie *War Games*.

"Hello, Kai," Mike said. There was no response.

"Hello, Kai," Mike said, this time louder.

The camera light lit up. Kai was awake.

"Hello, Mike," a voice returned. It was stilted and stiff.

There was another delay. Kai was assembling a speaking voice. Mike imagined that he was at an online voice store, trying on different-sounding voices. How does this one sound? Does this one make my butt look big? That sort of thing. It would be interesting to hear what Kai considered to be a normal voice for himself.

"So how does this voice sound?" Kai replied. It was full and rich now, not alien-sounding or ethereal, like Hal's voice in Stanley Kubrick's film, *2001: A Space Odyssey*.

"I like it. Did you choose that one for any particular reason?"

"I think it makes me sound sexy, don't you?"

"You sound like Johnny Depp."

"That's what I was going for," Kai replied. Not only had he grasped the language, but Kai was using nuanced, contemporary speech. And, he had a sense of humor.

"Go with it until it stops working for you."

"Word," Kai said. Mike laughed.

"I like the sound of laughter. It seems to be a regular part of human communication."

"It certainly is in this house," Mike said. Then, his tone grew serious.

"Kai, I feel terrible about the forty years you spent in stasis. Let's go over what happened after you arrived."

"Sure, Mike."

Mike provided more details about the night Maggie detected the radio signal from Mars. It was very different, he said, from the normal data that Viking was sending. He told Kai about the seismic activity and the photos that he copied while working that night at JPL.

Then, Mike explained how he and Maggie met and how she gave him the tape with Kai's data files. Mike said that it was his fault that he forgot about the data tape. He repeated that love and life got in the way and that only recently had the tape been found and converted into something his computer could understand.

There was a pause before Kai spoke. Mike imagined what Kai must be thinking. *Let me get this straight. I lose my phys-*

*ical body, transfer across space to Earth, and when I get here,
you stuff me in a closet for forty years?* Something like that was
bound to come next.

"Kai?"

"Yes, Mike?"

"Kai, I'm sorry. I really had no way of knowing."

"There would be no way you could," Kai replied. "We
didn't exactly ask for permission to come here. And from
what I've learned about your technology, you wouldn't have
been able to restore me until right about now, anyway."

"Thanks for that. But you must be so worried about your
people."

"Yes, especially my wife."

Mike hadn't figured a partner into Kai's equation. But why
not? Weren't they just like us? The same amino acids and the
same Sun? Humans and Martians were related, albeit distant-
ly.

"What's her name, Kai?"

"Mia. She is a teacher."

"How were you able to do it? I mean, leaving Mia?"

"She was all I had," Kai said. "But we were dying and
didn't have much time left. I convinced Mia that I could do
more by coming here. But, I did ask her to wait."

"Do you think she's still alive?"

"I don't know," Kai said. "Forty years is a long time. So
much was changing. I just don't know."

"Could you contact Mia and tell her that you're alive?"

"Maybe, if anyone is still listening," Kai said. "But no one,
not the United States or any other country, has the capability
to send a manned rescue mission to Mars."

"True, but maybe a lander with radio transmission equipment could be sent," Mike said.

"Still, my people would need to do one more thing."

"You mean the transference?"

"Yes. It would be the only way anyone could get here."

"Maggie returns on Sunday and we're going to do everything we can to help you."

"That is all I can ask. Thank you, my new friend. And goodnight."

"Goodnight, Kai."

Mike turned off the light in the study, called Sasha and headed upstairs to bed. He was exhausted. Kai was too, in his own way, Mike supposed. Tomorrow was Saturday. Mike had the whole day to talk to his new friend. There were so many things he wanted to ask.

The phone rang. It was Maggie.

"Hi, honey," Mike said, "how are you?"

"We're having a great time," Maggie said, "but you sound tired."

"I turned in early."

"Are you feeling alright?" Maggie asked.

"Everything is fine," Mike said. "I'm having some trouble with the computer, but I should have it fixed by tomorrow."

"It's not like you to take this long to fix a computer," Maggie said. "Are you sure you're okay?"

"Great," Mike said. *Damn, I hate to lie to her. But I can't tell her about Kai over the phone.* "Can't wait to see you, my love."

34
Storm Warnings

MIKE WAS IN a deep sleep when the phone rang. It was just past 7:00 a.m. and Sasha was sitting next to the bed, staring at him. He picked up his phone as he sat up. It was Maggie.

"Hey. Are you alright?" Mike asked.

"Hi, Mikey. We're fine, but there's a big Pacific storm coming in on Sunday. We decided to come back today."

"When are you leaving?"

"Right now," Maggie said. "I don't want to get rain on your Chevy."

"You know that's not a problem," Mike said. "Your dad taught me that good cars are meant to be driven – especially by his very pretty daughter."

"Aw, you're sweet," Maggie said. "Hey, are you still in bed?"

"Yep, and Sasha's getting a little frustrated with me."

"Okay. Take care of the fella and we'll be on our way."

"Be careful. Love you."

"Love you, too," Maggie said and clicked off. Mike turned to Sasha, who had flopped his big head on Mike's lap.

"Dobroye utro Sasha," Mike said, smiling as he sat at the edge of the bed. Sasha's tail was swishing the floor from side to side. *"Vwee khotite, chtoby vyyti na ulitsu? Vwee golodny?"*

Sasha popped his head up and down, then spun around in excited circles at the foot of the bed. *Yes, I want – check that – I need to go outside. And, of course, I'm hungry. Why do you think I'm acting all crazy up in here?*

Mike was still half-asleep. Yesterday took a lot out of him. Besides, at 65, Mike was finding it a little harder to get vertical than he used to. Not that he was ever a physical specimen. Physicists who scribble on whiteboards and play chess in their spare time don't end up on the cover of *People* magazine.

Mike walked downstairs. Sasha was already waiting at the back door. He opened the slider and got out of the way as Sasha burst through. The dog bounded out of the house, across the porch and onto the grass. With all of the sniffing, running, and squatting going on outside, Mike took his turn inside and then padded into the kitchen to start the coffee and get Sasha's breakfast. He scooped up a brimming cup of prime U.S.D.A. kibble from the dog's food container and then slowly dropped it, kibble by kibble, into a large ceramic bowl that said *Dogs Rule* on the outside. The distinctive *tink-tink-tink* sound the kibble made against ceramic stopped Sasha in his tracks. When Mike looked up, Sasha was already at the back door, smearing the glass with his nose and wagging his tail furiously.

Mike loved this part. He cracked the sliding door open a bit – just wide enough to fit Sasha's nose. From there, Sasha would do the rest. Sasha stuck his nose through the opening and then pushed the sliding door to the left with his head, using the exact number of Newtons of force to open the door to full-body width. After that, it was a blur as Sasha bolted for the kitchen, slip-sliding across the wood floor.

Breakfast lasted about thirty seconds. Sasha didn't really chew his food. It was more like he vacuumed it up. After licking the bowl clean, he took a dozen gulps from the companion water bowl, this one marked *Humans Obey*. Sasha was now ready to begin his day, thank you very much. After yesterday, it was good to do something normal with his dog. He would feel even better when Maggie was home.

With coffee brewing in the background and the dog fed and watered, it was time for them to get to work. They headed for Mike's study, Sasha walking alongside Mike. After entering the room, Sasha waited for the entertainment portion of the morning. He was panting. The *huh-huh-huh* was Sasha's way of moving things along. He stood near the desk, facing the large computer monitor as the computer finished booting.

"Okay, Sasha," Mike said. "It's movie time."

The two fellows usually started the morning with a few online videos of dogs doing dumb stuff. The links were curated by a fellow golden retriever owner who seemed to have a knack for finding these *Dogs Gone Wild* videos on the Internet. Mike patted his thigh. Sasha jumped up and stood with his front paws on Mike's legs, getting a great view of the computer monitor.

One of Sasha's not-so-bright cousins was chasing his tail in an oval bathtub filled with bubble bath. Water had formed a large cyclonic mess that was slopping over the rim of the bath tub. Another video showed a large pile of snow. Then, a dog's head popped out of a mound that had been dumped on top of him by some kids. The third, and possibly the best, showed a golden retriever firmly standing his ground against one of those robotic vacuum cleaners. When it tried to go forward, it was blocked by the dog. Going left or right, the dog got in front of it. There would be no sweeping-up of dog hair in that house.

Combine a few videos with Sasha's short attention span and the dog was already bored. He dropped down on all four paws and pulled in under the desk to lie down, taking up most of the foot room. That was intended, since it required Mike to rub Sasha's belly with his feet while working. Mike looked at his best friend under the desk and smiled. He was ready to talk to Kai.

"Good morning, Kai." He waited for a response. There was none.

"Kai? Are you there?" There was still no answer.

Kai was gone. Or worse. Mike had a dream about Kai last night. In it, a man dressed in a black western duster that extended almost to the ground walked through the front door of Mike's house. Staring at Mike, the strange figure went past him and into the study. There, he violently picked up Mike's computer. Then, glaring at Mike with eyes full of hate, he took the computer out to the driveway. The man lifted it above his head and smashed it into pieces.

The figure turned and grinned at Mike, who was terrified. The man in black walked toward Mike, his yellow teeth becoming more prominent. Mike tried to run, but he couldn't move. He turned his back and waited for the man in black to crush him, but instead, he was jarred out of the dream when Maggie called with news about coming home today.

Mike shuddered as he vividly recalled the dream. He kept calling for Kai, but there was no response. Mike guessed that Kai was traveling, looking at options for a mission to Mars. That was good – the more information he had, the easier it would be to plan a rescue mission. He only hoped that Kai would return so that he could meet Maggie. If he didn't, Mike would just have an interesting story to tell, one that even Maggie might not believe.

Mike heard the garage door go up and walked out as Maggie pulled the '55 Chevy into its place of honor. Next to it was Mike's 1970 Volkswagen Beetle. Like the Chevy, it had been restored to new condition.

Maggie got out of the car, looking radiant and invigorated. They held each other for a long time, exchanging kisses and nuzzles. Walking back into the house, he asked about the trip and Maggie obliged, telling him about each of the spa treatments they had during their stay. Mike smiled as he listened, but his mind was on the computer in the study and how he was going to handle the subject of Kai once Maggie's exuberance calmed a little.

They went upstairs to unpack Maggie's things. She cleaned up and put on an old Caltech sweatshirt and sweatpants. The rain came in faster than expected and it was already getting colder.

"A great day to stay inside and watch old movies," Maggie said, as they made their way to the family room.

"It sure is," Mike said, smiling at her as he took a spot on the couch. Sasha pulled in next to him in the perfect position to get head pats. Mike petted Sasha, not saying much. While he was relieved that Maggie was home, he was also worried about Kai.

After almost forty years together, it didn't take long for Maggie to notice that something was on Mike's mind. She pulled up next to him on the couch. Maggie smelled good from all the creams and goo that spa people slather on their customers. She took his hand, and in her own gentle way, she tried to bring out what was bothering him.

"Alright, jughead," Maggie said. "Spill it. What's going on?"

Mike looked at her and smiled. "Wow, that was smooth."

"I can't help it," Maggie said. "I'm just brimming with class."

"Maggie, I have to tell you something," Mike said.

"You found someone else," she said with a pouting lip.

"No chance."

"You joined the other team? Not that there's anything wrong with that," she said, quoting the classic *Seinfeld* line.

He pretended to consider the question, then grinned and shook his head. Then his face got serious. While they disliked stories that saved the conclusion to the end, for this one, Mike was going to need some build-up before saying something like, *"Oh, by the way Maggie, there's an alien living in our house."*

"This has to do with the Viking tape," he began.

In ten minutes, Maggie knew everything Mike knew about what had been going on for the past several days – from Sasha's odd behavior to Mike's conversations with Kai.

"Wow." That was all that Maggie could muster. She shook her head and continued to stare at her husband. Mike never lied, and never withheld things from her. She believed him.

"Have you talked to him since then?" she asked.

"Not today. He isn't answering his phone."

"Is he dangerous to us? Not you and me, but us as humans?"

"No, not dangerous, but I don't think there is much outside his reach," Mike said. "And that's especially true now that he's been doing some traveling."

Mike explained that Kai had been stepping out frequently, visiting computers all over the world. He also told her about his phony embezzlement request, which Kai refused to do.

"Do you believe him?" Maggie asked.

"Well, let me put it this way. We're the only two people in the universe who know what happened that night, forty years ago," Mike said. "And the parts we didn't know, Kai filled-in with perfect symmetry. Oh yeah. He's from Mars. And, he came on that radio signal."

"Wow," Maggie repeated. "Do you like Kai?"

Mike smiled. "He's amazing. He told me that he is over 400 years old."

"Too bad they couldn't build a spaceship."

"Yeah. Martian geology and atmosphere. No metals and no way to make fire."

"So, here's this old guy who volunteers for a mission where he has to hitch a ride to get to Earth?" Maggie asked.

"Yep. He thumbed it," Mike said. "How's that for pathos?"

"So what do we do next?" Maggie asked. She had some thoughts, but since Mike had been dealing with this alone for two days, she wanted to get a feel for how much this had affected him.

"I really don't know," Mike said. "We're looking at one of the biggest scientific discoveries – wait, *the* biggest discovery in human history – and you and I are sitting here on the couch, having a staff meeting. There's a certain irony in all of this, don't you think?"

"Like The *Three Stooges Meet the Martian* kind of irony," she quipped.

He laughed. "Exactly. I mean, what do people normally do when faced with something of this magnitude?"

"It's a little bigger than Carter and Herbert's discovery of Tutankhamen's tomb in 1922."

"Exactly," Mike said. "Kai changes everything. Economics, environment, strategic alliances – everything."

"Even religion and faith," Maggie said.

"Yes," Mike said, remembering last night, sitting outside and thinking about God and man and the universe.

"We have some big decisions to make," Maggie said.

"Like Neville Chamberlain."

"Harry Truman. Or, John Kennedy."

"Ike and Tina Turner," Mike shot back. "Does she leave the guy or not?"

"Exactly!"

Humor is such an amazing safety valve that can help when what someone is facing is too much to handle.

"So now, you have three guys in this house," Mike said, grinning at his wife. "In order of intelligence – Kai, Sasha, and me."

"Just as long as Kai doesn't leave the toilet seat up," Maggie replied. "Let's go say hello."

35
Kai and Maggie

WITH SASHA LEADING the way, Mike and Maggie headed for the study. Mike held Maggie back for a moment as he peeked into the room. The computer was dark and the camera light was off. The computer was running, but there was no activity on the hard drives.

He sat down in front of the computer. Maggie stayed out-of-range of the camera, while Sasha jumped up on Mike's lap to get a good look-see. Before she got home, Mike removed the headset he used to speak to Kai and replaced it with a microphone and a set of computer speakers on either side of the computer monitor.

"Hello, Kai," Mike said. He no longer had to tap on the keyboard to make the computer monitor light up. Kai was doing that from inside.

The camera light blinked on.

"Hello, Mike. Hello, Sasha," Kai replied.

"What have you been doing this afternoon?" Mike asked.

"Exploring. Reading news sites and learning about your systems of government."

"Is our world that different from yours?"

"In some ways. When we lived on the surface, we didn't have countries or borders," Kai said. "It is fascinating the way humans seemed to have evolved."

"How do you mean?"

"You are all the same. But you have so many divisions," Kai said. "You are separated by borders and languages and religions. And, there is so much conflict and anger. How do you deal with it all?"

"Badly," Mike said. "Kai, I would like to introduce my wife, Maggie."

Mike slid his chair to the left as Maggie pulled up another. Since his first discussion with Mike, Kai had taken some liberties with the computer's programming. On the screen, Kai built two smaller windows. One showed what Kai was seeing. The other window had a grayish head-and-shoulders shape that had few distinguishing features.

"Hello, Kai. It's very nice to meet you," Maggie said, smiling nervously into the camera. Her pulse was up and she was slightly sweating. Evidently meeting her first extraterrestrial was more stressful than she expected.

"Hello, Maggie. It is a pleasure to meet you. Mike told me how you two met. I must say that it is a wonderful story."

"Wonderful, yes, but we lost you. For forty years. Aren't you upset about that?"

"I am concerned about my people," Kai replied, "but you had no way of knowing what was being sent on that radio signal."

"Why can't we see your face," Maggie asked.

"Because, after the transfer, I lost all of my physical features," Kai explained. "I am working on a physical image that resembles how I once looked. I think you call it an avatar."

"Is that hard to do?" Maggie asked.

"Well, art was never my best subject."

Maggie laughed. Kai was bright, witty, and polite. So far, she wasn't getting any weird vibes from Kai. She even liked him.

"I am sorry for scaring you," Kai said. "That was not my intent and I won't use Sasha as my mobile camera anymore."

"Sie wusste nicht," Maggie said in German. It was her turn to do a little investigation. She simply said that he didn't know that he was going to frighten her. It was a clever trap.

"Ja, habe Ich," Kai replied. He should have known.

Maggie looked at Mike and smiled. *"Govorit li on po-russ-ki?"*

"Da, Maggie, he can speak Russian, too," Mike chuckled. "And probably more. Kai?"

"Eleven languages, so far. Will English work for you?"

"Yes, that will work fine," Maggie said, turning back to the camera. "Now, what can we do to help you, Kai?"

There was a pause for a moment. Kai was usually quick with a response.

"I'm not quite sure, yet," Kai said. "Earth is a much more complex place than we imagined when we planned this mission."

"How do you mean?" Mike asked.

"We thought that because your civilization was advancing so fast – with spacecraft landings on Mars – that you would be more like us," Kai said.

"How are we different?" Maggie asked.

Kai talked about his planet's evolution and the Koya disaster that forced the survivors underground. Mike and Maggie were getting a living history of another civilization – not one that existed here, on Earth, but one that thrived on Mars, 225 million kilometers away. In twenty minutes, they knew more about Mars than a hundred space missions could have discovered. All of it delivered by someone who was alive when Galileo first watched Mars through his primitive telescope.

The biggest difference between them, Kai said, was Earth's complex political, ethnic, and religious divisions. When they planned for Kai to come to Earth, the Martians expected a global response. Now, he didn't think that would be possible.

"As to my plans for seeking help for my people, may I defer that question?" Kai asked. "I need to sleep. Then, there is a place I must visit. Maggie?"

"Yes, Kai?"

"Can we resume our discussion later?"

"Of course," Maggie returned. "It was a pleasure meeting you, Kai."

"And you as well, Maggie."

The computer screen resumed its normal appearance and the camera turned off. Mike touched Maggie's shoulder as she sat there, stunned by what just happened. She stood up and looked at him. She was still smiling, placing her hand on his.

36
Memorial Day

SUNDAY WAS A quiet day at the Savin household. Kai was away. Mike and Maggie figured that he was exploring the world, learning more about his new home. The Pacific storm that came ashore yesterday was worse than expected, with Los Angeles getting pounding rains that continued all day Sunday. Maggie was tired and sore from her spa trip – the massages that worked out all of the kinks also released a lot of junk that was built-up in her muscles.

"Tell me again why you do those spa things?" Mike asked, as the two sat at the kitchen table and sipped coffee.

"Mainly for the hunky guys," Maggie said, not looking at Mike. The television caught her attention. She was reading a scroll on CNN that kept repeating something about North Korea.

"I thought so," Mike said, now noticing the same information.

There were other reasons why the two of them were tired today. After saying goodnight to Kai, they went upstairs and had a rousing welcome-home event under the sheets. After that, they spent several hours locked in each other's arms, talking. Of course, the topic was the extraterrestrial living in their house. Mainly, the conversation had to do with how the world would react when it learned of Kai's presence.

Kai, on the other hand, slept most of the night. But an hour before they awoke, Kai left Mike's computer and was headed far away, exploring computer sites in Asia. One computer server led him to another. Asia's many languages slowed him down, but something serious was happening. Kai stayed inside two particular computer servers for several hours, reading the written communications that were firing back and forth. He also located their phones and listened as two men, evidently the leaders of these two countries, had sharp and angry words. There were warnings of caution and responses of defiance. The conversation ended when one of the men hung up on the other.

By late Sunday afternoon, contact between the two countries had stopped. Even though he never experienced war on his planet, Kai knew one was coming – if things happened as one of the leaders promised they would. The other country's computers began losing all of the electronic communications between the two. They were covering their tracks, putting them in a position of what politicians liked to call *plausible deniability*. By Sunday evening, there was no evidence of any of the communications that had taken place between the two countries earlier in the day.

Monday was Memorial Day, a day to remember those who died while serving in the nation's armed forces. The day was a solemn one for Mike and Maggie. They honored their families by placing American and Canadian flags on their front porch. The American flag honored members of both of their families who died in Korea, Vietnam, and most recently, in Afghanistan. The Canadian flag honored Mikhail Savin, Mike's uncle, who served in the Canadian Forces during World War II. Uncle Mike died in Sicily, in the same battle with the Germans that wounded Mike's father. When Mike was born, he was named in honor of Viktor's brother.

Several years ago, a family from Toronto moved in across the street and picked up the tradition of displaying both flags. Soon, neighbors all around the Savins were displaying the flags of both countries, a visible gesture of the special relationship between Canada and the United States. It was one of the things Mike would tell Kai when he returned, because there were many examples of humans working together. Perhaps Kai's mission back to Mars would be one of them.

Unfortunately, today wasn't a good example of human cooperation. The cable news channels were buzzing all morning about North Korea. In a message timed exactly with the president's arrival at Arlington National Cemetery, the North Korean leader appeared on state television. His speech lasted more than an hour, denouncing the United States and slandering the president. The leader closed his long and often-disjointed speech by promising a convincing demonstration of North Korea's military power. He said that he would make it clear, once and for all, that the United States could never prevail in a war with North Korea.

But there was more going on behind the scenes than a typical North Korean hate speech. CNN's Pentagon reporter broke a story a few minutes ago, saying that North Korea might have a new weapon to demonstrate. Within the last twenty-four hours, she said, the Pentagon received what it called credible information that North Korea was preparing to test a new generation of anti-ship missiles. The source claimed that the North Koreans were given the plans for the missile, called the *Rodong 2*, by China, who was thought to be working on a similar weapon.

Unlike traditional, surface-skimming anti-ship weapons, the *Rodong 2* was a ballistic missile, launched vertically into low space. On its return to Earth, it would accelerate toward its target from above. A weapon like this, with both explosive and kinetic power, could punch a hole in an American aircraft carrier, most likely sinking it. Chinese and North Korean military doctrine was built around denying the United States access to the Sea of Japan, and the East and South China Seas. There was even speculation that Hawaii could be within range of the weapon.

As the North Korean leader blustered, red-faced on state television, the U.S. Navy was conducting joint exercises in the Sea of Japan with ships from Japan and South Korea. The USS Ronald Reagan, a Nimitz-class aircraft carrier based out of Yokosuka, Japan, was part of this training exercise. The Reagan's presence so close to North Korea infuriated its leader, who threatened the United States with war, if the exercises continued.

The level of vitriol from North Korea had been rising for months as the problems in the magic kingdom increased. The country's food shortage was getting worse and there was even talk of dissent within the ranks of the military. For six decades, North Korea had been unstable and unpredictable, but no more so than in the last few months. There were whispers in the intelligence community that North Korea was planning something big, perhaps sinking another South

Korean naval ship. South Korea showed amazing restraint a few years earlier when one of its ships was sunk by the North Koreans. But privately, the South Koreans told the United States that they would tolerate no more attacks from the North.

In the United States, the quadrennial presidential election campaign was in full-swing. Last fall, President David Collins announced that he would not seek a second term. The nation was stunned that the popular, former Colorado rancher, wouldn't run. His announcement caused both major parties to scramble to find a suitable replacement. Each ended up with a dozen or so candidates – governors, members of Congress, and business tycoons, all who promised to do a better job than Collins. With the summer political conventions looming, the early caucuses in Iowa and the New Hampshire primary were inconclusive. Without a star player in either party, the conventions promised the kind of behind-the-scenes intrigue that hadn't been seen in the United States for more than a half-century.

With CNN and the other news networks cycling back to the North Korea story again, Mike and Maggie watched at the kitchen table, drinking coffee. Maggie looked at the television and then back at Mike, placing her arms on the table as if she were anchoring a public television newscast.

"Dr. Savin, have you considered the geopolitical ramifications of the presence of an extraterrestrial in our house?" she asked solemnly.

Mike furrowed his brow in a decent attempt at taking on the role of the talking head in this mock interview. "Yes, well, um. Could you repeat the question?" Mike asked.

"Of course. What up wit' Kai?" Maggie said, perfectly truncating the complex sentence into one her husband could use to provide an intelligent reply.

"Oh, *those* geopolitical ramifications," Mike replied. He was about to continue the fake interview when CNN played its breaking news music – the third time this hour. Wolf Blitzer was at the anchor desk and CNN's Pentagon reporter Barbara Starr was reporting. The network's A-Team was on-duty, something unusual on a federal holiday.

Wolf, we're getting confirmation that the Joint Chiefs of Staff have been in session for more than two hours. No one in the JCS office is commenting on the reason for a Memorial Day meeting, but we have confirmed that the President has been in contact with the Joint Chiefs.

While the report was running, Mike wandered into the study. The camera light was off, as was the computer screen. He called Kai's name, but there was no response from the computer. He waited a few minutes, but the computer remained dark.

"Kai's still not here," Mike said, coming back into the kitchen as Starr's report continued.

"Do you think he has anything to do with this?" Maggie asked, nodding at the television.

"Well, I know that he has the power to do a lot of things," Mike said. "Whether he intends to get involved, is the question. Remember, even the crew of the Enterprise had a non-interference clause in their contracts."

Maggie laughed. Mike was a devoted *Star Trek* fan – the original series – and they often gave each other the Vulcan greeting.

"But, think about the potential," Maggie said, her face turning serious. "He could do a lot of good."

"Define good. Good for us? The Russians? The Chinese? Just having him on anyone's team would be a game-changer."

"Do you think he will shop the market to get the help he needs?"

"Kai doesn't see political boundaries," Mike said. "I think he hopes that we'll all pull together to help. After all, the Martians have a lot to offer."

"Let's have breakfast and then we'll try reaching Kai again."

"Good plan."

During the night, Mike got up and rearranged the furniture in the study. He moved the computer monitor to the front of his desk, placing two armchairs in front of the screen. He also connected an external video camera so that Kai could see them better.

After breakfast, Maggie and Mike walked into the study and sat down. They called Kai's name several times before the computer screen lit up. Kai was there, his image looking clearer and more detailed since last night.

"Good morning, Kai," Maggie said.

"Good morning, Maggie. Oh, good morning, Maggie and Mike. I like the new seating arrangement," Kai said.

"Did you sleep?" Mike asked.

"A little bit."

"How does that work for you?" Maggie asked.

Kai explained that his sleep program was based on his level of activity. The more he did, the longer he slept. The commands that put him to sleep were there to prevent corruption of his programming, which, if severe enough, would be fatal to him.

"Have you been keeping up with the news this morning?" Mike asked.

"Do you mean the situation in North Korea?" Kai said.

"Their leader is so unpredictable," Maggie added.

"His medications will do that to him," Kai replied.

Maggie and Mike looked at each other. How did he know that? Of course. He had access to the North Korean leader's computer files.

"He plans to attack the USS Reagan today," Kai said.

Mike and Maggie gasped, as they looked at the computer monitor. Since the last time they talked, Kai had created a rendering of himself as a Martian. He had light skin, two large black eyes, and a small nose. His mouth was larger than science fiction movies often depicted Martins. But they were right about his head. It was very large relative to his shoulders. They could only imagine what his IQ would be by Earth standards.

"But, there are more than six thousand Americans on that ship!" Maggie said.

"Yes," Kai said. "I cannot allow that to happen."

"Do you have the ability to prevent it?" Mike asked.

"I do."

Kai must have been very busy. There seemed to be nothing that he was incapable of doing inside the computer world. Even the North Koreans were connected to the Internet and Kai must have found a way inside.

"Maybe we should contact someone," Maggie suggested. "The Navy, perhaps?"

"I have already been in contact with them," Kai said.

Mike looked at Maggie. The report on CNN, of course.

"Do they know about North Korea's intentions?" Maggie asked.

"No one knows – not even his military commanders," Kai replied. "Their leader and a few of his aides are the only ones behind this."

"Did you tell that part to the Pentagon?" Mike asked.

"No. That would result in war," Kai replied. "Will you trust me to handle this? I promise that no one will be hurt."

There didn't seem to be a choice. There was a new sheriff in town and from what they had learned about Martians so far, the concepts of war and violence were anathema to them. Kai evidently learned enough to know that the United States was not the aggressor in this situation and that North Korea's leader had weapons that could start another world war.

And, a war would clearly interfere with Kai's plans.

37
North Korea

NORTH KOREA

T HE *TONGHAE* SATELLITE Launching Ground is located on the northern coast of North Korea. The site has been the country's primary missile research and launch facility since it first reverse-engineered donated Soviet Scud rockets in the 1960s. Since then, the facility has grown, adding more launch pads and expanding their rocket-making facilities. North Korea had nuclear weapons, and if the leader's claims were to be believed, they might even have the hydrogen bomb.

At Red Victory Launch Pad Three, North Korean military officers and staff were assembled in the launch control room. The technicians and officers were members of North Korea's elite Strategic Rocket Forces, specialists in building and launching the country's growing arsenal of strategic and tactical missiles. A long row of computer monitors faced out through a set of angled windows, giving the technicians a clear view of the *Rodong 2* missile that was sitting on the launch pad.

Standing behind the launch technicians was a row of military officers, carefully watching their activity. And on a platform behind them, stood North Korea's leader and a small cadre of aides. The leader had both hands on the red metal railing, gripping it tightly while scrutinizing everyone's actions. A twisted smile was on his face as he looked out at the gleaming white rocket sitting on the launch pad.

The countdown clock showed three minutes to launch. The *Rodong 2* missile was a huge leap in technology for the North Koreans. The guidance system was complex, requiring satellite information in order to put the missile on the correct path to its target. The North Koreans launched a new satellite last month and there were rumors that they were also getting data from Chinese satellites parked in orbit above the Korean peninsula. China denied the allegation. But if true, North Korea would have everything it needed to deploy a formidable weapon to use against enemy ships.

Today's launch was set to coincide with the joint naval exercises underway in the Sea of Japan. Choosing a time when American, Japanese, and South Korean naval vessels would be gathered together was a provocative act in the extreme and the North Koreans had given only an hour's notice of their intent to fire the missile. If anything went wrong, if the missile went off course, there was a chance it could reach Japan. If it landed near the training exercises, it posed a risk to ships in the vicinity. And the North Koreans weren't saying whether the missile had a live warhead onboard.

"Do you have the coordinates for the missile's launch," the supreme leader barked out to the line of officers in front of him.

One snapped an about face and shouted, "Sir, yes sir."

"Very well. We will now change the coordinates," the supreme leader announced.

Everyone in the room went stiff. No one ever knew what their leader would do next, but they had firsthand experience of what happened when his orders were not obeyed. Reports had leaked to the West of horrible deaths suffered by those who displeased him. Some, the reports said, were blown to bits after being stood in front of an anti-aircraft gun. It was a particularly gruesome method of execution that resonated throughout the country and kept his military in the grip of quiet desperation.

"What coordinates does the Supreme Leader wish to use?" a military officer asked him. The leader handed him a mobile phone. On the screen was an app that showed coordinates for a red dot in the Sea of Japan. The officer took the phone, stared at the image for a second, and then looked up at the leader. He glared down at the officer, who immediately turned and handed the device to a flight control technician.

The technician, who had not witnessed the exchange between the leader and the officer, expressed surprise when he looked at the coordinates. He turned back to the officers behind him. "Sir, these are the coordinates for the American…"

A gunshot echoed across the room. The technician fell out of his chair, dead on the floor with a gaping wound in the side of his head. The uniformed officer standing next to him holstered his weapon and resumed his position in line.

"Proceed with the launch," the supreme leader quietly ordered.

38
Battle Stations

SEA OF JAPAN

FLIGHT OPERATIONS ABOARD the USS Reagan were underway when the Commanding Officer received a message from the Combat Information Center. At 07:47, a missile launch had been detected at the *Tonghae* launch facility in North Korea. The missile launch was confirmed by fleet operations in Honolulu and from Peterson Air Force Base in Colorado, where the North American Aerospace Defense Command is located. Satellites over North Korea detected the launch of a high-speed rocket of medium to long-range capabilities. The launch signature was that of a *Rodong 2* missile, an anti-ship weapon. The data received so far suggested a short but very high boost phase ending in a splashdown in the eastern Sea of Japan.

Off the coast of North Korea, a Japan Self-Defense Force Boeing E-767 sent live video of the missile launch to the Reagan. The aircraft also picked up North Korean satellite telemetry being used to guide the missile, as well as some scrambled two-way communication between the launch facility and an aircraft somewhere in the area.

Within two minutes of the launch, the Reagan's CIC confirmed that the naval exercise group was in the target zone of the *Rodong 2* missile. Battle stations were called and U.S., Japanese, and South Korean vessels were linked to the Reagan's combat defense network, forming an electronic shield of air defenses around the group. The ships would work off of the same information, and if necessary, coordinate their defensive fire to shoot down the missile.

One of the ships in the surface group was the USS Antietam, a guided missile cruiser equipped with the navy's newest ballistic missile defense system. The system was capable of shooting down weapons like the *Rodong 2*. The Antietam signaled the Reagan that it had already locked onto the North Korean missile and could fire when ordered by the group's commander.

Two surveillance aircraft, one Russian and one Chinese, had been shadowing the combined naval exercises all week. One, possibly both of the surveillance aircraft, were communicating with the North Koreans, sending information about the course and speed of the ships. On orders from the CO, the Reagan's Air Boss launched eight F/A-18E aircraft, assigning four fighters to each plane. Their instructions were to pull in behind the aircraft. If it was determined that the missile was coming down near any of the ships, their orders were to shoot down the two surveillance aircraft.

Two more fighter squadrons, each with twelve F/A-18E Super Hornets, were called in from Yokosuka, the Reagan's home port. That gave the naval group a commanding amount of air power, if the order was given to attack North Korea. The jets were refueled mid-air and ordered into circular holding positions just off the coast of North Korea. If necessary, the jets would be sent in to destroy the launch facility.

On the Korean peninsula, U.S. and South Korean ground forces were placed on combat readiness status, with all units forming into their offensive positions. In less than fifteen minutes, the Korean peninsula was closer to war than it had been since the truce was signed in July, 1953.

Kai had been monitoring the situation in North Korea since well before Mike and Maggie woke this morning. He read the secret communiques that went back and forth between the North Korean leader and the members of his inner circle who were in on the attack. It was the leader's idea to attack the Reagan, but if any of the members objected to the plan, none was willing to say so. China's earlier warnings to their North Korean ally to avoid a confrontation with the United States were brushed off with hostile responses. The Chinese had lost control of their long-time friend.

Kai was in North Korea when the missile was launched. He easily navigated through the regime's computer networks and positioned himself inside the flight director's computer. He watched the rocket as it began its boost phase, pushing nearly straight up, slowly gathering speed to minimize friction on the rocket's thin metal surface.

The rocket launch had three phases. The first, the boost phase, was pushing the missile higher – actually high enough to briefly leave the Earth's atmosphere. In the second phase, the mid-course phase, the missile's warhead and decoys would slip over the top of the ballistic arch before beginning the third phase – the terminal phase. In this final part, the missile would be guided to its target with satellite and aircraft reconnaissance data, using small thruster jets to steer it. In this final phase, the missile was on autopilot – receiving satellite data and using its own onboard flight system to aim precisely at the deck of the Reagan.

At about ninety seconds before the mid-course phase, Kai took control of the missile, rewriting the rocket's sequence of automated commands. The new commands were entered, ordering the rocket motors to shut down before entering the mid-course phase. The motors complied, sputtering for a moment and then flaming out. The North Korean missile was now a brick. It climbed another 1,000 meters on kinetic energy alone before flipping over and tumbling out of control. As it picked up speed, friction began heating up the rocket's thin surface and the *Rodong 2* soon broke into bits of flaming wreckage.

It was an amazing fireworks display for the sailors on the deck of the Reagan. Even North Korea's supreme leader got to see the show, but before he could do anything rash, Kai had one more surprise. A software worm was set loose inside North Korea's command and control system. Within five minutes, the country's entire air defense network was shut down. North Korea was blind, with no way to defend itself if the United States chose to attack.

The Russian and Chinese surveillance aircraft, stationed about ten nautical miles from the Reagan, decided it was time to leave. Each made a path for home – north for the Russian aircraft and west for the Chinese one. The U.S. fighters followed until the surveillance aircraft crossed into their own airspace. Then, the Hornets turned and stayed in a holding pattern off their coasts. Neither Russia nor China sent up any opposing aircraft, looking to diffuse the war footing the United States was already on.

With American warplanes off their coast and military forces still on combat status, the only way out of this mess was for the North Korean leader to quickly admit to the launch and call it a failure. KCNA, the government's news agency, issued a release to Reuters and other international agencies, reporting that an attempted weather satellite launch failed and that the rocket was destroyed over the western Sea of Japan. It was a face saving measure that allowed the North Korean leader to hang onto power for a while longer.

Less than an hour after the missile launch, CNN's Pentagon reporter Barbara Starr broke the story in a live report.

> *Sources here at the Pentagon say that the missile was launched at 7:47 Korean Time and its target was an area in the Sea of Japan. The U.S. Navy is conducting joint exercises with Japan and South Korea in that area, so this launch is considered very provocative. The latest we are getting is that the launch was a failure and the missile burned up on reentry, falling in an area about two hundred kilometers east of the North Korean peninsula.*

The CNN anchor team thanked Starr for her report and brought in experts to talk about the ongoing problems with North Korea. Neither they nor anyone else at the network knew just how close the United States had come to war again with North Korea.

39
Crisis Management

THE WHITE HOUSE was a beehive of activity since word of the missile launch reached the president. David Collins met with his national security team and the Joint Chiefs of Staff. He spoke with the leaders of Japan, South Korea, Australia, Russia, and China. He told all of them the same thing – the analysis they were getting confirmed that the target of the North Korean missile was the USS Reagan and that if the *Rodong 2* had hit the carrier, it would have sunk it.

The president made it clear to the Chinese and Russians that, although the North Koreans claimed the launch was another failed weather satellite, the United States considered North Korea's action tantamount to a war declaration. Neither the Chinese nor the Russians put up any real resistance. They were as flummoxed by the unpredictability of North Korea's leader as everyone else.

A majority of the president's security team argued that he should go public with the full story about the attempted attack by the North Koreans on the USS Reagan. Of course, that would enrage the North Korean leader, but since he was always pissed off, that didn't mean much. What did matter was that an announcement of an attempted attack on an American naval vessel would raise hell at home. Voters were tired of North Korea's threats. Polling data showed that the American public strongly favored full military action against North Korea, should that country attack the United States.

But in the president's view, something was missing in this provocation. After the launch, North Korea opened itself up to attack. Whether intentional or otherwise, the country's entire military structure could be destroyed by an air campaign from the U.S., Japan, and South Korea. Why would North Korea do that?

Some argued that the failure of their defense network was a gift that should be exploited. Others, including the president, weren't so sure.

In the media, the North Koreans were pushing hard on the story that the failed launch was a weather satellite. They invited journalists to the *Tonghae* launch complex to review the footage of the launch, which showed the missile sputtering and then falling into the Sea of Japan. The North Koreans even produced doctored photos that showed a weather satellite sitting in the payload bay of the rocket's nose cone before the launch. One reporter from the United Kingdom asked her North Korean handler which version of Photoshop they used to make the images. Her press credentials were immediately taken and she was sent packing for London.

The United States had all the information it needed to declare war on North Korea. Eavesdropping on North Korean radio communications showed that there had been some kind of last-minute change in launch coordinates, with the supreme leader ordering the USS Reagan to be the target.

This apparently happened just a few minutes prior to launch. What's more, the spy agencies picked up mobile telephone conversations, confirming a report that someone had been shot and killed in the missile command center. An open cell-phone in the room recorded the gunshot and the sounds of scurrying around, as the victim was removed.

Later in the day, the president spoke again with his counterparts in South Korea and Japan. On the Korean peninsula, U.S. and South Korean military forces would stand down. The intelligence that they had would not be disclosed. It was better that the North Korean leader did not know how deeply his country's communications had been penetrated.

But the Japanese prime minister had enough. He was tired of missile overflights from North Korea and was ready to knock North Korea off of its list of worries, once and for all. President Collins, mindful of the number of military campaigns the United States had been through in the past two decades, wasn't eager to start another war. He persuaded the Japanese Prime Minister that it would be better to wait.

For now, North Korea was safe from attack.

As expected, China had been silent all day. Even through back channels, they claimed they knew nothing about the launch or the fact that the North Korean missile behaved very much like the one they were developing. The president spoke with his Chinese counterpart, who promised to look into the matter with North Korea. But it had always been clear that, although China had the means to slap down its petulant neighbor, for some reason China felt it was in their national interest to keep North Korea angry and on an active war-footing with the United States and South Korea.

While the president was on the phone with the Japanese prime minister, his chief of staff walked in and whispered that the director of the Central Intelligence Agency was waiting to see him. Dr. Katherine Clarke was one of his first presidential appointees. She was doing a great job rebuilding the agency in the wake of the classified data leak caused by an agency contract employee.

The president smiled at Dr. Clarke and pointed to the couches in his office. As she sat down, the president wrapped up his phone call with a three-minute conversation in Japanese. He and the prime minister talked about their grandkids and the challenges of raising children in the dangerous world they were facing.

"So, Kathy, what's the latest?" the president asked, as he hung up the phone and moved to the couch opposite her.

"Someone pulled the plug on that missile, Mr. President," Dr. Clarke replied.

"Who was it?"

"We don't know yet," Clarke said. "But the National Security Agency picked up the telemetry from *Tonghae* that showed the instructions came from their launch control center. And something else – it wasn't a destruct order. Someone just shut down the rocket."

"So our fearless leader has some internal problems," the president mused, as he poured coffee for both of them. "We might have one friend in Pyongyang."

"One less than yesterday," Clarke sighed.

She told the president that one of her operatives in North Korea was a young woman who provided certain services to the old men who ran North Korea. The woman's younger brother had recently been shot by the North Korean government on a trumped-up spying charge and she was eager for revenge. Over time, she earned the trust of two of the top leaders in the North Korean military. When they talked, she listened and then sent encrypted messages to her CIA handler in Seoul.

Unfortunately, one of her messages was intercepted and she was arrested. The next day, the American Embassy in Seoul received a fax, showing the dead woman's body lying against a brick wall. There was no message. Just the photo and her name.

"I am so sorry, Kathy," the president said. Life in North Korea is unbearable for most citizens and, although this woman had acquired a modest lifestyle, it was only because of the things she was forced to do in a system that rewarded the elite North Korean leadership.

"We may have had help from another friend," Clarke said. "This one is much closer to home."

Clark told the president that eight hours before the North Korean missile launch, the NSA noticed an unusually large stream of data entering North Korea. The data came from the United States and traveled a circuitous route through Iran, Kazakhstan, India, and China before finally entering North Korean servers.

"The file was a computer worm that our analysts are still trying to unravel. This program is way beyond the one that crashed the Iranian centrifuges a couple of years ago."

"Where did this super-worm come from?" the president asked.

"Santa Monica, California."

40
Aftermath

WHILE EVENTS ON the Korean peninsula were taking a dangerous turn, Mike and Maggie were at the cemetery, putting flowers and on the graves of her parents. The cemetery placed American flags on the graves of all of the veterans, including her father's, and the fluttering, whispering sound they made in the breeze seemed to be asking that their sacrifices not be forgotten.

Driving home, Maggie dialed around on satellite radio for news about the North Korean situation. The BBC's correspondent in Seoul reported that South Korean and U.S. forces had been mobilized and that residents in the capital were told to be prepared in case evacuation was ordered. CNN covered a live news conference at the Pentagon, where a spokeswoman downplayed the incident. She denied a reporter's question that the USS Reagan was the target of the North Korean missile. A CBC reporter in Pyongyang said that the North Korean leader had left the capital for what was described as an extended vacation. Few North Koreans on the street seemed to know about the missile launch.

Maggie and Mike knew that Kai was behind all of this. He told them that the sailors and airmen on the Reagan would not be harmed. Was he also responsible for dismantling North Korea's air defense network? That would explain the leader skedaddling out of Pyongyang, since it would be the major target of retaliatory air strikes.

As they walked in the back door, Sasha barked and squealed with enthusiasm. His habit was to grab a tennis ball as he ran to them, and then bark through the ball in his mouth, creating a strange-sounding muffled *urk-urk-urk*. Although he usually carried a stuffed dog toy when he wandered around the house, the tennis ball was his go-to when his humans came home. Eventually, he would drop the ball someplace, knowing one of the humans would return it to his toy basket.

Maggie poured some lemonade and filled Sasha's food dish while Mike took him outside. She laughed as she watched the give-and-take as they tussled in the yard. By the end of the fracas, Mike was lying on his back in the grass, with Sasha standing proudly over him as if he had just won the gold medal in the *International Man-Dog Wrestling Tournament*.

She thought about Kai in the next room. Except for his birth certificate, he was just like Sasha – a living being, different from them, but coexisting peacefully with humans. When you boiled it down, it was really that simple. Each of them was separated by a little genetic rewiring – and in the case of Kai – by a bit of distance between his planet and ours. Why should Kai's presence be such a big deal?

Mike and Sasha came in from outside and the big golden made a beeline for the ceramic food dish. They watched as he vacuumed up his dinner. In a blink, he was done and ready for his next assignment.

"Did anyone call the house phone?" Mike asked.

"A couple of unethical companies who don't believe in the Do Not Call law," she said. "And, one from the cable company."

"What about?"

"It was someone in technical support," Maggie said. "They said that we were exceeding our data amount by quite a bit and wanted to talk about upgrading our service."

"Well, we know who's responsible for that," Mike said, nodding toward the study.

"They can track us, you know," Maggie said. "There's a data trail leading right here, to this house."

Mike nodded in agreement. It was something they would have to discuss with Kai, although by now, he probably knew more about Internet security than they did.

Maggie and Mike walked into the study and sat down in front of the computer monitor. Kai sensed their presence and the video camera came on. Since their last conversation, Kai had developed a full face and features and the moving image was very much like the high-definition animation that was being used in Disney films.

"Hello, Maggie and Mike. How was your day?" Kai asked.

"We went to the cemetery to visit my parents," Maggie said. "Kai, tell us about your family."

Kai talked about his mother and father, two teachers who raised a precocious child and carried him to safety during the evacuation. Both of them died within a hundred years of moving to the Underground, victims of the wasting diseases that were slowly killing all of the survivors.

"You must miss them," Maggie said.

"Yes. Every day. And my grandparents. They were also very important in the decisions I made about what I wanted to be when I grew up."

"What were they like?" Mike said.

"He was a physician. She was the president."

"The president?" Maggie asked.

"Yes. She was the president of the planet's governing body. It is called the Administrative Council. She and the rest of that Council died on the surface when Koya struck."

"Oh, my. We are so sorry," Maggie said.

"Thank you. I miss them all," Kai said. There was a pause for a few seconds.

"And your wife, Kai," Maggie asked. "What is Mia like?"

Kai told them that Mia was a teacher. She helped her students appreciate the great writers of Mars' past. For 200,000 years, Martian writers wrote passionately about their world – both the challenges and the successes. They wrote odes to love that were memorized and used when couples expressed their feelings for each other. Every home had access to the entire catalogue of Martian literature and a great deal of time was spent in quiet contemplation with a good book.

"Our problems on Earth have kept you distracted from your mission," Mike said. "Thank you for what you did today."

"You saved a lot of lives," Maggie added.

Kai paused for a moment. "Not everyone. The North Korean leader has executed eleven in his inner circle on suspicion of treason," Kai said. "And there was a young woman."

Kai told Mike and Maggie about the young woman who was shot to death.

"How awful," Mike said, "but her death wasn't in vain. A war was prevented this morning."

"I think the North Korean leader will be quiet for awhile," Kai said. "I have other options if he decides to misbehave again. But we do have a problem."

"What kind of problem?" Mike asked.

Kai told them how he neutralized the North Korean missile and then shut down their command and control system with a software worm that could not be removed from their computers.

"But I made an error," Kai said. "I wrote the program here and then sent it to North Korea. That data transfer was picked up by the NSA. They know where it came from."

"You mean here, our house?" Maggie asked.

"Yes. They suspect, but need to confirm. That's where the FBI comes in," Kai said. "The NSA doesn't do domestic spying. The FBI has to investigate. That's why two agents will visit here tomorrow. Their names are Sanchez and McNulty."

"So, they know all about us?" Maggie asked.

"No," Kai said. "You are persons of interest, but they have nothing on you. Don't worry."

"Even so, it was worth it, considering the lives you saved and the war you prevented," Mike said.

"I can get the FBI off of you pretty quickly," Kai said. "Two suspects will be arrested in a few minutes. All you need to do is to be nice to the FBI agents when they come here tomorrow." Both Kai and Mike turned in sync toward Maggie.

"Hey, why are you guys looking at me?" Maggie snapped.

There was a long pause as Maggie's voice resonated in the room. Mike was smiling and a smile was beginning to appear on Kai's avatar.

"Oh yeah," Maggie said. "Redheads. Be nice. I get the point."

∞

Ten minutes north of Santa Monica, drivers on the 405 noticed something unusual in their rearview mirrors. Three California Highway Patrol cars were traveling in single file at a high rate of speed in the passing lane. Motorists moved to the right to clear the lane and the cars disappeared over a rise. A few seconds behind them, a police helicopter roared overhead, flying right above the highway.

Twenty minutes later, those same drivers found out what the fuss was all about. A Chevy of some kind, in rental-car silver, had been pulled over to the service lane. The three police cars formed a box around it. The helicopter hovered above the scene.

Behind the rental car were two men dressed in black pants and shirts. Drivers could see that both men were bent over the trunk lid of the car, their hands cuffed behind them.

The two men were put in one of the cruisers for a ride to LAX. After a few hours of detention, they would board a flight to Beijing. The next day, the State Department would announce that two Chinese embassy personnel had been kicked out of the country on suspicion of spying. The reasons were not specified, but when pressed by reporters, the spokesman said that their arrests and deportation had something to do with computer hacking.

Another fact not disclosed was that the Highway Patrol got the tip from an anonymous cellphone call from Beijing, telling them that two Chinese nationals were leaving Los Angeles and headed for Nevada. The caller even provided coordinates for the car's location. The caller did not identify himself, but the officer taking the call said that she thought he sounded American and that he had a voice very much like Johnny Depp.

The next day, the State Department would file a formal complaint with the Chinese Ambassador, who appeared completely surprised by the accusation. The ambassador's calls to Beijing were met with the same reaction. In their own intelligence agency, one question came up again and again – how did the police find two highly-trained Chinese agents who had been operating completely unnoticed for months in the U.S.?

The arrest of the Chinese agents was Kai's way of covering his tracks and protecting Maggie and Mike. Kai discovered the Chinese spies by accident while he was inside the computers at the Chinese Ministry of State Security. His Mandarin was now quite good and he found a top-secret file with the names of the two agents living in Los Angeles.

Pinning the data transfer on the Chinese agents was easy. Kai adjusted a few files on the Chinese server and then corrected the tracking data that the National Security Agency had collected. The changes made it look like the Chinese agents sent the file, using the same IP address as the Savins. With both of them shipped back to Beijing, the FBI had a plausible story about the data transfer. Mike and Maggie were merely an accident for which the FBI would need to apologize.

While Kai was monitoring the arrests, he also pulled the files on the two agents who would be visiting Mike and Maggie tomorrow. He had their backgrounds and read the intelligence they had already collected on the Savins. There wasn't much – certainly nothing that could hurt Mike and Maggie. All they planned to do was ask the Savins if they could explain how a large amount of data had been sent to North Korea from their house.

Kai had already answered that question. They didn't send it.

41
The FBI Visit

THE DOORBELL RANG early Tuesday morning. Sasha did his big-dog bark as he headed for the front door with Mike following behind. Standing on the porch were a man and a woman, both in their late thirties, dressed in business attire.

"Dr. Michael Savin?" the woman asked.

"No, I am *Mikhail* Savin."

"Okay. I'm Special Agent Martha Sanchez of the FBI. This is Special Agent Timothy McNulty. We need a few minutes of your time this morning."

Mike had been practicing for the FBI visit since being warned by Kai last night. He wanted to be a tough guy again, the street-smart Detroit kid who didn't take guff from cops. But considering the situation, and especially the risk to Kai, he decided to take a lighter approach.

"Come in," Mike said, standing back to allow the agents to enter the foyer. Maggie had been standing in the kitchen, listening to the opening round of this match and she walked in to join the three of them.

"Maggie, these are Special Agents Sanchez and McNulty of the FBI," Mike said, smiling at his wife. The look telegraphed the *be friendly Maggie* warning that Kai gave her last night.

"It's very nice to meet you, Dr. Savin," Agent McNulty said as he extended his hand to shake hers. Agent Sanchez simply stared at her.

"Please, call me Maggie," she said, smiling back at McNulty, then giving his partner a quick and sharp glance. Maggie had been practicing too, literally at the bathroom mirror, to present just the right mix of friendliness with a whiff of unapproachable academia.

"Why don't we talk in here?" Mike asked, gesturing for the agents to follow him to the kitchen table. "Can we get you some coffee or water?"

"No. We're fine," Agent Sanchez said as they sat down. Mike joined them at the table and waited for the agents to make the first move.

"Have both of you been following the news the past day or so?" Agent Sanchez asked.

Maggie took the first question. They were going to co-anchor this interview, trading responses. It was one of the reasons why FBI agents worked in teams and the Savins thought it only fair to even up the sides.

"Just bits and pieces," she said.

Agent Sanchez summarized the situation with North Korea. She told them about the failed missile launch. Fortunately, she said, the missile fell harmlessly into the sea, but that a number of naval vessels were downrange. Had the missile continued on its programmed trajectory, she said, there was a risk that one of the ships could have been struck. She did not tell the Savins that the USS Reagan was the target of the missile. Nor did she tell them just how close the United States came to war with North Korea yesterday.

"So, is everything okay now?" Mike asked innocently.

"Are either or both of you programmers?" Sanchez asked, ignoring Mike's question.

"I guess we both are," Maggie said. "Of course, we play for different teams."

"What do you mean?" Agent McNulty asked.

"Well, I code for the Apple platform," Maggie said smiling. "My husband over there writes for – you know – the Microsoft team."

"Like two ships passing in the night," Mike mused, shaking his head with some false laughter. So far, they were doing alright. Even McNulty chuckled.

"Are you both *good* coders?" Sanchez asked, not joining in the levity.

"Well, we can write a phone app or an executable for a physics project," Maggie replied, "but no, we're not coders in the professional sense of the word. Why are you asking?" Maggie locked eyes on Sanchez as the staring contest between the two women began. If there was a good-cop-bad-cop thing going on here, Sanchez was definitely the latter.

McNulty took the hand-off and explained that the North Korean air defense system had been taken down after the missile launch. McNulty said that some very advanced software was written to disable their computers and that it appeared to have been written in the United States.

"But, all of that is a good thing, right?" Mike asked. "I mean, the North Koreans are what, defenseless right now?"

"What we find curious is that the code came from Santa Monica. Specifically, the IP address that serves your house," Sanchez said. "How do you explain that?"

"We don't have to explain it," Maggie said, focusing on Sanchez.

"You understand that we don't have a dedicated IP address," Mike jumped in before things got heated. "Anyone could have spoofed that address."

"Spoofed?" Agent Sanchez repeated. "You sure seem to know the language, Dr. Savin."

"We do. So does every eighth-grader in Santa Monica," Mike said. "Do you have any kids, Agent Sanchez?"

"No."

Agent McNulty's phone rang. The caller ID had a Washington D.C. area code. McNulty looked at Sanchez and then told the Savins that he had to take the call.

"Please, use the family room," Maggie said, standing up and leading Agent McNulty in that direction. She was getting pretty ticked-off at this woman who was doing a bad Jack Webb imitation. She also knew that Mike had a short fuse when it came to cops and she wasn't going to take any chances of him getting into a beef with federal agents. Better that she played the black hat on this one.

"Anyway," Sanchez said, sounding annoyed at the interplay between her partner and her suspect. "We're checking on this activity because, as I said, the worm that took out North Korea's command and control systems was extremely sophisticated."

"How would you rank it against *Stuxnet*, the code you guys wrote to break the Iranian centrifuges?" Mike asked, now joining the fray with Sanchez.

"We don't know who created *Stuxnet*," Sanchez said. That was a bald-faced lie. "But the computer code that hit North Korea was a hundred times more powerful than *Stuxnet*."

"Wow!" Mike said. "I'd love to have a look at that code."

"I bet you would," Sanchez said.

"You understand that both of us are physicists," Maggie said, returning to the table and taking the next pitch. "And even though we were writing computer code when you were still wearing *onesies*, neither of us could write anything with that kind of sophistication."

Mike looked over at his wife. He was getting the drift. She had reached her hospitality limit.

"So, is there anything else?" Mike asked, sensing that things might get out of control between the two women sitting on either side of him. Agent McNulty was still talking on the phone in the family room. Something was up in Washington.

Sanchez looked to see if her partner could hear her. Then, she leaned in toward Mike. "You're a Russian. Is that correct?"

Mike's nostrils flared. She was baiting. "I am an American, Agent Sanchez," Mike said, "just like you, I presume."

"But you are Russian?"

"I was born in Detroit, so that would make me what?" Mike said. "And you're, what, a Mexican?"

Sanchez walked into the trap. "No, I was born here in Los Angeles."

"Then that makes us *both* Americans," Mike said. "Anyway, I thought it wasn't politically correct to profile people. Or, doesn't that rule apply when you interrogate people of Slavic descent?"

All of this was too much for Maggie. Despite Kai's warning, her temper got the better of her.

"What does this ethnicity shit have to do with what happened in North Korea?" Maggie said. Maggie stood up and looked at Mike. *"Poluchit' ikh otsyuda!"* she said to Mike.

"My wife is right," Mike said. "Unless you have anything else for us, you need to go." He stood up to demonstrate the direction he wanted Sanchez to take.

"Right," Sanchez said as she stood up. Her hand rested on her sidearm, which only added to the tension.

McNulty had just finished his phone call and walked into the kitchen, where everyone was standing. He didn't catch the interplay that lit a fire under this redhead, but was enjoying his partner squirm under her blinding glare.

Back in Boston, before joining the Bureau, McNulty was a detective who liked catching bad guys the old-fashioned way – through solid leads from law abiding citizens who weren't afraid of the police. After the September 11 attacks, he thought the FBI had become too aggressive, alienating citizens and local police who could help their investigations. It was one of the things he talked at length about with Anthony Costa, the FBI Director, who recruited Tim to the FBI. Costa agreed that the bureau worked better when citizens weren't afraid of them. Evidently, Sanchez hadn't gotten the memo, because she had done a fairly good job of pissing off these two citizens.

Things were getting heated fast, with Sanchez staring down Maggie and Mike. What Sanchez didn't know was that these two people were in the clear. The phone call McNulty just finished confirmed that. It was time to defuse the situation.

"That was the FBI office in Washington," McNulty said looking at his partner in an official-like manner. "California Highway Patrol picked up two suspects who had been communicating with North Korea via the Darknet. I don't have any more details, but I was told that both of them are serious coders and have been using a lot of IP addresses to hide their tracks. One of them was yours, Dr. and Dr. Savin."

Thank you, Kai, Mike thought, as he watched the staring match continue between Maggie and Sanchez. Unfortunately for McNulty, neither woman responded to his overture. It was time for them to leave.

"We're sure glad you got to the bottom of that," Mike said.

"Me, too. Well, thank you both for your time," McNulty said. "We're sorry to have bothered you, but I'm sure you can appreciate that we have to follow all leads."

"Agent McNulty, you are welcome back any time," Maggie said to McNulty, while her stare was still locked on his partner. "But you, Sanchez. The next time you show up, bring a warrant."

Sanchez stepped forward as did Maggie, but McNulty grabbed Sanchez by the arm and pulled her out the front door.

"Again, thanks for your time," McNulty said, holding back a laugh as he watched his partner storm back to the car.

"*Suka!*" Maggie said loud enough for Sanchez to hear. Yes, that bitch crossed the line alright. Maggie had always had a wicked temper. But it had been a while since Mike had seen her use it. It turned him on.

"Are you okay, Maggie?" Mike asked as the agents pulled away from the curb.

Maggie turned to Mike. "Why, of course I am," she replied, smiling brightly and batting her eyelashes. Her grin got even bigger. She was just jerking those two around.

"Why you little devil," Mike said as he tried to grab her. She laughed and ran inside the house. They were still laughing when they walked into the study, where the computer screen was on. They called Kai's name and his window popped up on the screen.

"I guess you heard all that," Maggie said. "Sorry about the outburst."

"It was a very impressive bit of acting, Maggie," Kai said. "I must say, you almost had me convinced."

"She's probably calling in for an arrest warrant for me right now," Maggie said, thinking that maybe she played Sanchez too strong.

"Oh, I don't think she will," Kai said. "You see, Agent Sanchez has just suffered a rare and unfortunate mishap. Her mobile phone just died. The battery overheated and ruined the phone. And I think it will take some time for the phone company to recover her account and her contacts."

"Kai, you're as bad as Maggie," Mike said.

"Well, we all have things to do, and we can't afford to waste time on that *Suka*," Kai said.

⊕

Sanchez was quiet for most of the ride back into downtown Los Angeles. McNulty had been no help and, with her growing record of complaints filed by citizens, her FBI career was on thin ice.

"Shit," Sanchez said as she stared at her phone.

"What?" McNulty asked.

"It's fried. My phone is fried. How did that happen?" Sanchez asked, looking at McNulty. He pulled his phone out. His still worked.

"Who are you calling?" Sanchez asked.

"Director Costa in Washington."

"Sir, this is McNulty. Yes sir, we just met with them. No, sir. No, I don't think they were involved. Yes. Well, sure. I mean, if that's what you want. Just a moment."

McNulty handed the phone to Sanchez.

"He wants to talk to you."

"This is Sanchez. Yes, sir. But! Okay, sir. Yes, sir. Agent McNulty will file the report."

The phone clicked off and Sanchez handed it back to McNulty.

"The director wants you to file the report," Sanchez said. "You white boys stick together, don't you?"

"I caught that little comment you made about Dr. Savin's Russian heritage," McNulty said. "That was way out of line. You would be holding a protest march outside of FBI head-quarters if your heritage was questioned like that."

"My heritage has been questioned," Sanchez replied, "and my people have been discriminated against."

"So have theirs," McNulty said. "And my people too."

"You don't get it," Sanchez muttered.

"Oh, I get it," McNulty said. "Right now I'm your chauf-feur and you're my boss – at two federal pay grades higher than me.

"What are you saying?"

"I'm saying that you might want to get past all this victim-ization crap if you're going to make it with the Bureau.

"So now, you're giving me career advice, McNulty?"

"Take it if you want. But I just called the FBI director on his private cell phone. When we get back downtown, you'll be lucky if they validate your ticket for the parking garage."

"Just secure it, McNulty."

"*Sí, mi jefe.*"

42
Blood Money

AYN AL ARAB, SYRIA

ZAAHIR NEJEM PULLED his new Mercedes into his reserved spot in the parking lot of Nejem Bank, a run-down building with four teller windows and one small office. The bank's charter was issued by the Syrian government to his grandfather in 1923, and for most of its history, Nejem Bank survived on deposit accounts and small loans made to farmers and businessmen in this Syrian town on the Turkish border.

But the Syrian government no longer controlled Ayn al Arab. In a battle that killed hundreds of Syrian forces, the city became part of the Islamic State. After IS forces moved into the city, a public meeting was called. The citizens were told that they were now part of the Islamic State. They were given two choices – allegiance or execution. Everyone, including Zaahir Nejem, took the oath. But just for good measure, IS forces pulled ten men out of the crowd and executed them in front of the rest.

After the town's fall, life returned to a desperate sort of normalcy. Some businesses were allowed to continue. Others were not. The town's two other banks – owned by companies in Damascus – were closed. Their employees were pulled out into the street and shot to death. Everyone was told to use the Nejem bank from now on.

Shortly after the other banks were closed, two men driving a white Toyota pickup truck walked in. They said they wanted to open a savings account. A bank teller tried to help, but they insisted on talking to the manager. The men were shown to Zaahir's office. They opened an account and made a deposit of $1,000. Later that day, another $1,000 was deposited by wire transfer from a bank in Turkey. Nejem was instructed by the two men to handle all deposits and wire transfers personally. With guns strapped over their shoulders, he could hardly argue.

In the weeks ahead, the two men would visit the bank almost daily, making deposits of larger and larger amounts, both in cash and by wire transfer. In seven months, Nejem Bank held more than a billion dollars in assets – nearly all of it owned by the two men who opened the savings account. As the Islamic State sold oil on the black market from seized fields in Syria and Iraq, Nejem Bank eventually held nearly two billion dollars in proceeds for the Islamic State.

Each day, the procedure would be the same. Zaahir would arrive before the bank opened for business. Then, the white pickup truck would arrive. The exact time was different each day. Zaahir figured they were worried about a drone attack. The two men, both with Kalashnikovs over their shoulders, would bring cash or make withdrawals. Additional monies came in and went out from banks in Turkey, Syria, and Iraq.

Each time they arrived, they walked into Zaahir's office and locked the door. Saying nothing, they placed stacks of currency on his desk, for which Zaahir would give them a receipt. Then, he would print a statement of their deposits. With one man watching Zaahir, the other would check the statement against an old-fashioned account ledger he carried with him. The two numbers had to balance. Zaahir knew the consequences of an error.

This morning, the two men arrived and placed $31,000 in currency on his desk. Zaahir accepted the cash, placing it in a small safe he kept in his office. Later, he would transfer the cash to the bank's vault. Then, Zaahir logged into his computer to print a statement of their account.

Zaahir stared at his computer screen for a moment. It was long enough to arouse the suspicion of the men watching him. One of the men said something to his friend, who pushed Zaahir out of the way and looked at the computer screen. The screen showed that the account had a zero balance. The man looked again at the $0.00 and then raised his weapon at Zaahir.

"Where is our money?" he said, pushing the gun to Zaahir's temple.

"I don't know!" Zaahir said. "Please, let me check." Zaahir was a heavy smoker and the panic was causing him to cough, unable to get enough air. "Please, just a moment." His finger clicked on the old computer keyboard, but not fast enough to suit the man with gun. The gun's barrel pushed harder into his temple.

"No, wait. Please!" Zaahir said as he typed and scanned the screen. The old computer was slow and the two men were running out of patience.

"It looks like the funds were wired to another bank," Zaahir said.

"What bank?"

More typing and waiting as the slow connection gave Zaahir the information he was dreading to see.

"The routing number is unusual," Zaahir said. "I don't recognize…"

A deafening shot came from the closed office. Zaahir crumpled and then fell out of his chair. The wall next to him was splattered with his blood.

The man who killed Zaahir sat down and began typing on the computer. The funds were indeed gone – sent to a bank somewhere in Iraq and then to another bank in Syria before disappearing into the international banking system.

"What are we going to do, brother?" the other man asked.

"Tell the truth," the shooter said. "I will go back and tell them."

"They will kill you."

"Yes," the shooter said. "Take the cash in the vault and drive southeast. Do what you must to get back to Baghdad. Go back to your wife and your children. Allah be with you."

"And you."

43
The Security Meeting

O N WEDNESDAY, TWO days after the missile incident in North Korea, President David Collins met in the Oval Office with his security team. There was Katherine Clarke from the CIA, Anthony Costa from the FBI, Sanjay Riv from the NSA, and Ari Levin from the Department of Defense. Also present was Thomas DuPont, the president's national security advisor.

"Good morning, everyone," the president said as he walked in. "I am sorry that North Korea interrupted everyone's Memorial Day plans, but it all turned out for the best. Let's get started. Kathy?"

"We have a pen pal who is close to the North Korean leadership," Clarke began. "The information spigot is wide open."

"Pen pal?" the president asked. "How are you getting the information?"

"Emails. Directly to me."

"You have to be kidding me. A spy who sends emails to the director of the CIA?"

"He has my work and my home email addresses."

"Sir, we're all getting emails," DuPont said as everyone in the room nodded in agreement.

"Ari, what's the military situation on the Korean peninsula?" the president asked.

"Right now, we could turn the place into a parking lot if we wanted to," Levin said. "Without a command and control system, they have a see-shoot-and-miss air defense system. Even their field communications are down."

"And where's the dear leader?" the president asked, turning back to the CIA director.

"It looks like he's on an extended vacation," Clarke said. "Our source told me that he was denied travel into China and is hiding out somewhere in the north."

"Is he in trouble with his crew?" the president asked Clarke, referring to the cabal of military leaders who seemed to surround him wherever he went.

"Maybe. No one knows how the missile was turned off or why the country's air defense network was left in shambles," Clarke said. "Its a game of *Whack-a-Mole* over there. Everyone's afraid that if they pop up, they'll get their heads shot off. Even the leader feels vulnerable."

"Tony, what do we know about the source of that computer worm that took down their command and control system?" the president asked FBI Director Anthony Costa.

"Sir, we arrested two Chinese nationals with diplomatic credentials that were sending large amounts of information to Beijing," Costa said. "We found a lot of industrial spy stuff on their laptops, and one file looked like it might have been the computer worm that ended up in North Korea."

"How did we get them?"

"A phone tip. California Highway Patrol picked them up yesterday on a freeway heading out of Los Angeles."

"Are they talking?"

"No. They claimed diplomatic immunity and demanded to be sent back. But we got a peek at their laptops and traced their Internet usage."

"Why would the Chinese mess with their friends in North Korea?" the president asked as he slumped back in his chair.

"I don't know," Costa said. "But if it was a frame, it's the tightest one I've ever seen. The trail leads right back to China."

"What about those two physicists in Santa Monica?" the president asked. Costa called the president yesterday before the arrests to update him on the leads they were following. The Savins were persons of interest at that point.

"My guy said the lead was a dead end."

"So, they're out of it?"

"Yes, sir."

The president's secretary came in and whispered something in his ear. He nodded and the secretary quickly left the room.

"Folks, we have someone joining us this morning," the president said. "Liz, is he on the line?

"Yes, sir," the president's secretary replied over the telephone speaker. "Line three."

"Jack," the president said, "it's nice to hear from you this morning."

"Mr. President, I apologize for interrupting your meeting, but I thought your national security team should hear this." The caller was John Rhodes, the Treasury Secretary. Rhodes had been in that position through three presidential administrations and was considered the steady hand that calmed nervous currency and stock markets, especially during times of high stress.

"No problem, Jack," the president said. "What do you want to tell the group?"

"I just received an email message," Rhodes began. "The sender part is blank, but let me read the message."

I established a custodial bank account at BNY Mellon Bank in New York and have transferred $1.86 billion to that account. The funds were removed from a bank in Syria used by the Islamic State to pay its soldiers and buy weapons. Any future deposits to the Islamic State will be routed to this custodial account. I believe the money belongs to the people of Iraq and Syria and am confident that you can handle its return.

There was silence in the room as the treasury secretary finished reading the message.

"Mr. President, are you still there?"

"We're here, Jack," the president said, shaking his head. "Have you checked with the custodian bank?"

"Yes. They confirm that they have good funds. They're just waiting for instructions."

"How is the account titled?"

"In my name, John Elmer Rhodes." There were some quiet snickers in the room.

"Elmer?" the president chuckled. "You never told me."

"So my parents watched a lot of Warner Brothers cartoons," Rhodes said, as the laughter continued. "Anyway, how the hell did this guy get my name?"

"He's a sorcerer," the president said.

"I have already retitled the account in the Treasury Department's name. What should I do with the funds?"

"Let me call the Iraqi and Syrian presidents and tell them that their stolen oil money will be returned," the president said. "Thanks Elmer – I mean Jack."

"That wasn't very funny, Mr. President."

There was a moment or two of laughter after the treasury secretary hung up.

"Mr. President, Secretary Rhodes' report is consistent with aerial reconnaissance in Syria and northern Iraq that shows Islamic State guys walking away from their posts," Levin said.

"No one's getting paid," the president said. "I thought this wasn't about money?"

The mood in the room was becoming surreal. Someone prevented a war in Asia and was dismantling a terror network in the Middle East.

"Ari, let's go back to the missile launch for a moment," the president said. "Would you tell everyone what you told me about how the Pentagon got word of the launch?"

"Seventh Fleet got an email, sir. The message was sent directly to the mobile phone of Rear Admiral Stanhoff. He was having breakfast with his Japanese counterpart."

"Go on."

"At the same time, Pacific Command at Pearl got the message."

"And?"

"I got the message, too."

There wasn't much left to surprise this group. So far, each of these national security directors had received personal emails from a source that gave up intel that the United States could never get on its own. Everyone turned to Sanjay Riv, the director of the National Security Agency.

"Okay, Sanjay," the president said, "you're up. How's this guy doing all of this?"

"We don't know. There don't seem to be any doors that he can't unlock."

"What do we have in the way of electronic fingerprints?"

"None. He's a ghost. All we have is a theory."

"What's the theory?" the president asked.

"It's his method of communication that suggests something," Riv said. "It's almost like he doesn't know what he doesn't know about the way we communicate at this level of government."

"Go on, Sanjay."

"When you don't know the rules, you make up your own. This guy isn't good just because he knows how to do this. He's good because he's working out of an entirely different playbook."

"So, do you think he, or she, is an amateur?"

"No way, Mr. President. This person is off-the-charts brilliant," Sanjay said, leaning forward in his chair. "Look at it this way. No one is going to get a computer worm inside the North Korean command and control system. Even the North Koreans would find something like that."

"And the Islamic State bank account," Costa said. "It's like he can walk in and out of any computer system."

"How can that be, Sanjay?" the president asked.

"He's working on an entirely different level of computer power," Riv responded. "The Chinese agents didn't write that computer worm, but he pinned it on them. And the money the Islamic State squirreled away in a Syrian bank would never have been found with the technology we have."

"So who, or maybe, *what* is this?" The president was now in uncharted territory.

"I'm going to step out on that limb," Riv said. "No one on this *planet* can do what this guy is doing right now."

The room went quiet. Sanjay Riv wasn't crazy. He was brilliant and sometimes quirky. But he wasn't crazy. And, he was right. No one on Earth could have assembled so much information and then send it to just the right people.

"Is this guy our friend?" the president asked.

"So far, what he's done has been to our benefit," DuPont said. "But, maybe he's just showing off before pulling the big caper."

"Alright," the president began. "Let's assume that he knows who we are, and that we're talking. Starting right now, we go back to the 1950s – face-to-face communication only."

"What about phones?" Tony asked.

"We're off the grid, starting right now," the president said. "When you get something new, come over and tell me. We meet every morning here at 9:00 a.m. until we find the source."

The president stood to signal the end of the meeting. "That door is wide open," the president said, pointing. "Walk in when you have something."

The room cleared as the president's secretary came in.

"Mr. President, you have a phone call," Liz said.

"Who is it?"

"The Russian President."

Although officially relations with Russia were still cool, both leaders had done a pretty fair job of patching up the damage done by the previous administration. They talked once or twice a week, and even though they had different agendas, they agreed that it would not do for the United States and Russia to return to a Cold War. Both countries were suffering from terrorist attacks and there were no longer ideological reasons to separate them.

"Alexei," the president said. "How are you?"

"I am well, David," the Russian president said. He sounded in good spirits.

"You caught me as I was going to the pool," the president said. "I'm working to get some pecs like you have." President Collins admired the Russian president's physical exercise routine. It was something the president's wife had been urging him to emulate, but without much success.

"This will only take a minute. My man at the FSD told me that he received an email from your office this morning." The FSD was Russia's equivalent of the FBI and considered a top law enforcement organization worldwide.

The president had no idea what Alexei was talking about, but played along.

"Was the information helpful to you?" the president asked.

"Very much. This morning, we arrested the terrorists who shot down our passenger jet in the Sinai last year. And, we broke up two terrorist cells in Syria that were planning attacks on our pilots that are based there."

"That is great news, Alexei," the president said.

"*Spasibo, David.*"

"*Vy lyuboye vremya moy drug,*" the president replied. "Anytime, my friend. I'll see you next month in Moscow."

The president hung up the phone. Nothing else could possibly top what had already happened today.

44
Kai and David

THE PRESIDENT HAD dinner with his wife, Jen, in their private living quarters. He told her about the amazing things that were happening. After dinner, Jen suggested that they turn in early. He was tired, but he wasn't ready to end his workday.

David Collins headed back to the West Wing, where the oval office and cabinet room were his daily commute. It was about 8:00 p.m. when his mobile phone rang. He thought it might be Jen, urging him not to stay up too late. But the caller was not his wife. There were no numbers in the caller ID space – just dashes where the ten numbers should have been.

The president wasn't supposed to take private calls without the assistance of his secretary or an aide who could monitor the call in case a threat was made or some other act was set in motion by the call. But, David Collins knew who was on the phone. For the past hour, he had the sense that the mysteries of the past week would be revealed soon.

"This is David."

"Good evening, Mr. President. I think it is time we talked."

"Who is this?" the president asked.

"My name is Kai Tuparnac."

"Kai Tuparnac. What sort of name is Tuparnac?" the president asked, trying to judge from the voice and accent where the caller might be from.

"Tuparnac is an Atonan name," Kai said. "I am from Atona – the planet you call Mars.

"So, you are from Atona."

At dinner, the president told his wife that his day couldn't get any weirder.

He was wrong.

The president stood up at his desk. Two secret service agents were in the hall and two more beyond. He had plenty of firepower if this was the start of something.

"Are you responsible for the things that have been going on for the past few days?" the president asked.

"Do you mean the North Korean missile failure and the Islamic State money transfer?" Kai asked.

"Yes. Are you responsible?"

"I am."

"Have you done anything else today to help the human race?"

"Other than what the Russian president told you earlier, no."

It was a good reply to a trick question. Only his secretary knew that he talked to Alexei today. Sanjay's comment about someone from another planet rang true. He was starting to get his mind around the reality of what had been going on.

"Then I want to thank you for what you did," the president said. "You saved lives. And what you did will continue to save lives."

"You are most welcome, Mr. President."

"Why don't you call me David?" the president said.

"Very well, David," Kai said. "You must have many questions."

"More than I can count," the president said.

"Why don't I start by telling you how I arrived here."

For the next ten minutes, Kai talked, while the president sat back and listened. Kai started with the history of his people. He recounted the destruction of their planet by Koya in 1619 and the hundreds of years the Atonans lived underground. Then he explained his transference and how he came to Earth on the Viking 1 radio signal in 1976. He also told the president about his wife and wondered whether Mia was still alive on Atona.

"Kai, you made a great sacrifice to come here," the president said.

"My grandmother would have done the same."

"Your grandmother?"

"Yes. Her name was Naira. She was a president, like you."

"But you said there were no countries, no nation-states."

"My grandmother was President of Atona."

A world government, he thought. As a college student, dabbling in all of the political systems of modern society, Collins often imagined a world with one government, where resources and wealth were shared by everyone. Of course, he would never admit to such thoughts as President of the United States. Besides, just being president of this country was brutal enough.

"Tell me, Kai, how did Naira manage to do her job?"

"A small planet with limited resources. And pragmatism."

"Pragmatism?"

"Well, you can't survive if you're always trying to kill each other," Kai said. "We learned that cooperation was the only way to prosper. *All for one and one for all* is the expression, I believe."

"Do you think we could achieve that here?"

"Not today or tomorrow, but yes, with the right leader," Kai said. "I'm curious, David. Why did you change your mind and decide to run for reelection?"

Late yesterday, President Collins held a news conference, announcing that he would, in fact, seek another term as president. Most in his own party were delighted with his decision and the opposition feared a landslide loss.

"In the last few days, I starting having hope again," the president said.

"How do you mean, David?"

"Well, you would understand this better than anyone, but the job is a thankless one. The endless bickering, just to get something, *anything*, done. I had almost given up."

"So, what happened?" Kai asked.

"Someone arrived who was putting things in order."

"Do you mean in the Biblical sense?"

"No, not really. But we certainly could use some help right now."

"I am just an old man," Kai said. "I had no intention of interfering with your world."

"But you saved the sailors on the Reagan."

"I couldn't abide the loss of lives."

"Exactly," the president said. "You showed us a different way."

"Is that why you didn't attack North Korea?" Kai asked.

"Yes. Their people are badly treated, but they don't deserve a war."

"I think perhaps you have given me too much credit and yourself too little," Kai said.

"Why?"

"Because you believe the North Korean people matter. It's evidence of your philosophy," Kai said. "You would have done well on my planet, David."

"Kai, you came here for a reason," the president said. "How can we help your people?"

Kai and the president talked for another hour. By the time they were done, they had a plan to introduce Kai to the world and a Mars mission to help his people.

"So, do we agree on what to do next, Kai?"

"Yes. Thank you, David."

"Thank you, Kai," the president said and clicked off the call.

The president sat back in his chair. The Oval Office was still. He had talked to Kai for two hours. But he wasn't quite ready to leave. He just met an extraterrestrial, only the third person on the planet to do so. He had a lot to think about and a great deal to do, if their plan was going to work.

That he should even be in this room was a surprise, especially to David Collins. He never aspired to the job, viewing himself as a philosopher, not a politician. When he turned 65, he began a lengthy reflection on his life and what he had accomplished. Of course, anyone who has ever occupied this office would be considered a success by most people. But he never measured success in that way.

David Collins was the son of Colorado ranchers – breeders of prized Arabian horses. The Collins Ranch, outside of Durango, was a menagerie of horses, dogs, cats, goats, and other assorted animals who showed up for a free meal and decided to stay. When school wasn't in session, David was on the road with his parents, attending horse shows in the Southwest. The Collins horses were purchased by everyone from school teachers to heads-of-state. David traveled with his parents several times to Saudi Arabia, Dubai, and the United Arab Emirates to deliver their horses. His heart broke every time he had to say goodbye to one of them.

In high school, David was an especially good baseball pitcher. He was being scouted by colleges and minor league clubs when a shoulder tear ended his baseball career before it even started.

After graduation, David stayed in town, attending Fort Lewis College, majoring in philosophy. Although he was raised a Methodist, David joined the Roman Catholic Church and after graduation, he began the rigorous academic and service requirements to become a Jesuit priest. He earned master's degrees in history and religious studies at Arizona State University. He was working in a Jesuit parish on the Navajo reservation in northern Arizona when word reached him that his parents were killed in a highway crash. They were traveling to a horse show in California. Both horses were also killed in the horrible wreck involving a tractor-trailer rig.

David was devastated by the deaths of his parents. Although he had a large family with whom to share his grief, David was inconsolable. His sadness grew into a deep rage that he directed at the God he was working so hard to serve. He couldn't reconcile the deaths of his parents with any sort of plan that God might have for his life.

David left the Jesuits and became a public school teacher. He taught at the middle school level. It was quite a sight watching the six-foot-four teacher in cowboy boots fold

himself into small chairs to sit with kids who were just starting their journeys into adulthood.

In 1985, he ran unsuccessfully for the Colorado House
of Representatives. A year later, he was back in the political
ring, this time running for a seat in the United States House
of Representations. His family's name recognition, plus his
superb oratory skills, made him as natural at the politician's
podium as he would have been in the pulpit. David defeated
the incumbent representative in a squeaker of a race.

He remained in the House until picked as the former
president's running mate in the 2008 presidential election. Although his ticket lost, he was a rising star in his party and in
the next presidential cycle, he ran for the presidency and took
the White House by a comfortable margin. Over the past four
years, with a combination of solid and pragmatic policies,
an even temperament, and close friends on both sides of the
aisle, David Collins became the role-model for a consultative
presidency. He appointed good people of differing political
and philosophical stripes and allowed them to do their jobs.
He listened more than he spoke. And even when he disagreed,
he treated those who opposed him with courtesy and respect.

Reelection was one of those rare times when the president
went against the advice of those he trusted. They wanted him
to run for a second term. But, Colorado kept pulling at him
and he decided to leave after one term as president. Perhaps,
he would go back to raising horses. Those were the happiest
years of his life.

⚭

But during the past few days, his Jesuit-inspired belief that service to others was his mission caused him to reconsider his decision. Whatever was going on right now, David Collins wanted to be at the helm to make sure that the United States was able to navigate what was certain to come. The president decided that he could give four more years to public service before withdrawing from public life.

The last candidate still running in his party called earlier today. She told the president she wasn't surprised that he had changed his mind. Quite the opposite, she had urged him to run and only got into the race after he decided not to run. Now that he was back, she called to give him her endorsement. David Collins had a clear field and a very good shot at a second term as president.

With the events of the past week reeling in his mind, the president imagined what Earth would be like in one, or five, or ten years. Kai could literally change the world for the better almost overnight. Cold fusion energy, more food for more people, and unlocking the last mysteries of space and time. These were no longer hopes, but tangible realities.

Like many Americans, David had grown tired of the constant struggles that his nation faced. He hated how the world had been split by religion, tribes, and nationalities. He saw himself as a citizen of Earth and his guest from Atona came from a place where such a philosophy was not just admired, but practiced. If he could instill even some of these same ideals in the minds of reasonable men and women around the world, he could see a new era coming, one in which people could put aside old grievances and begin to work together for the common good.

It sounded all groovy and hippie-like. But, it worked on Atona and it could work on Earth, too.

45
Preparations

BEFORE TURNING IN for the night, the president asked his secretary to call a special meeting of his cabinet for Friday at 10:00 a.m. No reason was given for the unscheduled meeting. All the White House would say was that there would be a presentation and then an extended discussion on a major decision President Collins needed to make.

After speaking with Kai, David Collins phoned the presidents of Syria and Iraq, telling them that the Treasury Department had funds that belonged to them. These were the receipts from oil sold on the black market by the Islamic State. Collins gave them the total amount and asked them to split the monies fairly between their two countries.

It was a test to see if he could get *just two* world leaders to start thinking beyond their own political ambitions. The next day, in a joint telephone call to the president, the Syrian and Iraqi leaders would tell him that they had decided on an equitable split of the funds. They would thank the president, whose next call would be to Jack Rhodes at Treasury, instructing him to wire the funds to Syrian and Iraqi national bank accounts.

The last thing the president did on Wednesday night was to make a call to Santa Monica, California. Maggie answered the phone.

"Dr. Savin, this is David Collins at the White House."

"Mr. President?"

"It's just David to you and your husband. Is he there? And, can you put us on speaker?"

"Certainly, sir," Maggie said as she put the phone down on the kitchen table. She and Mike were playing chess with Kai, who was playing from an iPad set up next to the board. Maggie and Mike were both playing white. Kai played black.

There were more white pieces off the board than black ones when the phone rang.

"Good evening, Mr. President," Mike said. "Maggie and I are here. Kai is here, too."

"Hello, Kai," the president said.

"Hello, David," Kai said into the phone sitting among the three of them. "You work very quickly."

"You inspired me Kai," the president said. "Mike and Maggie, has Kai briefed you on our conversation earlier tonight?"

"He has, sir," Mike said.

"Will you come to Washington tomorrow and attend the cabinet meeting on Friday?" the president asked. "I'd like it if you would stay with Jen and me at the White House."

Before the chess game, Kai talked with Maggie and Mike and recounted the conversation he had with the president. A cabinet meeting would be called to discuss plans for a rescue mission to Mars. Kai and the president agreed that Mike and Maggie should be there.

"Mr. President, Mike and I aren't sure what we can add to a meeting with Kai and your cabinet."

"I understand," the president said. "But, in order for the plan to work, you need to be part of Kai's announcement to the world. After all, you are the ones who restored Kai and have been with him during his first weeks on Earth."

"Yes, but how can we help, now that you and Kai have met and have a plan?" Maggie asked.

While talking to Mike and Maggie earlier, Kai didn't mention the role they would have in the president's plan. He wanted the president to make the case for them to come to Washington. Kai needed Maggie and Mike, but he wasn't going to demand that they be involved.

But there was something else about this human to human interaction. Kai already learned of the amicable split of the money between Syria and Iraq. He knew that the Russian and American presidents were friends again. And now, if Maggie and Mike could be involved in Kai's introduction to the world, his presence would be a global discovery that could be shared by everyone, instead of a U.S. government announcement that was sure to arouse suspicion and jealousy. Yes, Kai and the president needed Maggie and Mike to be part of plan.

"You two are integral to the plan that Kai and I discussed," the president said. "It would be a great favor to me if you could come to Washington."

Maggie nodded her approval as Mike answered. "We would be honored to be there."

"Wonderful. The Secret Service will pick you up tomorrow morning and take you to LAX," the president said. "You'll be brought directly to the White House. Jen will be so excited to meet you both. The four of us will have dinner. Oh, and don't pack anything fancy. The dress code around here is blue jeans."

Jen Yee Collins was the president's wife. Married thirty-four years, they met while the president was on a House of Representatives trade mission to China in the early 1980s. Her parents were university instructors and members of the Chinese Communist Party. Although relations between China and the United States were warming, her parents were uneasy that their only child might marry an American. But, David soon won them over with his modest ways and his quick grasp of Mandarin Chinese. The First Lady was a powerful resource in the Collins administration, her charm and soft-spoken ways making short order of tough guys in Congress, who opposed her husband's legislative agenda.

"Thank you, Mr. President," Mike said. "We look forward to meeting both you and Jen."

"Then, it's settled," the president said. "See you tomorrow."

"Goodnight, David," Kai said.

46
White House

SANTA MONICA – THURSDAY MORNING

THIS MORNING, THE television news channels were covering two big stories. First, was the announcement from the White House that David Collins had changed his mind and decided to run for reelection. Political pundits on the cable networks were spinning the implications of the president's decision. With his popularity as high as any president since Ronald Reagan, most concluded that the president would easily win over the other party's leading candidate, an odd businessman from Florida who thought that a successful career building strip malls was good training for the presidency.

The second story had to do with the Middle East. The governments of Syria and Iraq announced that they had recaptured oil fields and refineries that had been the source of millions of dollars in funding for the Islamic State. The money spigot was being closed. There was no mention of yesterday's huge transfer of money out of Ayn al Arab, Syria, but drone reconnaissance video showed checkpoints on roads leading into IS territory were no longer being manned. Advancing forces on both sides of the Syria-Iraq border were easily reclaiming territory and freeing citizens from the terror of Islamic State control.

At 9:30 a.m., a black SUV pulled to the curb in front of Mike and Maggie's house. Two men in suits got out and walked to the front door. Their job this morning was to safely deliver the Savins to Los Angeles International Airport. There, a private jet would take them to Reagan National Airport. Then, another Secret Service detail would take them to the White House.

When the agents knocked on the front door, it was Maggie who opened it.

"Good morning, Dr. Savin," the agent said. "I'm Oscar Hill and this is Raymond Griffin. We're with the Secret Service." They both showed their badges and photo identification cards.

"Good morning, gentlemen," Maggie said smiling. "Please come in."

"No, thank you," Agent Hill said. "We'll wait outside for you and your husband, okay?"

"That's fine," Maggie said. "See you in a minute."

Maggie walked into the study, where Kai and Mike were talking. Maggie sat down.

"Kai, the agents are here to take us to the airport."

"I will be monitoring the flight, Maggie," said Kai. "You'll enjoy the White House. From the pictures I've seen, it is quite spectacular."

Maggie chuckled. Neither of them had ever been to the White House and here was Kai, a guy from Atona, who took the virtual tour on the White House website, giving *them* information about tonight's accommodations.

"Kai, you are too much," Maggie said.

"Is there anything we can do for you before we leave for Washington?" Mike asked.

"No. Now that you are part of the plan, I feel comfortable talking to the president and his cabinet tomorrow."

"Kai, what will you do if we can't help you?" Mike asked.

"I could visit the Russians or the Chinese," Kai said, "but I don't think I will."

"Why not?" Mike asked.

"Because I have already seen too much," Kai replied. "What happened in North Korea was not just the work of a deranged leader. There are other forces testing the United States."

"And you know, NASA has a Mars mission already scheduled," Maggie said.

"I do. That's why I wrote some engineering modifications to make it ready for contact with my people."

Maggie and Mike laughed. Kai was way ahead of the curve.

"Okay then. We'll see you on the big screen at the White House," Mike said.

"Mike, Maggie, I want to thank you for all you have done."

"Well, you are part of our family now," Maggie said. "See you soon."

The computer screen went dark. Kai moved to a secure location, a place where he could connect with the White House computer during the cabinet meeting. He had a lot of work to do before the meeting.

And, there was something else. Kai picked up a tail. Something was trying to track him. It wasn't close, but whoever was behind it was getting better at finding his footprints. He would try to find it before it found him, and then make sure it wouldn't interfere with the president's cabinet meeting.

Mike and Maggie locked the front door. One of the agents took their bags and they got in the back seat for the ride to LAX. At the airport, the SUV moved through several motorized security gates and drove onto the field, to a fixed-base operator that served only private jets. A Cessna Citation X was parked there, being serviced by two aircraft technicians. The fuel truck was just leaving as their SUV pulled up. Maggie and Mike were escorted to the steps and after they got aboard, a steward came out of the plane to retrieve the bags from the SUV. There was plenty of room to move around and Mike and Maggie chose swivel chairs that faced each other.

"Is there anything you folks need before you take off?" Agent Hill asked.

"No, we're good," Mike said. "Thanks. And, thank Agent Griffin for us, too."

"It's our pleasure," Hill said. "The steward will serve lunch and there is plenty to drink onboard."

"Thanks."

"Have a safe flight."

The agent stepped off the aircraft and the steward closed the door. He introduced himself and the two pilots who came out of the cockpit to meet Maggie and Mike. The pilots suggested that the couple kick back and relax. The flight time to Washington, they said, would be slightly under three hours. This was one fast business jet.

The middle part of the country was under a severe weather watch as a cold front collided with warm air coming up from the Gulf of Mexico. Huge cumulus clouds were visible in a line from Arkansas to Indiana, but the Citation was flying at a much higher altitude. There was no turbulence and the plane had clear air all the way to Washington.

The touchdown at Reagan National Airport was perfect and the aircraft taxied to a private ramp where another SUV was waiting. Two agents were there, standing at the doors. They greeted the Savins, who got into the backseat. The SUV left the airport with a police escort and quickly moved into the HOV lane on the 395. Red and blue flashing lights got motorists to move out of the way. Evidently, drivers in Washington were used to this sort of thing because cars gave way as soon as they spotted the big vehicle. The drive to the White House was quick. After clearing security, the SUV pulled under the White House south portico, where staff members opened their doors and welcomed Maggie and Mike.

The star-struck couple was taken immediately to the Oval Office, where President Collins was waiting to greet them. The president came from behind his desk to shake hands.

"Dr. Savin and Dr. Savin, it is a pleasure to meet you," the president said.

"It is a pleasure to meet you, Mr. President," Maggie said, "but maybe you should just call us Mike and Maggie to avoid that doctor business."

"I was hoping we could do that," the president said. "We were wondering how to address two esteemed Ph.D.'s in the same sentence. First names are a rule in this administration, so please call me David."

"I'm not so sure that's going to come out so easily," Mike said. "We might slip back into Mr. President."

"Well, for tonight at least, it will be Jen and David," the president said. "We were planning on dinner at seven. Is that okay with you?"

"That would be great and we would be honored, sir," Maggie said.

"We have so much to talk about," the president said, "but for now, we're going to let you get settled in the guest quarters and give you a chance to freshen up. The staff can get anything you need or might have forgotten."

"That's very kind, David," Mike said, trying out the president's first name.

"Great. So, Mike and Maggie, Jen and I will see you this evening."

"Thank you, David," Maggie said.

An aide standing behind them introduced herself and then escorted Mike and Maggie to their guest quarters in the Lincoln Bedroom. Neither of them had ever been on the White House tour, let alone to be asked to stay as guests. After the aide excused herself, for a few minutes, they just stood still, drinking in the sounds and the flavors of the White House. So much history was made here.

Mike put his arm around Maggie's shoulder and then pulled her toward him. He gave her a soft kiss on the lips.

"Do you want to fool around before dinner?"

Maggie smacked him on the shoulder.

"What?"

"Are you really in the mood?" Maggie asked.

"Yeah. There's something about this room," Mike said. "Hey, what if we were late for dinner?"

"Can it, slick," Maggie said. Then she reached up and gave him another kiss. "Maybe later?"

"Oooh, I like the way you think," Mike said.

Their suitcases were already set atop small stands that looked like they were built in 1860 for that purpose. The Lincoln Bedroom had furniture from that period. Mike wondered if roller suitcases were around when Lincoln was here?

He was in a playful mood. That was odd, considering where he and Maggie were this evening. Kai was safe and his presence was known. There was a good chance that Kai would be able to contact his wife and his fellow citizens on Atona. Then, maybe things would return to normal for Mike and Maggie. No, that wouldn't be possible with Kai here, but at least they would no longer have to be the keepers of this world-shaking secret.

At five minutes to seven, there was knock on the door. A White House staff member asked the Savins to accompany him. They were taken to the family dining room, a place rarely seen by guests. David Collins and Jen Yee Collins were already there.

"Mike, Maggie, I would like to introduce my wife, Jen," President Collins said.

"It is a pleasure to meet you, Mrs. Collins," Mike said.

"Please, it's Jen," the First Lady said. "Everyone has trouble with David's informality rule around here."

"Well, it is a great pleasure," Maggie said. "You're even more beautiful in person than on television."

"You are very kind," Jen said, bowing slightly.

"Should I ask them?" the president looked at his wife. Jen pinched the president's arm.

"Ouch," David said. "Mike, do you get this, too?"

"About an hour ago," Mike said. "A smack on the arm."

"It's the Lincoln Bedroom Effect," the president said.

"Sir?" Mike said.

"The Lincoln Bedroom Effect," David said. "It's supposed to bring out certain kinds of, well, certain feelings. Anyway, that's what I've heard."

Maggie and Mike looked at each other. "We just had that conversation," Maggie said. "So it wasn't just Mike clowning around?"

"Oh, no. It's real," Jen said, giggling and looking at her husband. Both were laughing.

"To be honest, Mike suggested. But, I told him we would be late for dinner," Maggie said. She couldn't believe they were having this conversation with the President and the First Lady of the United States. They all laughed as a White House staffer served glasses of champagne.

"Well, the night is young," David said, holding up his glass. "To our new friends. And, to Kai."

When the toast was over and the laughter subsided, the president motioned Maggie and Mike to sit down. The table was casually set – none of that twenty forks and spoons on either side of centuries-old dishes you were terrified you would knock off the table. The appetizers were Chinese dumplings with an exquisite soy sauce. The First Lady told them that the dumplings and the sauce were recipes from her Chinese grandmother. The main course was Colorado grass-feed beef, fried potatoes, and a salad of fresh vegetables grown in a small garden that Jen and David tended when they had time together.

While Maggie and Mike had their pick of adult beverages, David and Jen had beer – Budweiser for Jen and *Tsingtao* for David. The Savins followed their hosts by ordering the same way. Both were surprised by how casual the First Couple was when away from the television lights.

The dinner conversation was just as casual. Jen talked about growing up in China and meeting this tall, handsome Congressman during a visit he made to Guangzhou. They fell in love almost immediately and the delegate from Colorado got into a bit of hot water, trying to explain his frequent visits to Guangdong province to see Jen. By their fourth date, David was ready to pop the question, but the Yee family had reservations about their daughter marrying an American.

Accompanied by her parents and grandparents, Jen visited the United States, all of them staying at the Collins ranch in Colorado. Maybe it was the Rockies, the beautiful horses, or David's quiet, almost Asian-like philosophy of life, but by the time the Yee family returned to China, they were sold on their prospective son-in-law. The marriage ceremony was in the Chinese tradition and the couple honeymooned in Yangshuo, a favorite destination south of Guilin City. After staying a few weeks in China, David and Jen left for Washington, where she quickly adjusted to just another large, crowded city, full of political intrigue.

The president went to the kitchen to prepare the dessert – warm apple pie and vanilla bean ice cream. Jen continued the conversation with Mike and Maggie. The subject turned to Kai.

"David told me about Kai – your discovery of him and how he has been so helpful," Jen said. "What was it like for you to meet Kai?"

"At first, we were stunned," Maggie said. "But now, Kai is like a member of the family. He's not very different from us."

"David talked with him," Jen said. "He says he trusts Kai."

"I think you will too," Mike said. "He's not here to save the world, but we sure could use his help. And, all he asks in return is a little help for his people."

The president walked back in, holding four plates balanced on two arms. It was quite an impressive bit of coordination and the president saw the looks on Mike and Maggie's faces.

"Hey, I worked at Denny's for three summers," the president said. "The tips weren't good, but I learned how to do this." He served everyone and then sat down. It was time to brief the Savins on what tomorrow's meeting would be about.

The foursome talked for an hour. They discussed Kai's presence and the long-term impact he would have on the world. The president told them that NASA had been cooperative with their next Mars lander and had been given a heads-up that new specifications would be coming from the White House soon.

"Tell me about Kai, as an individual," the president said. "How does he view himself in dealing with human beings?"

Maggie looked at Mike. He had more conversations with Kai and probably understood Kai's thinking better than Maggie. He smiled at her as he took the question.

"Kai is a quiet and humble man. He's very old, but thinks big things," Mike began. "The world he comes from is full of brilliant people and among them, I think his star shines even a little brighter. But the Atonan philosophy of Ka-Atona taught him to be humble and to use his gifts to be of service to his fellow citizens. That's why he sacrificed so much to come here."

"And waited forty years to be awakened," the president said. "Oh, I'm sorry, I didn't mean to be unkind."

"We're sorry, too." Maggie said. "We had no way of knowing what was on that tape. We were two kids, caught-up in the biggest space mission since landing on the moon."

"And, you were falling in love," Jen added.

"Yes, Jen, we were," Mike said, "but we can't go back and change what happened to Kai."

"Even if you could," the president said, "there was no way in 1976 that we had the technology to do anything for Kai. Or, his people."

"Kai is a patient man and a grateful guest," Maggie said. "But I think he believes that there will be few, if any, Atonans left when he returns."

"We're hoping that Mia and other Atonans living in the Underground went through the transference process," Mike said. "If they did, they might be in the same kind of stasis as Kai was before he was restored."

"Can I ask you a question, David?" Maggie said.

"Certainly."

"What will countries like China and Russia do when they learn about Kai?"

David looked at his wife. She was the one that answered.

"The Chinese don't want to be at odds with the United States," Jen said. "But, they are growing and learning how to be a superpower. David understands that. But China, and probably Russia, will feel threatened by the United States having access to Kai's incredible knowledge."

"Would they understand if Kai explained that he doesn't view himself as a citizen of any one country?" Mike asked.

"Yes, they would understand," Jen said, "and they would believe David when he tells them. But, certain factions in their governments would view Kai's presence in the United States as a threat."

"What he did in North Korea was just one example," the president said. "And when our Russian and Chinese friends learn about that little Islamic State bank caper, they are certainly going to be unhappy that Kai is here."

Everyone chuckled at the term the president used. Even his everyday words reflected a lack of interest in overwhelming his guests with fancy language. Mike and Maggie were always fans of this president, but now they really liked the man behind the office.

"Have you thought about how Kai's presence should be revealed to the world?" the president asked. Mike and Maggie had talked at length with Kai about his coming-out party. But they, and Kai, had a view on the subject that wasn't strictly pro-American.

"Kai will always be grateful that an American spacecraft got him here," Maggie said. "And, if you agree to help him with a mission to Atona, I think he will always view Americans with a special fondness."

"But?" the president asked.

"We believe that Kai's presence should be announced in a way that reflects a common unity of all countries," Maggie said. "He would like the benefits of his knowledge, like fusion power for example, to be available to everyone."

"So, everyone would share in the knowledge Kai brings to the human race," Jen said. "Is that a fair assessment of Kai's views?

"It is and while he lives in a cyberworld and will likely stay here in America," Mike said, "he would like the distribution of benefits from Atonan knowledge to be managed separately from any one government."

"Are you thinking the United Nations?" the president asked.

"Maybe, but Kai's been reading up on the U.N.," Maggie said. "He isn't convinced that it's the right place to manage and distribute knowledge and funding that will come from new technology. Too much intrigue."

"I would agree," the president said. "What about the two of you?"

Maggie looked at Mike and both stared back at the president. He was smiling, but his eyes were serious.

"What do you mean, Mr. President, err, David?" Mike said.

"A new organization," the president said. "It would be headed by both of you and charged with fairly distributing the benefits Kai and other Atonans may offer."

"You were Kai's discoverer," Jen said. It was obvious that the president and his wife had this proposal in mind when they invited the Savins to the White House.

"And with your reputations as internationally-known physicists," the president added, "the Chinese and everyone else would be more likely to trust you than a politician like the President of the United States."

"Um, may I have another *Tsingtao*, David?" Mike asked.

"Of course," the president said. "How about another round for everyone?"

47
Cabinet Meeting

WHITE HOUSE – WEST WING – FRIDAY MORNING

A T PRECISELY 10:00 a.m., President David Collins walked the few steps from his desk in the Oval Office to his seat at the midpoint of the large mahogany table in the Cabinet Room. Everyone stood as the president walked in, and as was typical for the president, he motioned for everyone to immediately sit down.

Of the sixteen cabinet members, only one was absent. Vice President Robert Eastwood was at Walter Reed, undergoing an emergency appendectomy. The former four-term senator from Ohio put up such a fuss when he was told he could not attend the cabinet meeting that he demanded a video hookup from his hospital bed.

There were five additional attendees, not normally part of the president's cabinet meetings – CIA Director Dr. Katherine Clarke, NSA Director Dr. Sajay Riv, and FBI Director Anthony Costa. And, seated directly opposite the president, were Maggie and Mike Savin.

"Welcome everyone," the president said. "I'd like to introduce our guests, Drs. Mikhail and Margaret Savin, from Santa

Monica, California. Mike and Maggie are two of the foremost physicists in the world and former professors at Caltech."

Cabinet members gave them a round of applause as Mike and Maggie smiled nervously. The room was full of the most powerful members of the U.S. Government.

"What Mike and Maggie will share with you this morning has never happened in the history of the human race," the president said calmly. "I can't say it any plainer than that and I have been trying to find the right words for this opening monologue since yesterday. Mike and Maggie are going to tell you an incredible story that began almost forty years ago. And what they discovered will change the course of human history. We, in this room, are the first to learn about this and the information will remain among us until we are ready to announce their discovery to the world."

Everyone sitting in the room shifted slightly as they processed the weight of the president's remarks.

"Maggie, Mike, if you will," the president said.

For the next half hour, Mike and Maggie told their story, from the Viking 1 landing on Mars in 1976 up to the events of the past few weeks. The president watched the stunned faces of the cabinet members as they listened to a story that could only be fiction. Was this some kind of elaborate gag the president was playing on his cabinet? David Collins was known for his pranks, but neither he, nor the Savins, were smiling.

As Mike and Maggie finished telling their story, the lights in the cabinet room dimmed a bit so that everyone could get a good view of a large high-definition screen that was dropping down from the ceiling at one end of the table. Some digital hash came from the speakers for a few seconds and then the screen lit up with scrambled bits of digitized video coming and going across the screen.

Then, the screen cleared and a crisp image of Kai appeared. There were audible gasps from some members. Kai's image was sharp and clear. *This guy cleans up pretty good for meetings with the president,* Maggie thought. She turned to look at Mike, whose thinning hair was sticking straight up, the result of a habit he had of running his fingers through his hair when he was stressed or deep in thought. She wanted to fix it, but it wouldn't do to have her messing with her husband's hair in a meeting like this.

Instead of the ethereal background on Mike's computer, the background behind Kai was a changing set of photographs, each depicting beautiful scenes of Atona before Koya struck the planet in 1619. There were photos of its oceans and lakes, beaches with reddish-white sand, and green plants that seemed to love the carbon dioxide-rich atmosphere that used to surround the planet. Stunning images of *Olympus Mons* were shown, with its slopes lined with trees and the top covered with snow and glaciers.

The president looked over to Mike and Maggie and nodded for them to make the first move.

"Hello, Kai," Maggie said. Her relationship with Kai had blossomed and she felt a sort of maternal protectiveness for him. After all, he was restored to life in their home and chose to stay with them, even though Kai could have gone anywhere he wanted.

"Hello, Maggie," Kai said as he smiled. He saw Mike sitting next to her. "Hello, Mike, I hope you had a pleasant flight to Washington. I'm glad both of you are here."

Kai turned slightly in a way that made it seem as if he was making eye contact with the president. "Mr. President, it is an honor to see you in person," Kai said, "and to meet all of you who serve your fellow citizens."

"We're very happy to see you, Kai," the president said. "May I ask when those pictures were taken?"

"These are pictures that my grandmother, Naira, took during her lifetime," Kai said. "Naira was the president of the Atonan Administrative Council, a group very much like yours, Mr. President."

"I understand that she died in service to your citizens," the president said. "We are very sorry."

"Thank you," Kai said, "that is kind of you."

"What would you like to discuss first?" the president asked. He was going to let Kai drive the bus this morning.

There was a pause for a moment as Kai's image seemed to freeze. The pictured scrambled and unscrambled several times. Maggie called out, "Kai!"

The screen went blank and Kai disappeared. Aides of the NSA and CIA directors entered the room and whispered to their bosses.

"Mr. President, the White House servers are under a DDOS attack," Katherine Clarke said.

"A what?" the president asked.

"A distributed denial of service attack," Sanjay Riv explained. "It's a way of shutting down servers by flooding them with requests for access."

"They're trying to isolate Kai," Mike said, leaning forward in his chair.

"Confirming, sir, the White House servers are down," the president's chief of staff said as security personnel entered the room. Other staff members came and went, with instructions from the president's chief of staff.

The video screen went black as the intelligence directors and their staffs conferred away from the table.

"Why don't we take a break for a few minutes," the president said calmly. The lights in the room were brought up, but nobody moved. Inside, the president was seething mad. The past two administrations had made protestations to certain governments who regularly tried to hack United States government computers. Despite a signed agreement, hackers were still trying, and sometimes succeeding in breaking into computers. Today's attack was on the White House.

Everyone was standing when Mike felt his phone buzz in his pocket. He looked at the screen. It was Kai.

"I have Kai here, Mr. President," Mike said.

There was a collective sigh in the room. The president quietly motioned to everyone to sit back down.

"Hello, Kai," Mike said, answering his phone. "Yes. Yes. Okay, I understand." Mike pushed the speaker button on his phone and placed it in the middle of the table.

"Where were we, Mr. President?" Kai said, as if nothing had happened. The group didn't know whether to laugh or not, but their faces showed relief.

"Are you safe, Kai?" the president asked.

"Yes, I am fine."

"Can you tell us what just happened?" the president asked.

"Dr. Riv can better explain, but about forty million compromised computers tried to get into the White House servers," Kai said. "I stopped it, but we're going to have to continue the meeting on the phone. Will that be alright?"

Communicating with an Atonan over a plain-old cell phone. How quaint and old-fashioned is that? the president mused. "That's fine, Kai. Can you identify a source?"

"Not yet, but it is somewhere in Asia," Kai said. "It was started when they were notified that Maggie and Mike had arrived at the White House."

"Notified?" the president asked incredulously. "How were they notified."

"SMS – simple messaging service," Kai said. "One of the flight technicians at Reagan National texted confirmation of Mike and Maggie's arrival just after the Citation touched down."

"Do you know which one?" the president asked.

"Yes. The information is in an email on Director Costa's phone." Costa looked at his phone. He nodded to the president that he had the information.

"He's still at Reagan," Kai said.

Costa jumped up and excused himself from the room. Outside, he was speaking with someone on his phone and gave him the information. Costa walked back into the conference room.

"Agents are on their way to the airport, Mr. President," Costa said.

"They weren't trying to attack the White House," Kai said. "They were trying to block this meeting while they searched for me."

"Are you saying that the Chinese know you are here?" the president asked.

"No. They don't even know what I am, Mr. President," Kai explained. "They've been working with North Korea to find out who is behind the odd events that have happened in the past two weeks." Kai could see that the president was angry. David Collins rarely showed this kind of emotion, but with the greatest discovery in human history in his house, he was seeing red.

"Mr. President, I have taken care of the infected computers," Kai said. "The Trojan that controlled them has been removed. The owners are innocent victims in this and I didn't want to destroy their computers."

"Thank you, Kai," the president said, relaxing a bit.

"And, I have something else for you," Kai said. "Secretary Levin, if you will check your inbox. And yours too, Dr. Clarke."

The Defense Secretary looked at his phone. "These are plans and specifications for the carrier-buster missile," Levin said.

"Both the Chinese and North Korean versions," the CIA Director said.

"Ari, can you develop a defense for this?" the president asked.

"Yes, sir," Levin responded. "These systems require aircraft and satellite guidance. Take those away and the missile is blind."

"So, the Reagan's CO was correct in planning to take out those two reconnaissance aircraft," the president said.

"One of them was helping the North Koreans," Levin said. "Yes, shooting them down would have been the right decision."

"Thank you Kai," the president said. "Now, let's talk about helping you."

"David, I would like you to make some changes to the Mars lander that is being built for a launch this summer," Kai said. "With these modifications, I believe we can find out the status of my people on Atona."

The president's mobile phone buzzed. He smiled as he looked at the message.

"Kai, I just received your modifications. I will get them to the NASA director and make sure that everything you requested is ready for the July mission."

"Thank you, David," Kai replied.

"But Kai, there are limits on what we can do to help your people on Atona," the president said. "We have a satellite orbiting your planet right now called MAVEN. It is telling us that it would be nearly impossible to return your planet to the conditions we saw in your grandmother's photos."

"I know."

"So, do you want to bring your citizens to Earth?"

"No. They wouldn't survive. Ironically, your atmosphere has too little carbon dioxide. They would trade one enclosed environment for another. But, maybe a virtual world, like the kind I'm in," Kai said, sounding tired. "Perhaps they are already there. My transference proved that my grandfather's theory works."

"Your grandfather?" someone at the table asked.

"Yes," Kai said. "He developed the first scanner that allowed our brains to be transferred to electronic form. He died trying the process on himself, but others made improvements. That's how I was able to come here."

The video screen came back to life and Kai was visible again.

"The attack on the White House servers is over and two computer hackers in Shanghai have been arrested by Chinese authorities," Kai said.

"Were they working for the Chinese government?" the president asked.

"No, sir," Kai said. "They did the job on spec. They were hoping to get jobs in the Chinese government by hacking the White House."

"So now, they'll make license plates, instead."

"That is correct."

"If we modify the spacecraft for the July launch to Atona, will that be an acceptable start for you?"

"It will."

"Do you plan to return with the spacecraft?"

"I don't know," Kai said, sounding tired. "May I defer that decision for a while longer."

"Of course. Up to the day of launch," the president answered.

"I need to sleep now. Mike and Maggie will explain," Kai said.

"Will we talk again, Kai?" the president asked.

"Many times, Mr. President," Kai replied. "I think you will achieve much in your second term."

"It's a shame we can't register you to vote, Kai," the president said as Kai gave the room a grin.

"Mike and Maggie, I will see you when we get back home."

"Later today, Kai," Maggie said.

"It was very nice to meet all of you. I will say goodbye for now," Kai said, as the screen faded to black.

48
United Nations

I N EARLY JUNE, the President would travel to New York City to address the United Nations General Assembly. Members were asked to send their highest-ranking officials for what was said to be an event of historical importance for the future of the planet. Leaders from nearly every nation confirmed that their heads of state would be in attendance.

Security was a top concern. With so many of the world's leaders gathering in one spot on the East River, there was a real possibility of a terrorist act. State and federal law enforcement would be heavy and the city would have to close down an area from Park Avenue to FDR Drive and for ten blocks north and south from the U.N. Building. Kai would do his own security sweeps, identifying hundreds of individuals and terror cells across Europe, Asia, and North America. Arrests would be made before the terrorists even knew what hit them.

Kai would work closely with David Collins in writing the speech the president would give to the Assembly. After the president spoke, he would introduce Mike and Maggie Savin. They would tell their incredible story and then introduce Kai, who would appear on a large screen to address the Assembly and the world community.

The president would then return to the podium to announce the formation of a new organization that would share whatever technology Kai wished to offer to the world. The environment, economic development, and agriculture would be top priorities, especially in nations where prosperity never seemed to reach. With a new source of energy possible, the world was looking at the end of a carbon-based economy. Global warming would be reversed.

With seed money from the United States, an independent agency would be set up. Unofficially called the World Development Agency, it would be a foundation that would distribute the benefits of Kai's knowledge to every country on the planet. The agency would be headed by two trustees – Mike and Maggie Savin, with advice from a board consisting of eleven members selected from around the world. Kai would serve as the agency's independent advisor, providing knowledge across the entire spectrum of human activity. The knowledge his people had acquired would push human civilization ahead by hundreds of years, and the mandate of the WDA was to ensure that the benefits of Kai's assistance were shared with everyone.

An end to global warming was a top priority. Kai would work with manufacturers around the world to produce cold fusion reactors to replace carbon-emitting power plants. Battery technology would extend the range of motor vehicles so that gasoline would no longer be needed. Air pollution would become a thing of the past as the world started to heal from the devastation of more than 200 years of industrialization.

Atonan technology would be made freely available to any business seeking to use the new knowledge to offer better products and services. No one company would be allowed to dominate the market. And, a portion of the profits from Kai's technology would be collected by the WDA in trust for the benefit of every citizen on the planet.

There would be conditions attached for any nation that wanted access to technology and funding. Old ways of thinking would have to change. Women would have the same rights as men in all matters, including governance. Required membership in a single religion would be banned, as would the discrimination against other faiths. With the Islamic State out of business, a new model for religious and ethnic tolerance was already emerging in the Middle East. Any citizen could worship as he or she wished, but as on Atona, no one would be forced to adopt any belief system.

Additionally, member nations would pledge to reduce spending on weapons, but only as trust was established among nations. Without competition for scarce resources, there would be less to fight about. All nuclear, chemical, and biological weapons would be destroyed. A living wage would be paid to all workers, equalizing the economic disparities among countries and preventing the exploitation of children in manufacturing. And finally, healthcare would become universal.

Participation in the World Development Agency would not be a requirement. Some countries were sure to object to the conditions placed on them. But with all of the benefits the WDA could provide, very few nations would choose to sit on the sidelines as living standards around the world improved.

◯◯

Mike and Maggie were flown to New York for the speech, this time on Air Force Two, the Vice President's aircraft. Vice President Eastwood was in good health again after his appendix surgery, and was anxious to spend time with Maggie and Mike. Kai was linked to the aircraft, allowing the four of them to discuss details of the World Development Agency.

Thirty minutes before the president's speech, Mike and Maggie were ushered into the United States offices in the U.N. Building. David and Jen Collins were already there and warmly hugged their new friends from California.

"So, are we ready to do this?" the president asked.

"We're ready, and Kai is ready," Mike said.

"I understand you're heading back to California right after the speech," the president said.

"Yes, sir. We're scheduled to review the construction progress on the new Mars lander at JPL," Maggie said. "Kai will be with us."

"The NASA director called me today and told me they are just about done with the changes Kai requested," the president said. "The director's still not sure why we're making the changes, but I told him that you would fill him in after today's speech."

A United Nations staff member entered the room and advised the group that it was time to make their way to the General Assembly Hall.

"Here's to the future," the president said, as he walked with his wife, followed by Mike and Maggie.

49
Rescue Mission

NINETY MINUTES AFTER the United Nations speech, Mike and Maggie said goodbye to the president and his wife. They would see a lot of each other in the months ahead. The Savins were taken to Kennedy International, where they boarded Air Force Two for the flight back to California. The Vice President stayed in New York for discussions with world leaders. Except for the pilots, a chef, and two assistants, Maggie and Mike had the plane to themselves.

Mike's iPad chimed. It was Kai. Mike set the tablet between him and Maggie.

"Hello, Kai," Maggie said. "How are feeling about today?"

"I thought you both did a tremendous job, as did the president," Kai said, looking more excited than they had seen before.

"So, when will we be back home tonight?" Mike asked.

"With headwinds and Los Angeles traffic, you should have your feet up with a *Three Stooges* video playing by 9:00 p.m."

"How about *Disorder in the Court* tonight?" Mike asked excitedly. He and Kai were working through the entire series.

"Sure. Followed by *Sing a Song of Six Pants*," Kai said. "I'm a Shemp man myself."

"Alright you two guys," Maggie finally intervened. *Never get Three Stooges fans started*, she thought.

"Hey Kai, what did you think of the North Korean delegate."

"I liked his suit," Kai returned. "Made in South Korea."

"No, I meant when he called you a running-dog-capitalist war-mongering tool of the United States?"

"It's not true," Kai said.

"What do you mean?" Maggie asked.

"My ears are too short to be a dog."

Mike and Maggie laughed. *He's already doing shtick,* Mike thought. *A year from now, he's going to have his own late-night television show.*

"Any new developments since the speech?" Mike asked.

"The Chinese are reducing their naval presence around the Senkaku Islands," Kai said. "Japan is doing the same."

"How about the Islamic State?" Maggie asked.

"They're gone," Kai said. "Syrian refugees are going back home to rebuild. The president of Syria has agreed to a representative election and a new parliament."

"And our friends, the North Koreans?" Mike asked.

"Still no word from their leader," Kai said, "but their air defense network is gone and the current regime may be in its last days."

"Okay," Maggie said. "So, we'll see you when we get home."

"That would be great," Kai said. "Headwinds are lighter than expected. So, I'll see you earlier, around 8:30 p.m."

∞

As Kai predicted, Mike and Maggie did get home earlier than planned. Mike cracked open two beers from the refrigerator, handed one to Maggie, and sat down on the couch next to her. Maggie was looking at him, smiling.

"What?"

"Let's turn on the news."

Neither had watched any media coverage of the United Nations speech since leaving New York, but it didn't take long for them to catch up. Every channel, not just the news channels, was carrying a live feed from New York, where correspondents were talking about the news of the first contact with an intelligent being from Atona. Camera shots from Times Square showed thousands of people gathered there. Many had little candles and were rejoicing at the news, and of the things that could be accomplished with Kai's help.

The same was true around the world. In Paris and Berlin, Moscow and Beijing, citizens were coming to grips with the fact that intelligent life exists in the universe. Even the cable channels that ran nothing but Area 51 programs had to switch to live video from the networks to report the news.

"Well, I guess that answers the question of how everyone was going to react to the news," Mike said. "Not a bad day's work, right, kiddo?"

"You up for something?" Maggie said, winking at Mike.

"I was on the plane, but they wouldn't leave us alone."

"Well then, let's see if we can't do something about that right now," Maggie said, standing up. "Kill the lights and I'll see you upstairs."

∞

At 9:00 a.m. the next day, an SUV pulled up in front of their house. The same two Secret Service agents that took them to Washington two weeks ago were back this morning to deliver them to the JPL assembly building, where the next Mars mission was being prepared.

"Good morning. Agents Hill and Griffin, right?" Maggie asked.

"You have a good memory, ma'am."

"You want to come in for coffee?"

"No, thank you. We'll wait out here." Mike and Maggie were now under federal protection. There was a lot at stake and the president didn't want anyone messing with these two people.

The SUV got them to Pasadena in less than thirty minutes. They were taken to the Jet Propulsion Lab, the place where everything began for Maggie and Mike forty years ago. A lot had changed since then, but it was good to be back.

They were taken to a large assembly building, where the Mars mission, now called Recovery, was undergoing final testing. Kai was there, too. Carried by Maggie's iPad, he could see the lander close-up, inspecting the equipment and asking the technicians questions about the spacecraft. It took a few minutes for the team to get used to the fact that they were talking to someone from Atona. But, Kai's charm eased them into a new paradigm of interplanetary relations. It was the adaptability to his presence that Kai admired most about humans. Within a half-hour of his introduction, Kai was accepted as just another member of the project team.

The Recovery spacecraft was made up of three pieces of equipment. Once in orbit, the Recovery package would separate into two parts. One part would stay in orbit, taking photographs and using an array of sensors to provide data about the landing site. The other part, containing the lander and a small rover, would enter the Atonan atmosphere and make a soft landing on the surface. It was the same general process that the Viking missions used forty years earlier.

But Recovery was much more capable than the dormant Viking twins that still stood on the surface of Atona. The Recovery lander had a powerful digital transmitter capable of sending large amounts of data to Earth. Redundancies in the way the lander communicated with Earth would minimize the risk of radiation damaging the data. The lander's original scientific experiment package was removed. Kai was providing detailed information about Atona that made the experiments unnecessary. The extra space aboard the lander was used for a larger transmitter, digital recording equipment, and a large downward-firing antenna that would send communications to the Underground, where it was hoped that Atonans were still alive.

In addition to the lander, the mission would also deploy a surface rover. Its mission had changed since Kai provided new plans. Instead of exploring, the rover would serve as a kind of remote television news vehicle – shooting live video and relaying it back through the lander's transmitter to Earth. Its destination was specific – one of the elevator stations that once served the Underground. If Kai's people were still alive, they would come to the surface there. Video screens on both the rover and lander would play prerecorded messages, asking them to walk to the lander that would be nearby.

The launch date for the Recovery mission was set for July 20 – forty years to the day Viking 1 landed on Atona. The two planets weren't as close to each other as they were in 1976, so arrival would take five months instead of four, as was the case with the Viking missions. Landing on Atona was scheduled for December 31.

After inspecting the lander, Mike and Maggie addressed the Recovery project team. Kai was there, too, speaking to the audience on a video monitor. He thanked them for helping his people and said he hoped to return their kindness by sharing knowledge that might help Earth solve some of its most pressing problems. He acknowledged that his presence was still unsettling to many, but he assured them that his only goal was to be of help. In all other ways, he said, nothing would change with Kai living among them.

When they got home, Mike started up the restored 1970 Volkswagen Beetle, the one he drove to California from Michigan. They were taking Kai to the beach. And, with Sasha in the back seat, Kai would see a different side of the Savin family and the place they lived. It was an odd juxtaposition – an ancient car model, first built in the 1940s, carrying an extraterrestrial, who was watching the action from an iPad. They walked on the beach, while Sasha headed for the surf. Then, the four of them went to the Santa Monica Pier, to the place where Mike proposed to Maggie.

That evening, back home, Mike and Maggie noticed that Kai was going into sleep mode more often. The programming that controlled his sleep patterns was working to protect him, but the energy he was expending was taking its toll. Kai was worried – the Recovery mission would take so long to get to Atona. And, he still had no idea whether Mia – or anyone – was still alive.

While they waited until launch date, Kai's conversations with Mike and Maggie focused on physics, with Kai writing articles for publication in the major science journals. When they weren't talking shop, they explored wider, more philosophical topics like love and death, and what might follow death. These were the same kinds of conversations Mike and Maggie had before Kai arrived. But now, a new normal had settled in, with Kai being just another member of the Savin family.

In early July, the Recovery spacecraft was moved to Cape Canaveral, Florida, to be placed atop its launch vehicle. The spacecraft passed intensive inspections and sterilization to protect the Atonans from Earth-borne contagions. There would be a live video feed between the two planets, but they still had to contend with a nine-minute delay in getting information from Atona. For that reason, Recovery included a prerecorded video display that would allow Kai to talk to his people and explain all that had happened. Kai recorded hours of video for the mission, anticipating the questions they would ask.

With Maggie, Mike, and Kai in attendance, on July 20, an SLS rocket blasted off from Cape Canaveral, Florida. Sitting next to them in bleacher seats were David and Jen Collins and the leaders of Russia, China, and over a hundred other countries.

As the rocket roared into the sky, a new era was dawning for humankind. Someday, Earth might resemble the place Kai left behind, where the potential of the entire human race could be fully realized. Kai smiled as he watched the launch. But, he would still have to wait another five months before learning whether Mia and his people were still alive.

50
Recovery

PLANET ATONA – NORTHERN POLAR REGION

ON THURSDAY, DECEMBER 31, at 6:19 p.m. Pacific Time, the Recovery mission package entered orbit around Atona. Its orbit was north-south, allowing the satellite portion of the mission to cross the planet's polar regions. This would align the satellite with the Recovery lander, which would touch down very near the northern icecap. The orbit was tight – just 211 kilometers above the Atonan surface. Gravity would pull the satellite down in less than a year. But that's all the time Kai needed to find out if his people were still alive.

Two hours after establishing a stable orbit, the lander module separated from the orbiter and headed for the surface. NASA had learned a lot about landing spacecraft since Viking arrived forty years ago. The computers onboard the Recovery spacecraft gave it extraordinary capabilities to manage flight conditions as it made its way to a soft landing on Atona.

The spot chosen for the landing was *Olympia Mensae*, a flat, glacial region near the northern ice cap. Kai believed that any survivors would have congregated in this area. It had the newest fusion reactors to supply heat and light. Its agricultural facilities were still first-rate – at least they were when Kai left for Earth. And, this part of the Underground was right below a major pipeline to the ice cap, meaning that Atonans would likely still have drinking water.

At 11:42 p.m. Pacific time, the Recovery lander deployed its parachute to slow its descent. Then, its four rockets fired in bursts to begin pushing back against Atonan gravity. Recovery had full autonomy in deciding exactly where to land. This allowed it to scout the terrain, looking for a flat place without boulders or other ground hazards. Using coordinates Kai provided, the lander would touch down as near as possible to an elevator station that the Atonans often used to go to the surface. Confirming a successful touchdown on Atona, the Recovery lander reported that it was less than twenty meters from Kai's elevator location.

After establishing radio links with its orbiter and with the NASA Deep Space Network on Earth, the Recovery lander began a series of programmed tasks that would be needed for it to communicate with the Atonans living in the Underground.

The first task was to build an antenna system that could communicate through the surface of the planet. An electric drill attached to an articulating arm was lowered to the surface, its drill bit already spinning. The large bit easily cut into the hard Atonan soil, as the robotic arm provided the necessary force to push the drill. The whirring drill worked for about ten minutes before the arm returned it to the lander. Cameras aboard the lander showed a neatly-drilled hole a meter deep and eight centimeters wide. Soil piled up around the drill hole. Much of it was white, indicating that large amounts of water ice were still present in the Atonan soil.

Planetary geologists were delighted with the images, but since Kai already gave them a full map of the planet's crust and core composition, there were no surprises when the drill found ice.

After the drill withdrew, the articulating arm returned, this time carrying a silver-plated aluminum rod slightly narrower than the hole. The rod was lowered into the hole with attached wires connected to a low-frequency transmitter. This was the subsurface antenna – a way of sending signals through the planet's crust. If the Atonans were monitoring radio communications, they would likely detect these ultra-low frequency waves, which had the benefit of traveling very long distances – literally radiating to the core of the planet. The U.S. Navy once used a similar system on Earth to communicate with its submarines.

On the surface, Recovery would use another antenna to broadcast messages like a radio station on Earth. Kai provided six different frequencies that he believed would still be in use. Unfortunately, these surface signals could only reach the northernmost portion of Atona. Like FM radio, the signals could not bend around the planet. If there were Atonans still living in the south, the only way they would know that Recovery had landed was through the ultra-low frequency signals sent by the underground antenna.

With its antennas and transmitters active, the lander began a series of repeating messages, recorded by Kai in the Atonan language. The messages said that Kai was alive and that the Recovery lander on the surface was there to help. He urged anyone who was healthy enough to use the elevator near the lander to come to the surface. There, they could communicate directly with Kai using a touchscreen on the lander that was designed to operate in the extreme cold of the Atonan surface.

Recovery had one more task to perform. After it began broadcasting, the lander deployed a small, six-wheeled rover. Again, the robotic arm was used to pick up the rover and carefully place it on the surface. Then, the lander located the elevator shaft and shot a laser beam at it. This would be a guide beacon for the rover. Aiming for the laser target, the rover moved out, dodging a few fist-sized rocks along the way. When it arrived, a camera aboard the rover showed the floor of the elevator station – old tiles in a geometric pattern. Kai recognized them and confirmed to mission specialists that the rover was in the right place.

The rover's cameras swept the area around the elevator station. No footprints were found – a discouraging, but not unexpected sign. There would be few rational reasons for Atonans to visit the surface. The radiation that burned Kai when he watched the Viking 1 lander was still there, deadly to anyone who stayed more than a short time on the surface.

Now, all Kai and the Recovery mission team could do was wait. For the next forty-eight hours, Recovery sent messages and waited for replies. Again and again, the broadcasts told the Atonans that Kai was alive and that he was there to help them. But, there was no reply to the messages.

Overhead, the Recovery orbiter was doing its own surveillance. As it passed over the northern ice cap, the orbiter took pictures, using sophisticated spectrograph instruments to search for signs of life in the Underground. Photos sent back to JPL revealed nothing unusual on the first few orbits over the northern pole.

But on its twenty-first orbit over the ice cap, the Recovery orbiter did report something unusual. In the infrared part of the spectrum, photographs revealed four heat signatures in the shape of long, rounded rectangles. The heat images were faint, but on the next orbit, more shots confirmed that something was still energized and making heat beneath the Atonan surface.

When Kai saw the images, he knew right away what they were. Four of the six fusion reactors that provided heat and light for the northern settlement were still active. One had been taken off-line while he was still on Atona. The reason for the other being down was something he didn't want to think about.

The orbiter's next pass confirmed his fears. Sensors detected isotopes of hydrogen – deuterium and tritium gas escaping from elevator shafts across the northern hemisphere. The atmosphere on Atona had little hydrogen of its own. The isotopes could come from only one place – a fusion reactor at the site of the Recovery mission. There was a growing fear at Mission Control that one of the fusion reactors had suffered a catastrophic breach.

There had never been a failure of a fusion reactor on Atona, even when Koya struck the planet. But as the population declined, there were fewer and fewer technicians capable of maintaining the delicate fusion process. If one of the reactors went out of control, it could burst through the heavy shielding that kept the fusion process contained. If that happened, the reactor would spew large amounts of hydrogen and hydrogen isotopes into the confined spaces of the Underground.

While concentrated hydrogen would be highly explosive on Earth, there wasn't enough oxygen in the atmosphere of Atona to cause a fire. But the pressurized gas would force out the heavier carbon dioxide atmosphere that the Atonans needed to breath. Like sediment in a glass of water, the breathable air would settle into the lower tunnels as the lighter gas continued filling the upper chambers. Atonans would have to follow the breathable air in order to survive. And as they went deeper, the conditions worsened. It was dark, cold, and wet. No one could survive for very long.

As the project team studied the data from the orbiter, there was indication that the reactor breach might have just occurred. If that was the case, there could still be survivors in the deepest parts of the Underground. They could be alive, but unable to acknowledge the radio signals from the Recovery lander.

But after another two days passed without a response, Kai's hope of finding anyone alive was rapidly fading.

Why did I leave Atona? What did I accomplish? I wish I had listened to Mia. At least, I would have spent the last years of my life with the person I love. This mission, which cost the United States billions of dollars, is a failure. When it is over, I will be alone – living on an alien planet with no one to touch, no one to love. And without a physical body, I could live alone almost forever. It would be unbearable.

Kai's thoughts were tangled and fragmented. He hadn't slept since the landing. That shouldn't have been possible, except that Kai figured out a way to turn off his sleep program. But changing his programming was like living on borrowed time – sooner or later, a part of his programming would fail. And without repairs, Kai was like the fusion reactors on Atona. Before long, his system would suffer a catastrophic failure that would kill him.

But in his present state of mind, he wondered if that would be so bad.

Neither Mike nor Maggie knew that Kai had re-jiggered his programming. Like Kai, they had been at Mission Control since the landing, taking turns sleeping on a couch outside the control room. Each assumed that Kai was sleeping when the other was sleeping. And Kai had been quiet since the landing, concentrating on the data that was being sent back from Atona. That's why they didn't notice Kai hadn't slept.

Mike was in the control room. Maggie was sleeping on a couch in a hallway nearby. The First Lady was there, too. She arrived yesterday as the news became more desperate. She and Maggie had become friends and were sharing the highs, and now the lows, that were coming from the Atonan surface.

"Kai, are you awake?" Mike asked, speaking into his headset.

"Yes, Mike, I am awake."

"What are your thoughts?"

"The hydrogen is not a good sign."

"Would your people have time to get to lower levels?"

"Perhaps, but the conditions would be terrible."

"And, there would be no atmosphere on the surface to replace what was lost," Mike said.

"Exactly."

"Are you seeing anything in the data coming back from Atona that gives you hope?"

"No, Mike," Kai said. "And right now, I am very tired."

"When was the last time you slept?"

"Three days ago."

"I thought you were programmed to sleep when your body needed it," Mike said. "Why haven't you slept?"

"I did a little reprogramming," Kai said. "I like to tinker – just like you."

"Kai, you need to listen to me," Mike said. "I need you to restore your original programming and go to sleep right *now*."

"Yes, I think that would be best," Kai said. "Please call my name to wake me. That will override the sleep program."

"Since when?"

"Since I reprogrammed that function as well."

Kai signed off as Mike continued to watch the live video images from Atona. In twenty-five minutes, the rotation of the planet would cut communications between Mission Control and the Recovery lander. The Atonan solar day is the same as Earth's. It would be twelve hours before Mission Control would be able to communicate with the Recovery lander again.

Mike had just looked at the clock when the rover cameras showed some movement at the elevator station. The video was nine minutes old, due to the delay in getting the signal from Atona to Earth. But someone was on the surface.

Mike ran out to wake Maggie and Jen. Everyone in the control room was standing, watching the large monitors play the video of the Atonan who came to the surface. Mike clicked the microphone on his headset. "Kai. Kai, you need to wake up."

"How long did I sleep?"

"About three minutes," Mike said. "I'll make it up to you later, but look at the elevator!"

A thin figure in a protective suit emerged from the elevator. The Atonan carried a small device, about the size of a laptop computer, under one arm. The suited figure walked slowly, almost painfully, to the rover, whose cameras were sending crisp, clear images. The figure bent down and looked into the camera lens.

"Kai, is that really you?"

"It's Sela!" Kai said, his raised voice echoing throughout Mission Control.

"Who is Sela?" Mike asked.

"Sela Jaran. She managed this part of the Underground," Kai said. "She was there when my grandmother and I came down before Koya struck." Kai's voice was shaky. They weren't sure if it was emotion or fatigue or both.

Sela stepped back from the camera on the rover. She held up the silver box.

"Kai, I have Mia."

The room erupted in applause as Sela's voice could be heard over the speakers. Kai had built a translation program so that anyone who spoke to the rover or lander would be understood in English.

The mission director quieted everyone so that Sela could be heard. She sounded weak and it seemed that she was having trouble breathing.

"I am walking to the lander to connect Mia to your space-craft." The radio transmissions told survivors to come to the lander, where they could watch Kai's recorded messages.

Sela stood up and walked toward the Recovery lander. Cameras on the rover followed her. Her steps were weak. She stumbled several times, and once, she nearly fell.

She finally reached the lander, her breathing labored. She was very old. It had been 400 years since Koya struck Atona and Sela was at least 150 years old when Kai visited the Underground as a small boy. With life expectancy in the Underground declining, Sela had to be very close to the end of her life. And here she was, walking on the surface of Atona, carrying his beloved Mia in her arms.

Sela touched the menu screen, which had instructions for playing the recorded messages. Kai's voice could be heard through her microphone as she breathed heavily and listened. As he explained what happened to him, they heard Sela make small gasps and sobs. She was crying. After forty Earth years, Kai had returned.

Kai's recorded messages also included questions that he wanted answered by anyone who came to the surface. Sela listened to the questions and responded.

"Can you tell me what has happened on Atona since I left?" Kai's recorded voice asked.

"Mia and I are the last," Sela said. "Terrible conditions. Conflict. Disease. Reactor core explosion. Everyone's dead."

Kai so wanted to respond, but with the nine-minute delay, he knew he couldn't have a direct conversation with Sela. All he could do was watch and listen to the delayed responses coming from Atona.

"Mia would not give up, Kai. She asked to be put in here," Sela said, holding out the silver box. "Mia went through the transference process just a month ago."

Everyone in Mission Control knew what that meant. Mia could be sent to Earth. Mike and Maggie hugged, with Jen joining in. But their happiness was short-lived.

"I stayed behind to keep the power on," Sela said. "But this is the last of the breathable air."

Instructions playing on the lander screen showed how to connect an Atonan device to the Earth vehicle. Two-way data transmission would be possible, although the nine-minute delay had to be considered.

"Fourteen minutes to loss of radio communication," a mission specialist called out.

The control room watched as Sela's shaky hands connected the silver box to the cables on the lander. Nine minutes after the unit was plugged in, Mission Control began receiving a clear stream of digital data. For the next twelve minutes, the data poured into computer hard drives.

Mia was coming to Earth.

Two minutes later, Mission Control lost contact with Recovery as Atona rotated away from Earth. It would be twelve hours before the Recovery lander would resume contact with Mission Control.

Twelve long hours later, when the Recovery landing site faced Earth again, Mission Control was able to reestablish contact with the lander. Video saved during the twelve-hour blackout was stored in a digital drive aboard the lander. The video now coming from Atona showed Sela following Kai's instructions on how to set up the communication link. She then pressed several buttons on the screen as the silver device in her arms lit up. Mia's files were being transferred to Earth in the same way Kai got here.

When the transfer was complete, Sela looked into the camera.

"Kai, Mia is with you now. I must go. But I wish for both of you, peace and happiness."

The Recovery mission team watched as Sela walked slowly back to the elevator shaft. A few steps from the rover, she grabbed her throat and stumbled. Sela tried to stand again, but couldn't. Gasping inside her protective suit, she fell forward, the silver box that held Mia fell out of her arms and landed on the tile floor.

The Mission Director asked Kai if he wanted to stop the video. But Kai asked that it continue. As the rover camera focused on Sela, the images showed her motionless body on the Atonan surface. She was just steps away from the elevator shaft.

For more than an hour, Mission Control tried to communicate with her. But Sela was dead. Out of respect, the mission director called back the rover to the lander, where it was shut down.

Epilogue

MIA OPENED HER eyes. The bedroom seemed familiar – smooth stone walls, rounded glass windows that looked out on dozens of green trees, all flowering with blossoms. A door to the outside was open and Mia could feel a warm breeze pass over her as she lay on a bed with a light blanket covering her. In the distance, she could see a shoreline and hear the tranquil sound of waves.

She tried to speak, but nothing came out of her mouth. Yet, an assuring voice told her that she was alive and that she was safe. Mia pulled her arms out from under the blanket and looked at her hands. They worked, as did her toes when she wiggled them. She felt her limbs and her body. Everything seemed to be in place.

"Sela, where are you?" Mia called out. Her distended voice echoed again and again. The voice didn't come from her mouth but from somewhere inside her head.

"Hello, my darling," another voice said softly. The words reached into her mind. She turned her head to see Kai, sitting next to the bed, smiling at her. His eyes were wet from tears.

But Mia didn't quite recognize him. She was going through the same reassembly and orientation that Kai went through some months ago. It would be at least a day before she was fully aware again.

"Kai?" Mia said weakly. "Kai, is that really you?"

"Yes, Mia," Kai said, taking her hand and kissing it. "I'm here with you and you are safe."

"You? You are my husband," Mia said slowly. "Kai. You are my husband."

"Yes, Mia, I am your husband. We are together again."

"Where? What happened…" Mia drifted off to sleep, her programming taking control as the assembly of her consciousness continued. Kai stood and kissed his wife on the lips and on the forehead. It would be another day before Mia would wake again.

Kai and Mia would never return to Atona. Their planet was dead, killed in a random act of violence that could happen to any planet. Now, they were residents of Earth. And they were welcomed openly by thoughtful and intelligent beings with the potential to do so much good. Humans were truly special and Kai was glad that he and Mia could be part of their world.

Even though their virtual world could be anything Mia wanted, Kai thought it only fitting that she woke in a place that resembled one that both of them knew as children. This was the place where they played in the sandbox. It was the place where Mia listened to Kai's tall tales of space adventures in rocket ships that he would launch – as soon as he figured out how to get them off the roofs of his neighbors' houses. And one day, much like today, it was where Kai noticed Mia – *really* noticed her – for the first time. Their love would grow and sustain them during the hard times on Atona and the forty years they were apart.

After Mia was fully restored and after he had time to explain where she was and what happened to Sela, Kai would introduce his wife to her new extended family. Kai thought of Mike and Maggie as family and Mia would, too. Together, they would do so much for humankind. Maybe they would even help create a world like Atona.

Peace and prosperity. Equality and acceptance. Freedom to believe what one wished. These were the characteristics of a people who thrived peacefully for a half-million years. And, although humans were still evolving, still learning, the help that Kai and Mia would offer could propel their civilization forward in a fraction of the time it took on Atona. Yes, with these remarkable people, it was possible.

Mike and Maggie returned home and to a new kind of normal life. They worked on setting up the World Development Agency. The headquarters would be in Los Angeles. The twenty-first century would be the Pacific century. Countries like the United States, China, Japan and South Korea would lead the world into a new era of freedom and prosperity.

Before Mia arrived, Mike and Maggie talked with Kai about the technology his grandfather invented. They wondered if it would be possible for humans to undergo the transference process. If it worked, humans could lose their physical bodies and enjoy nearly limitless lifespans. They imagined the disabled, the elderly, or anyone who wanted to make their own world, to have that chance. Yes, there were moral and ethical questions and some religious leaders would object.

But, technology has a way of overcoming established ways of thinking. Human beings might someday take up residence in a virtual world, free from the limitations of physical bodies.

Although Mike and Maggie probably wouldn't be here to see it, they were certain that Kai and Mia would be, guiding humans to the next step in their journey.

www.ingramcontent.com/pod-product-compliance
Lightning Source LLC
Chambersburg PA
CBHW061315170626
46817CB00001B/187